Andy checked his pockets. "What's this?" and he pulled out a ticket. Smiling broadly, he offered the stub to Cassie.

And so it came to pass, on a hot September night, Cassie O'Malley challenged Skeeter to the last dizzy bat race in Sand Skeeter history.

Bending over, Cassie rested her forehead on the knob of the aluminum bat, surprised by the spot of cool in the otherwise sweltering evening heat. Sneaking a peek at Skeeter, she prepared to spin. Cassie did not like to lose, not at life, not at love, not at Skeeball, not at dizzy bat racing.

On command, she began to spin, not too fast, not too slow, but just right to build up momentum for the race up the first base line. "You can do it," she told herself. "Just don't fall down," she counseled. As Cassie weaved toward first, she didn't see Skeeter as he staggered out to the pitcher's mound, falling in a heap, in mock exhaustion.

On cue, the team trainer ran out to the mound to check on the prostrate mascot. On cue, the trainer fanned Skeeter, waiting for his revival. On cue, the trainer waited. And waited. And waited. The crowd sensed the problem, just before the trainer looked back at the dugout, frantic now, yelling for assistance. Grabbing at the costume, he pulled off the mosquito head, but he had waited too long. Inside the costume, on a night of near-record temperatures, Skeeter was dead of heat stroke.

It starts by writing the best book you're capable of writing. It starts there, but it surely doesn't end there because writing a good book is an art, but publishing a good book is a business. The more the business changes, the more important it is for a writer to deal with people who understand the changing face of publishing.

My thanks to David Niall Wilson and to everyone at Crossroad Press who have helped me keep up with the changing face of publishing, first with eBooks, then with audio books and now, coming full circle, with this paperback edition of *A Minor Case of Murder*.

First Crossroad Press Edition

A Minor Case of Murder
A Cassie O'Malley Mystery

by JEFF MARKOWITZ

Crossroad Press

Now that I write murder mysteries, I see dead bodies most everywhere that I go. On more than one occasion, I have recounted for my wife Carol the details of her gruesome and untimely demise. Carol listens and smiles and encourages me to write. She is a lover of good murder mysteries and seems to count my stories among the good ones. Carol is not my most objective reader. But I didn't marry her for her objectivity.

To my lovely wife Carol, I dedicate *A Minor Case of Murder*.

Hot Cocoa with Mini-Marshmallows

It was a raw September afternoon on Godiva Beach, lonely and deserted, the wind whipping in off the water stinging Cassie's face—good weather, she told herself, for burying a friend. The church service in the morning had been small: twenty family and friends sharing their grief, saying good-bye, perhaps half that number continuing on to the cemetery to pay their last respects to the late Harrison T. Dicke.

Cassie hadn't seen the octogenarian naturist and amateur historian of White Sands Beach in quite some months, but that didn't lessen her sense of loss. Standing at the water's edge, Cassie wanted to laugh, but needed to cry. She told herself it was only the ocean spray moist on her face. Cassie was unprepared for the tap on her shoulder. Jumping at the stranger's touch, she nearly landed in the cold September surf.

"I'm sorry. I didn't mean to startle you."

Cassie examined the stranger closely. He was a good-looking gentleman in his thirties, handsome in a way no longer fashionable, not health-club handsome, not rock-star handsome, but Eisenhower-era handsome, Pillsbury-doughboy handsome, his hair cut by a barber rather than a stylist, his suit purchased at a discount warehouse.

"You were at Harrison's funeral this morning."

Cassie was unsure whether the stranger was asking or telling.

"I'm Andy MacTavish, Harrison's great-grand-nephew … I think."

Cassie realized she was looking at Harrison as he must have looked some fifty years ago. "I'm Cassie O'Malley."

"I thought you might be." Andy noticed that Cassie was shivering in the chill September air. "You must be freezing out here. Please, take my coat."

Cassie, in her slate gray funeral dress, was ill-prepared for the offshore wind. "Thank you. I'd like that."

"Would you like a hot cocoa?" Andy wondered. "I know a real nice spot in town."

Cassie thought she knew every restaurant in White Sands Beach, but Andy bypassed the trendy eateries along the water, instead going inland to Cubby's, a luncheonette untouched by time and tide, down to the wall-mounted jukebox at every table, and the music, The Big Bopper, The Chordettes, Patti Page, Bobby Darrin, The Everly Brothers, the "A" side hits mostly familiar, the "B" side tunes unrecognizable. Sitting at a small booth in the back, sipping hot cocoa with mini-marshmallows, listening to the Dell-Vikings—"Come Go with Me"—Cassie and Andy made small talk, picking their way carefully through the minefield of first impressions.

"I met your uncle when I was researching a story. I had no idea what to expect. No one warned me I was meeting an eighty-year-old nudist, but he truly was a charming gentleman. You know, there's a lot of Harrison in you."

"Thank you … I guess." And Andy blushed, imagining Cassie imagining him naked under a blue beach umbrella. "Just so you know…I don't share Harrison's…I mean…what I guess I'm trying to say is, I'm not a clothing-optional kind of guy."

It was Cassie's turn to blush. "I'm sorry…no…when I said you resemble Harrison, I mean…I didn't mean…well, you know what I mean."

Andy decided it was time to change the subject. "Harrison showed me some of your stories. He loved your stories, the more outlandish the better."

"Thank you. And you?"

Andy busied himself with his mini-marshmallows, as though somehow the hot cocoa might reveal the polite response. "I think you are a very talented writer."

"But?"

"But," Andy continued, "don't you think that the magazine you write for is just a little bit trashy?"

Cassie laughed. "I think the magazine is incredibly trashy. But that's its charm."

"I see." Actually, he didn't. Andy hit E2 on the jukebox and lapsed into silence. He sipped his cocoa, and, looking over the rim of his mug, allowed himself to consider the woman across the table. Andy reminded himself that a woman in her thirties, in our youth-oriented culture, is supposedly past her prime; but if she were, Andy decided, past her prime, Cassie was more impressive than most people's prime. She was of an age when women believed they were supposed to cut their hair, but Andy noted with satisfaction that Cassie looked great with her dirty-blond hair falling halfway down her back.

Cassie's taste in music ran toward the giants of jazz—Charlie Parker, Miles Davis, Dizzy Gillespie—and her taste in men…well, it had been so long, Cassie told herself, she could hardly remember. But sitting in the booth at Cubby's sipping hot cocoa with Andy MacTavish, listening to Dion and the Belmonts on the jukebox, she began to consider the possibilities. And when Andy asked if it would be okay to call her, Cassie said yes, and, for a change, she meant yes.

After her lunch with Andy MacTavish, Cassie decided to spend the chilly afternoon on the boardwalk. The boardwalk, like the town itself, was an extraordinary mixture of Victorian charm and carnival schlock, tearooms abutting tattoo parlors, ateliers tucked in alongside arcades. Cassie noticed a brand new storefront—Om Depot—a neon eyeball in the window—Madame Alexina, Spiritualist—and she decided to go in. Her editor had been pressing her for a new story idea, so she wouldn't be going in for any personal reason, she told herself, certainly not to learn about Andy MacTavish.

Madame Alexina, with her bright red bouffant hair and slight orange moustache, dressed in lime green polyester bowling shirt and pink capri pants, greeted Cassie warmly at the door. "Ah, my first customer. Please come in. Don't mind the mess—I'm still unpacking."

"That's all right. I can come back later."

Madame Alexina fixed her gaze on Cassie, her eyes like hazel tractor beams locked on Cassie's soul. "Ah, you met a man today."

Cassie took a seat and waited, while Madame Alexina searched for her crystal ball among the partially unpacked paranormal paraphernalia. Madame Alexina dumped the remaining boxes on the floor, revealing a veritable landfill of the sacred and the profane.

A worry stone. The I Ching. Hippie dog tags ("War is not healthy for children and other living things"). The Tibetan Book of the Dead. An iron cross. A rabbit's foot. Tickets from a Bruce Springsteen concert in Indianapolis. A *Life* magazine photograph of John F. Kennedy. A *Mad* magazine drawing of George W. Bush. *The Sayings of Chairman Mao.* The prophecies of Nostradamus. The wit and wisdom of Baba Booey. Zig-Zag rolling papers. Trail mix. Trojans. (Trojans?) Double-stuffed Oreo cookies. A Frisbee. A boomerang. Her unfinished collection of Zen limericks ("There was a Bodhisattva Kannon/Who was known for the men that she'd blown/With her eleven heads perched in ten different beds/She still had a mouth left to moan"). Two parking tickets. Three plantains. Four dried ancho peppers. Five golden rings. A balsa wood airplane. The New Testament. Support hose. An Ozzy Osbourne bobble-head doll. Her favorite fortune cookie ("Please disregard all previous fortune"). A gold tooth. A silver dollar. Her bronzed baby shoes. A stuffed rat. A rubber spider. Plastic vomit. *The Lord of the Rings* DVD. A black light. A blues harmonica. An autographed copy of *Steal This Book*. A ceramic cow. Chinese handcuffs. A Swiss Army knife. A French tickler. A Belgian waffle. A Led Zeppelin CD. Diet pills. Depilatory. A can of Sterno. A box of Red Zinger. A Louisville Slugger.

But no crystal ball.

"Damn, I was sure I had it in there. Wait, I've got an idea." And Madame Alexina bounded over to the closet, returning with her bowling bag. "I'll improvise."

Cassie imagined her editor's reaction when she turned in the story of the psychic kegler (or was it the kegling psychic?).

Madame Alexina began by gently caressing the ball, alternately stroking and tickling it, the foreplay to fortune telling. She explained to Cassie, "I've got to awaken her desires before the bowling ball will surrender her ebony defenses."

As Cassie watched, the bowling ball did seem to be losing some of its blackness. More precisely, it seemed to Cassie as if the ball were composed of a translucent shell containing an inky interior. Madame Alexina began to tease the bowling ball, tracing little circles around the finger holes. The shell was becoming steadily more translucent, the interior less dark, more liquid. Hesitantly, Madame Alexina slid her fingertips ever so slightly into the holes and, emboldened by the lack of resistance, began to probe ever more deeply and vigorously.

Sitting there, Cassie felt like a peeping Tom. She was fascinated, aroused, embarrassed and silently writing the first paragraph even as she watched. ("Woman has sex with bowling bowl. And sees the future!")

As Madame Alexina's pace quickened and her fingers grew more confident, the inky depths grew ever weaker, until, in a moment, the bowling ball surrendered itself—transparent, exposed, and vulnerable. She stared intently into the depths of the crystal-clear bowling ball, all the while rocking and quietly chanting. "Now we can begin," she announced, her words muffled in the eerie silence of the now-fetid storefront...

"You met a man today, yes?"

"Yes."

"And you want to know if he's the man, right?"

Cassie was not ready to admit that—not to Madame Alexina, not to herself. "Let's just say I'm curious."

Cassie spent the next half-hour chatting with Madame Alexina about love and death, about Andy MacTavish, but also about her late husband Rob, gone nearly fifteen years, and Harrison T. Dicke, interred just that morning.

At the mention of the morning's funeral, Madame Alexina again consulted her bowling ball. She chose not to tell her first customer that she saw many more funerals in Cassie's future.

The Developer's Daughter

Driving home to Doah in her rebuilt '67 Ford Mustang, the election just two months away, interspersed with small handmade signs promoting various local businesses—"Live Bait," "Authentic BBQ," "Small Appliance Repair"—Cassie couldn't help but notice the mass of political signage decorating the countryside. Nationally, interest was focused on the off-year elections and control of Congress. New Jersey was focused on a hotly contested campaign for governor. But in the Pine Barrens, the issues were more local and the contests more personal. And in Doah, the campaign that had captured the hearts and minds of the citizenry was Cheyenne Harbrough's independent campaign to unseat Mayor "Big Jim" Donovan.

Cassie was proud of her good friend and one-time Princeton roommate. When Cheyenne kicked off her campaign, no one, not even Cheyenne herself, believed she would unseat the popular mayor. But Cheyenne wanted to force the town to address the issue of development, an issue which sharply divided Doah, provoking otherwise rational officials to fisticuffs. The daughter of a controversial developer, Cheyenne was an articulate advocate for responsible development. Still, as the daughter of a developer, herself a part-owner of Harbrough and Daughters, the conventional wisdom was that Doah would never elect a developer as mayor.

For many in Doah, a rural town of pygmy pines and cranberry bogs, there are few epithets used with more disgust than "developer." And yet "developer" was only one of the derogatory labels that had been attached to Cheyenne Harbrough. For Cheyenne was not only a "developer," she was also a "homewrecker," it being well-known in Doah that Cheyenne lured married men to violate their sacred vows.

When Cassie got home to her condo in Doah, the answering machine was blinking hello. She was curious about the messages, but first, Cassie needed to get out of the funeral clothes. Ten minutes later, dressed comfortably in her black Princeton sweatpants with orange lettering and her Jameson t-shirt, a first shot of Irish whiskey already warming her and a second waiting patiently by her side, Cassie was ready to check the message.

"Hi, Cassie. It's me. Cheyenne. Don't forget, tonight's the mayoral debate. Shit, I'm scared. Remind me why I did this, okay? Anyway, call me."

Cassie dialed Cheyenne's apartment. "I'd like to speak to Mayor Harbrough, please."

"Hi, Cassie. I'm so glad you called."

"You're gonna do great tonight, Chey."

"I wish I felt that way. Right now, I'm pretty nervous."

"Relax, girlfriend. It's gonna be fun."

"Yeah. Okay. So tell me what you think, Cassie. I bought a new outfit for the debate. A black skirt, conservative but sexy, and a turquoise blouse. It should look great on camera. So, what I want to know is, is it proper to wear f-me pumps to the debate?"

"And to think I plan to vote for you, Chey."

"Yeah, me too. What am I thinking? Anyway, will I see you there tonight? Are you coming to the debate?"

"I don't think so, Chey. I'm sorry, but I'm kind of exhausted."

"That's right. I'm sorry. I forgot. How was the funeral?"

Cassie was stumped. Is there a right answer to *How was the funeral?* "Okay, I guess." Cassie paused for effect, savoring the next line, anticipating Cheyenne's reaction to what she was about to say. "I met a guy."

"At the funeral? Shit, Cassie, what is it now, twelve years? All this time I've been trying to set you up, trying to talk you into getting back into the game, and after all this time you go and pick up a guy at the funeral? Details, girl, I want details."

"It's Harrison's great-grand-nephew…I think. His name's Andy MacTavish."

"Not *the* Andy MacTavish!"

Cassie again was stumped. "I didn't know that there was a *the* Andy MacTavish."

"Wake up, Cassie. Don't you read *Barron's*? They say Andy MacTavish is worth millions."

"You know I don't have a head for business. Anyway, it must be another Andy MacTavish."

"Cassie, we have to talk. I'll meet you for breakfast. Okay?"

"Okay, Chey. Nine o'clock at the Eggery. And I'll be watching you tonight. Make sure they get your shoes on camera."

Cheyenne was nervous walking into the Municipal Building, but the evening started well, she decided, although, in truth, she had only a limited basis for comparison. She was pleased with the power of her footwear selection, recognizing even before she took her seat that sex and politics are nearly identical ambitions. She made a point of seeking out the township manager before the meeting was called to order, leaning in close to the young man, letting her scent linger in his airspace, drawing him into her sphere of influence. She greeted each of the council members warmly, councilmen and councilwomen alike. Cheyenne found the women to be polite, perhaps too polite, and vaguely suspicious. The men…well, Cheyenne knew exactly how the men would react: polite, perhaps too polite, and vaguely aroused, running awkwardly for the cover afforded by their seats behind the large council desk. She looked for an opportunity to say hello to Big Jim, but the mayor was already working the room, flaunting the trappings of incumbency.

At the manager's prompt, Mr. Caputo, the self-appointed watchdog and political pundit, moderator of the mayoral debate, outlined the evening's format. Joe Caputo, young and articulate, was known around the Municipal Building as the "Boy Barrister." Mr. Caputo was fiercely neutral, took great pride in the fierceness of his neutrality, and reminded the three mayoral candidates that he would not shy away from asking the tough questions. In her case, Cheyenne assumed that the tough questions would focus on land development and sexual innuendo. Feeling the power of her footwear, Cheyenne was determined that Mr. Caputo would not make sport of her.

Cheyenne gauged her opponents. Big Jim Donovan looked mayoral, tanned and relaxed, ten pounds thinner for the campaign and sporting a new toupee. He was prepared to run on his record. Only Councilwoman Beverly Becht appeared anxious, squirming in her seat and interrupting, then lapsing into silence. Public comment at the debate was unusually subdued. Big Jim was masterful, turning the chaos of his first term into a testament to participatory government and the triumph of ideals over partisan politics.

Mr. Caputo was making a point about the debate rules when Ms. Becht interrupted, unable to contain herself any longer. "Excuse me, Mr.

Moderator. I realize that I am speaking out of turn, but time does not permit me to delay. We are only a few months away from the holiday season, and with Christmas fast approaching, I am deeply concerned by the decision made by this township not to decorate the Municipal Building this year. I understand that it is on the advice of our attorney who has indicated that the courts have found such displays to be unconstitutional. I do not agree with his legal opinion and I am embarrassed by the cowardice being shown by the township on this issue.

"I grew up in this town. And I remember there were always two or three houses in Doah that bore no evidence of Christmas. Jews, my mother explained, decent but misguided citizens who would never pass through the Gates of Heaven into the Kingdom of our Lord. I always felt sorry for the people who lived in those houses, their souls as barren as their homes at Christmastime. I still feel sorry for those in our community who do not believe—the Jews, the Muslims and the Chinese, the homosexuals, the liberals and the atheists. But now, when I think about the Municipal Building at Christmas, dark and unadorned, I have to ask, 'Is the very town of Doah going straight to hell?' "

The witnesses to the councilwoman's diatribe, elected officials and local residents alike, sat there in stunned silence, embarrassed by Ms. Becht's outburst. Many residents shared her disappointment at the anticipated absence of the Nativity scene which had stood proudly on the front lawn of the Municipal Building for so many years, but even her supporters—especially her supporters—sat there in silence, appalled by her interruption.

"And in a town that has abandoned its Christian values…" Ms. Becht turned to stare at Cheyenne Harbrough, "…it seems that just about anyone believes they can be mayor."

But Cheyenne Harbrough would not be shamed into silence. Cheyenne seized the issue with a disarming, self-deprecating humor.

"Did you hear the one about the traveling salesman and the developer's daughter? A traveling salesman's car broke down, so he walked to the nearest house—it happened to be the home of a developer—and asked if he could stay the night. The developer told the salesman that yes, he could spend the night, but you'll have to sleep with my daughter. "So…" Cheyenne continued, "…the traveling salesman climbs into bed with the developer's well-endowed [here Cheyenne blushed] daughter and cautiously makes a pass at the young woman. She turns to the middle-aged salesman, warning, 'Stop that right now or I'll call my father,' but she gives the gentleman a kiss and rubs up against him and before long they are enjoying intimate relations. An hour later, the salesman finds himself ready to go again. 'Stop that right now,' the young lady again insists, 'or I'll call my father.' But, under the covers, she runs her fingers along the inside of his thigh. The story repeats itself each hour, on the hour, each time the young lady threatening to call her father, but in truth, the young lady instigating, controlling, and reveling in the coupling. Finally, at four in the morning, the young woman's naked body pressed up against the exhausted, middle-aged salesman. 'Stop that right now,' the salesman insists, 'or I'll call your father!' "

Watching the debate at home on her TV, Cassie poured herself another Jameson.

Three Web Sites and Two Jameson's Later

Some men like to conduct their business on the golf course, standing on the first tee or lining up a putt on the back nine. Big Jim was not a golfer and had no use for the business and political opportunities to be found on the links. He was more likely to be found at his regular table at the Eggery, the large round table that had come to be known as the mayor's conference table, sitting at the table with a plate of Jimmy Dean breakfast links and a coffee black, one sugar, finding fact, dispensing wisdom and cutting deals that would benefit Doah Township, and coincidentally, the mayor himself.

The Eggery was nothing special—that is, of course, unless you like your eggs over easy, thick slabs of homemade bread dripping butter, bacon extra-crispy, home fries extra-spicy, coffee so rich you can smell it from your car. You see what I mean: nothing special unless you like a waitress who knows when to leave you alone but who appears at your side scant moments before you yourself become aware of your desire.

Big Jim's desires were prodigious, but uncomplicated—mayoral acclaim served with a side of breakfast sausage. At the start of his first term, Big Jim made it a habit to eat breakfast at the Eggery the morning after every political event in Doah Township. He would meet with his shadow cabinet, official and unofficial advisors, political friends and foes alike, to discuss the wants and needs of the good citizens of Doah. Big Jim was truly bipartisan, welcoming the advice of his political opponents, who were, as well, his fishing buddies, bowling partners, drinking companions and lifelong friends and neighbors.

Cheyenne was not a regular at the mayor's conference table. She was not even an occasional participant at these breakfast meetings, but she recognized that spending a few minutes with the mayor was the perfect opportunity to gauge the impact of the debate. When Cassie walked into the Eggery, meeting Cheyenne for breakfast, she found Cheyenne sitting with the mayor, her hand under the table, resting lightly on the mayoral thigh and discussing campaign strategy. As Cassie approached the table, Big Jim rose in greeting, until half out of his seat the mayor froze, awkward and embarrassed by his too-obvious arousal. Cheyenne chuckled, giving the mayor a quick peck on the cheek before greeting Cassie with a hug. Cassie and Cheyenne excused themselves and found a private table in the back of the restaurant.

"So, Cassie, what did you think of the debate?" Cheyenne tried to hide a grin behind her coffee cup.

"I thought you did pretty well last night. Held your own with the mayor. Made some good points about land use. But really, Cheyenne, was the sex joke really necessary?"

Cheyenne's grin spilled out from behind the rich French roast. "I wasn't sure about it last night, but I'm feeling pretty good after talking to the mayor this morning."

"Yeah?"

"Yeah. Big Jim thinks that Beverly is such a whack job that I come across pretty normal. He wants the sex issue to be this big thing that's never discussed openly, this thing always lurking in the background, making it unseemly for me to be the mayor. But he doesn't want it out in the open where people will be reminded who it is I like to fool around with."

"Is that why you had your hand on his thigh this morning? To remind everyone?"

Cheyenne put down her cup of coffee. "To tell you the truth, Cassie, I like teasing the man. Anyway, enough about the debates. Tell me about Andy MacTavish."

Cassie didn't know where to start. "He bought me a hot chocolate with mini-marshmallows. We talked."

"And?"

"And he's kind of dorky. His clothes. His hair. His music. It's like he's stuck in the 'fifties."

"And?"

"And he asked if he could call me."

Cheyenne heard a lilt in Cassie's voice she hadn't heard since Cassie buried her late husband Rob. "And?"

Cassie's face reddened. "If he calls, I think maybe I'm ready this time."

Waiting for a man to call was harder than Cassie remembered. She needed to call her editor and discuss a story idea, but suddenly she felt like she was fifteen again, afraid to tie up the phone line and miss a call from Andy. She felt foolish, but on Monday afternoon she placed a call to her editor and pitched a series of stories about New Jersey psychics. Morris jumped at the idea, pleased that his star writer was thinking of multiple stories. He accepted the idea without argument, asking Cassie if she could have the first installment ready by the end of the week. She spent the rest of the day at her computer, trying, without success, to write "The Psychic Bowling Ball of White Sands Beach." Cassie went to bed, Monday night, waiting for a phone call from Andy MacTavish.

On Tuesday, Cassie searched the Web, intending to look for links to psychic phenomena in New Jersey, but she found herself Googling Andy MacTavish instead. A page of links popped up on her computer screen, but the idea of reading up on Andy made her feel like a Peeping Tom. Without opening any of the links, Cassie exited the screen, reverting to her psychic search. She was directed to hundreds of thousands of hits and sampled a few, reading about levitation, ghosts, astral projection, psychic pets, prophecies, magic, mythology and secret societies. There was no way for Cassie to systematically sample the sites. She scrolled through page after page of search results, bypassing hundreds of links, waiting for…what? Cassie was confident she would recognize the site that she needed amongst the endless scroll. And she did. As she read about military applications of psychic phenomena, her story began to take shape. Three Web sites and two Jamesons later, Cassie logged off the Internet and began to write her newly retitled story.

The Psychic Spy Network

Tucked away in a small kiosk on the boardwalk here in White Sands Beach, dressed in her lime green polyester bowling shirt and pink capri pants, chain-smoking Pall Malls, manning the express lane to psychic assistance (twelve questions or less), Madame Alexina remembers the Cold War.

"I was in graduate school then. Nineteen seventy-one, I think. Yeah, 1971 and I was studying paranormal psychology. You know, ESP, astral projection, dream research, and stuff like that. Anyway, I was sitting in the psych lab one evening running data on an old-fashioned Wang calculator, trying to demonstrate the validity of the trance state and growing frustrated by the analysis of variance. It was getting pretty late—the place was empty, just me and a few lab rats— when I was approached by two suits. You know

the kind, crew cuts, and shiny black shoes. I wasn't really into drugs—shit, I was having out-of-body experiences without pot, but it was 1971, so I figured they were narcs."

But they weren't narcs. According to Madame Alexina, she was approached that night by the CIA and recruited for Project Stargate. At first I was skeptical, but now I've seen the documentation. The Russians were already developing remote spies; the CIA was determined to develop their own psychic spy network.

"That first night, when they tried to tell me about their research priorities, well, I just threw them out of the lab. Anyway, they gave me an encoded access pass and went on their way. It was months before I decided to give them a call."

If you believe Madame Alexina (and I do), she spent the next two decades fighting Communism as a remote spy for the CIA. We can only guess about the ways in which her psychic abilities were employed. Madame Alexina was understandably evasive when I asked about specific assignments, but she seems to have spent a good deal of time keeping watch from afar on Communist activity in Cuba and South America. Madame Alexina maintains that she has never left the country; my own research confirms that she has never applied for a passport. Still she has a detailed knowledge of persons and places in Chile and Nicaragua that cannot be found in any book. And she has way too much information regarding Castro's toilet habits.

According to Madame Alexina, she left the CIA sometime in 1992, worn thin by the strain of two decades of remote spying. The transition to civilian life was not easy for her. Her academic approach to psychic phenomena no longer held her interest and she had great difficulty holding on to a job. She worked briefly in the Atlantic City casinos, spying on card counters and cheats, but she left when she found herself rooting for the cheats to beat the casino. On at least two occasions that she can remember, Madame Alexina was the state's guest at the Greystone Psychiatric Hospital.

On September 11, 2001, Madame Alexina was in the day room at Greystone watching TV when a plane struck the first tower. On September 12, Madame Alexina was discharged. Today, she offers psychic advice (and sunscreen) to tourists in White Sands Beach. I asked her whether that was all she was doing, but Madame Alexina chose not to respond.

You be the judge.

Cassie e-mailed the story to her editor, poured herself a Jameson and water, and turned on the TV. Channel surfing, she sampled a fashion makeover and a reality wedding before stopping to watch Hepburn and Bogart navigating the rapids in *The African Queen*. Cassie allowed herself to wonder whether Andy MacTavish might be her Humphrey Bogart.

Inspired by her tale of psychic spying, Cassie found herself wishing she, too, had Madame Alexina's gift, but hard as she tried, Cassie could not look in on Andy MacTavish in his home in White Sands Beach. Tuesday night, Cassie went to bed and, again, Andy MacTavish did not call.

On Tuesday night, Cassie fell asleep thinking about Andy MacTavish, but her dream that night, as always, was of her late husband Rob. The details might change from night to night, but the dream never changed, nor did the result.

They were twenty. In her dreams, Cassie and Rob were always twenty. They were at the seacoast. Not the Jersey coast; they were picking their way along huge granite cliffs, ancient, geometric slabs of granite, Ice Age sculpture. The tide was coming in, and they were wet and cold, victims of the collision of tide and cliff. Time was coming in, decades pounding against the granite cliff.

They were twenty. In her dreams, Cassie and Rob were always twenty. They huddled behind the granite outcropping, hiding from time and tide, seeking shelter from the fierce ocean spray. Soaking wet, Cassie pulled off her sweatshirt and shorts, laying them out on the granite to dry.

They were twenty. In her dreams, Cassie and Rob were always twenty. Huddled together in a glacial cave, surrounded by ancient slabs of granite, the crash of ocean on rock obliterating the world beyond, Cassie and Rob made love. Secure in the confines of their private granite universe, they made love and fell asleep.

They were twenty. In her dreams, Cassie and Rob were always twenty. Asleep in the glacial cave, Cassie dreamt of children, of grandchildren, of great-grandchildren. Cassie dreamt of Grandpa Rob and Grandma Cassie. They were seventy. In her dreams, Cassie and Rob were always seventy.

Suddenly, in her dream-within-a-dream, a seventy-year-old Cassie flew into a rage, screaming at a Grandpa Rob that would never be. In her dream, a twenty-year-old Cassie, still sleeping, was pounding on her husband, her pain echoing in the closeness of the glacial cave. And in a condo in Doah, a thirty-something Cassie sat up suddenly in bed, shivering in a sweltering heat, bug-eyed, exhausted.

Cassie yearned for the morning that the sun would rise before she did.

Her First Official Date

Wednesday passed by in a blur. Cassie remembered just enough of the dream to be discomfited all day. She was teetering on the edge and unable to focus. She made a list of her reasons to be cranky, actually wrote out a list, stopping at reason number 342, finally giving in to the truth, unable to avoid the one reason she had refused to write, had refused even to think. It was Wednesday and, still, Andy MacTavish did not call.

When Wednesday, mercifully, drew to a close, Cassie prepared for bed, dreading the dream she knew was waiting for her just on the other side of consciousness. But the dream did not come. Cassie enjoyed an undisturbed night's sleep, was still sleeping soundly when her phone introduced her to morning.

She mumbled into the wrong end of the receiver. "Guh mawnin."

"Good morning, Cassie. I hope I didn't wake you."

"Hunnnh?" Cassie looked at the receiver and tried again. "Is that you... Andy?"

On a beautiful Thursday morning in September, the sun warming her face, the phone call warming her heart, Andy MacTavish phoned Cassie O'Malley and asked her out on a date.

Cassie had waited for years to care again about a date. She had waited for days wondering if he would call. After an uneventful night's sleep, she lay in bed Friday morning counting the hours until she could drive to White Sands Beach for her first official date with Andy MacTavish. He had offered to pick her up in Doah, but Cassie wanted to drive. She needed to know that, at any point in the evening, she could simply say good night and head home. Certainly, she had no intention of spending the night with Andy MacTavish. After ten years of waiting, she would not have a man think she was easy. According to Andy, they would be going to a minor league ball game. Cassie could not honestly attribute her excitement to baseball.

Andy MacTavish dated infrequently. He liked to tell himself that his business responsibilities kept him too busy for meaningful dating, but late at night, alone and lonely, he would allow himself to face the truth—his business success was not the cause of his difficulty getting dates, it was the result. Even now, he would gladly cut back on his wide-ranging business activities in exchange for a social life. It had taken Andy most of the week to prepare himself to call Cassie O'Malley. Sharing hot cocoa after a funeral was not the same as dating. She was beautiful. She was sophisticated. She was ever so slightly disreputable. She would not be interested in Andy MacTavish.

By Thursday, Andy had run out of excuses to not call. And when he did call, she said yes. She said yes. And then suddenly, it was Friday evening, and they were meeting at the ballpark.

Cassie and Andy had agreed to meet at the main gate half an hour before game time. Driving down from Doah, Cassie knew she was going to be late; still, she took the back roads, enjoying the drive through the Barrens, Freddie Hubbard on trumpet, Hubert Laws on flute, enjoying especially the evening's sweet anticipation. When she arrived at the ballpark, Andy was waiting out front, chatting with the ticket takers. It was Cassie's first visit to the cozy brick ballpark; immediately she felt at home. The ticket takers greeted her warmly; as they walked to their seats, Cassie noticed that everyone at the ballpark, the ushers, the vendors, all the personnel, stopped to say hello as Andy hustled them to their seats.

The Sand Skeeters played ball in a 7,200-seat bandbox. Every seat was a good seat, close to the players, but some seats were better than others. Cassie was startled when Andy directed her to the best seats in the ballpark, the owner's luxury suite.

"Are you friends with the owner?" Cassie was curious.

Andy reddened. "I'm sorry. I thought you knew."

He didn't know what else to say, so he took the opportunity to offer Cassie a brief history of minor league baseball in New Jersey.

"When the Thunder relocated from London, Canada, to Trenton in 1994, the conventional wisdom was that minor league baseball would not succeed in New Jersey. This, despite a history of minor league teams in New Jersey, which extends back for more than a century. Even the casual fan is familiar with the storied Newark Bears whose 1937 team may have been the greatest minor league team ever. The experts all said that the small town appeal of minor league ball would not take hold again in New

Jersey, where south Jersey fans can follow the Phillies and north Jersey fans root for the Yankees or the Mets." Andy gulped for air. "I'm sorry. I hope I'm not boring you with all this."

Cassie was touched by Andy's enthusiasm for minor league baseball. When she fell in love with Rob, she had been attracted to him by the things they shared—their love for jazz, for sports cars, for power politics. With Andy, what she found attractive was how easily he allowed her access to new loves. What she found attractive was the melody in his voice. "No, please. Go on."

"Conventional wisdom said that minor league baseball would not survive, but try to tell that to the Thunder, or the Bears, the Jackals or the Cardinals, the Atlantic City Surf, Lakewood Blue Claws, Camden Riversharks or our own White Sand Skeeters.

"The name pays homage to the Jersey City Skeeters," Andy explained. "Believe it or not, the Jersey City team was named after mosquitoes. Apparently mosquitoes were a problem in Jersey City a hundred years ago. I guess some things never do really change. But the 1903 Skeeters were a great team, one of the best teams in the history of minor league ball."

In the top of the second, the Skeeters' shortstop misplayed a relay, allowing the first run of the ball game. In the bottom of the inning, the Skeeters strung together three consecutive doubles to take a two-one lead in the ball game. Cassie was enjoying the game, but even more, the activity between innings.

Pointing toward the field, Cassie wondered, "What's that?"

Andy chuckled. "That's our mascot, Skeeter. Watch this."

Three youngsters were called down from the stands to race against the mascot. Rounding the bases, Skeeter had a big lead, until, mugging for the fans, he tripped over third. Falling down hard, he was passed by two of the young fans. As he got back to his feet, Skeeter lost his balance, falling again, allowing the youngest of the racers to pass him by and sprint for home. The crowd roared its approval. All three children were crowned "Skeeter Beaters" and given official Sand Skeeter jerseys. Cassie cheered the three young fans and applauded Skeeter's losing effort. "This is fun."

Two innings later, Skeeter was back. "What's a dizzy bat race?" Cassie wanted to know.

"Watch."

Skeeter and a well-endowed female fan, chosen at random, were lining up near home plate. Standing a baseball bat vertically, with one end on the ground, they each bent over their bat, gripped the barrel with both hands, foreheads pressed against the knob end. On command, the two combatants began to spin in circles, the crowd laughing and cheering. Again, on command, they dropped their bats and tried to run a short course along the first base line. Dizzy from spinning, neither Skeeter nor his competitor could maintain a straight path. As the female fan weaved erratically along the foul line, Skeeter staggered out to the pitching mound before collapsing in a heap. In a mock show of concern, the trainer ran out to check on the mascot. After a tense moment, Skeeter struggled to his feet, waved to the crowd and congratulated the winner. Cassie howled in delight. "That looks like fun."

Andy had an idea. "Maybe next time, we'll pick you for the dizzy bat race."

Cassie was pleased to know that Andy was already thinking about a next time. "Maybe."

On Cassie's first date with Andy MacTavish, he took her to watch the Skeeters play baseball. Cassie knew surprisingly little about minor league baseball, but she was confident she would learn a good deal more if she continued to date the principal owner of the White Sand Skeeters.

The Skeeters lost the game that night, four to two, giving up a three-run home run in the ninth inning, but no one seemed particularly upset, not the fans, not Cassie. Even Andy seemed to take the loss in stride.

Andy and Cassie sat in the luxury suite, sipping coffee. Neither of them was ready for the evening to end, but neither were they prepared for the evening to continue. After an awkward pause, Andy invited Cassie to return for the final home game the following weekend. She quickly accepted.

As Andy walked her to her car, a young girl (Cassie sized her up, pegging her as twenty—pretty, but too young to be competition) stopped them for a moment.

"Tough loss tonight, Mr. MacTavish."

"Yes, but still, it was a very nice night."

"I guess. Anyway, good night, Mr. MacTavish."

"Good night, Donna."

As they continued on toward her car, Cassie was curious. "Who was that?"

"I'm sorry, Cassie. I didn't mean to be rude. That's Skeeter."

Midnight Birding

It was nearly midnight when Donna got back to her garden apartment. She was tired and achy from one too many dizzy bat races, grimy from one too many nights inside the mosquito costume. Still, her night was not yet done. She was supposed to meet Billy, who would already be down at the Point, midnight birding.

Donna took a quick shower, shimmied into her tightest size-six jeans and t-shirt, grabbed her iPod and a pint of peppermint schnapps and jumped back in her Miata. She had been skeptical when Billy first invited her to midnight birding, figuring it was just an excuse to suck face, alone in the salt marsh after dark. It turned out that midnight birding was not an excuse to suck face, but it was an opportunity, and she thought Billy was cute, so Donna had seized that opportunity.

Midnight birding had become their regular Friday night date. Driving down to the Point, Donna looked forward to the drinking and the sex, but also to the long periods of almost spiritual waiting, the long hours in the dark listening for the bird calls of the nocturnal migration.

Pulling into the parking lot, Donna recognized Billy's car and Heather's, and three or four more cars belonging to the midnight birders. There was an ancient VW minibus, with its expanding universe of rust overwhelming the original lime green paint job, Buddhist bumper stickers attached like surgical strips to the scarred side panels, offering commonsense advice and spiritual guidance (It is better to be pissed off than pissed on) and each one advertising the grand opening of the van owner's psychic superstore (Om Depot). There was a yellow taxicab, a Rambler, even older than the VW bus, sporting its own brand of bumper sticker wisdom, a short course in American political history (No one wins a nuclear war). The midnight birders were not well-liked by the birder establishment, who saw late-night birding as a threat to their more organized, better-regulated events.

Donna, especially, was disliked by the regular birders who considered her employment with the Sand Skeeters as a betrayal of sorts. When the proposal to build the ballpark had been before the council, most of the birders were opposed to its construction, maintaining that the ballpark would disturb the habitat of migratory waterfowl. The birders were not the only group that opposed the ballpark, but they were the most vocal. It seemed to Donna that the birders' real complaint was that the ballpark would disrupt their bird watching, rather than cause any real disturbance to the birds themselves. It was not an unimportant argument, Donna concluded, but hardly the same thing. Donna kept her opinions to herself, but when she applied for a job with the Skeeters, ultimately becoming Skeeter, the very embodiment of the team, the regular birders roundly disapproved. She was especially pleased to see her friend Heather's car parked at the Point. Heather, like Donna, was more of a party-birder.

Donna took the short path through the high grass to the platform in the marsh. She stopped to say hello to the spiritualist and the cabbie, but Madame Alexina and Spit were deep in conversation. Donna found it nearly impossible to follow as their discussion moved from WMDs to spider holes to judicial appointments to political action committees and back again to WMDs, all without taking a breath. Political analysis and peppermint schnapps were a poor mix.

Donna continued moving, spotting Heather and Billy nearly hidden in the high grass, sharing a blunt. Giving Billy a kiss hello, she drew in musky Billy scent, mixed with the pot and just a hint of Heather. If Billy felt any guilt about messing around in the marsh with Heather while he was waiting for Donna's arrival, he was not going to let it become a problem. He told himself if he was patient, he would soon be making time with both ladies. Donna took a hit off the joint and offered Heather the peppermint schnapps. Taking a long drink, Heather announced she was going back to her car to get more pot.

Billy, wearing a Rob Zombie t-shirt and cut-off jeans, his spiked hair tipped in green, was embarrassed by his fascination with birding and found, in nocturnal birding, a strategic accommodation. Middle America could identify birds by the light of day; it took a truly warped mind to spend the night alone in the salt marsh, or in the bayberry thicket, listening for the call of migratory birds. And it took a freakin' genius to parlay that midnight obsession into sex with Donna and maybe, before long, Heather too.

"C'mon, Billy, I'm exhausted. Let's just tell Heather we're splitting. Okay?"

Before Billy had a chance to respond, Heather came back up the path. Still Billy slipped Donna a glance as if to say, "Don't get jealous, Donna. You know you're my girl." Then he turned his attention to Heather, who was adjusting her bra strap for his benefit.

Reassured as to Billy's intentions, Donna announced that she needed to find a place to pee. She was barely out of range when Heather rubbed up against Billy.

Billy rolled another joint and passed it to Heather. Looking past the joint in his hand, Heather's gaze was fixed on another threatening to peek out of his cut-offs. Donna, returning quickly, still fixing her belt buckle, stepped between Billy and Heather.

Twee-twee-twee. Billy turned away from both girls to listen. "Do you hear that ladies. Yellow-rumped warblers. Cool, huh?"

Donna adjusted her belt. "Huh?"

"Yellow-rumped warblers."

"That's great, Billy. Can we go now?"

Heather poured herself another shot of peppermint schnapps, toasting the warblers. "Yeah, let's go to the diner." It was nearly morning, but the yellow-rumped warblers had changed Billy's plans. "Why don't you guys go on without me? I'll catch up." Donna, her arms now around Billy, gave him a kiss. "You really are a strange one, Billy MacTavish. Don't be long."

Donna and Heather sat at their regular booth at the diner. Donna ordered corned beef hash, eggs over easy, and Heather had a short stack of chocolate chip pancakes. Between bites, they talked about a lot of stuff, but mostly about Billy.

Heather was curious about Donna's relationship with Billy. "Billy told me you guys are going to the White Stripes concert."

"Yeah, I guess so. I don't know. I'm supposed to work Friday."

"So take the day off. No big whoop."

Donna's radar picked up the signal. "I don't know. It's the last game of the season. Everyone expects me to be there."

"C'mon, Donna. Get real. You run around in a mosquito costume."

"Yeah, I know it's lame, but it's what I do. Besides, Mr. MacTavish has been real good to me."

Heather was surprised by the formality. "You call him Mr. MacTavish?"

"He's my boss."

"Yeah? So? You're going out with his brother."

Donna tried to explain her work ethic to Heather. "Exactly. I don't want anyone saying I get special treatment." Donna reached across the table, spearing a bite of chocolate chip pancake. "Thanks."

Heather pondered the complexity of family relationships. "Billy and his brother don't have much in common, do they?"

"Well, there's a fifteen-year difference in their age. Mr. MacTavish, he's like your father."

"No way."

"Way."

"You and Billy look good together. When'd he do his tips?"

"Last week. I told him purple, but the green looks all right, don't you think?"

Heather thought Billy looked real cute. "If you decide you have to work, is it okay if I use your ticket?"

Heather pushed her pancakes around the plate. Donna picked at her eggs.

Once Upon a Time

Driving home to Doah, her first date with Andy MacTavish officially in the record books, Cassie could still feel the soft tug of his lips on her lips, the sweet taste of life rediscovered. She felt foolish, alone in the car, reciting the platitudes of new love, her life changed completely at a minor league baseball game.

On a back road in the Pine Barrens, sometime after midnight, Cassie remembered a joke her father used to tell.

"How do you pronounce M-a-c-H-e-n-r-y?"

"MacHenry."

"How do you pronounce M-a-c-D-o-n-a-l-d?"

"MacDonald."

"How do you pronounce M-a-c-T-a-v-i-s-h?"

"MacTavish."

"How do you pronounce M-a-c-h-i-n-e?"

The very air in the car reminded her of Andy MacTavish.

It was well past midnight when Cassie let herself into the condo, her answering machine beeping a friendly hello. She turned off the machine without bothering to retrieve the message. It would be Cheyenne checking in, wanting the latest gossip from White Sands Beach. Cassie wasn't ready to talk about her date, even with Cheyenne. Instead, she brewed herself a pot of chamomile tea and pulled out a photo album.

It had been quite some time since Cassie had allowed herself to look at the old photos. Rob playing tennis; Rob on skis; the vacation in Vermont; Rob in his sports car, tanned and fit; the both of them at Princeton graduation, beaming, ready to take on the world; Rob in law school, buried behind his books; the apartment in D.C., Rob smiling for the camera. But his eyes, in all the photos Cassie could see the look in his eyes, or rather the look Rob tried to keep hidden behind his eyes: the fear of going to sleep, the night terrors. She was so young then, too young to be married, much too young to be widowed. Once upon a time everything was possible. And then nothing.

It was time to let go of the guilt, to allow herself another chance to be happy. It was time to fall in love again. That night Cassie dreamt she played third base for the Jersey City Skeeters. With a runner on third and one out, Cassie was alert for the suicide squeeze, when she was distracted by a ringing in her ear. As play continued, the manager walked toward her at third, carrying a telephone. "It's for you," he explained, but the ringing continued. Cassie tried to stay focused on the batter, on Roosevelt Stadium, on Jersey City, on the race for the Eastern League Championship, but gradually it all slipped away, replaced by her own familiar bedroom.

She answered the phone. "Hello?"

"Hi, Cassie." With Cheyenne's cheerful greeting, Cassie was fully awake. "How was Andy MacTavish?"

"It's all good."

"Details, girl, I need details."

Cassie shared enough of the story to keep Cheyenne at bay before changing the subject. "What's happening in the campaign?"

"Oh wow, Cassie. Last night, I spoke at a meeting of the Friends of the Library and I opened with, listen to this—'Did you hear the one about the traveling salesman and the developer's daughter?'—not the whole joke, mind you, just that line, and most of the audience responded warmly. I'm starting to believe I might actually win this thing."

Cassie gave that some thought before asking, "Do you want to?"

"Maybe. It's not that simple. You know who else asked me that, just last night?" Cheyenne paused for effect. "Rocki."

"Mrs. Big Jim? She came to your event?"

"Yeah, how cool is that? After the meeting, she asked me if I was serious. Asked me to get out of the race, if I was just in it for show. For all the BS he's put her through, she still loves her husband." Cheyenne thought for a moment. "She's okay."

Cassie knew Rocki from when Rocki was a suspect in the death of a lover. "I guess I never saw her at her best."

"I guess."

Cassie suddenly remembered the phone call of the previous night. "Anyway, Cheyenne, I'm sorry I didn't call you back last night. It was late and I was tired."

Cheyenne was startled. "Sorry, girlfriend. If you got a call last night, it wasn't me."

Cassie barely had time to hang up the phone before it began to ring again.

"Hi, Cassie." Her editor, as usual, preferred to be nameless. "I read your piece about psychic espionage. Great story, Cassie. Really awesome."

"Thanks."

"I'm gonna revamp the whole next edition. 'New Jersey remembers the Cold War.' Bomb shelters, air raid drills. Did you know that 'the button' was made in New Jersey?"

"Really?"

"Does it matter?"

"Morris, did you try to call me last night?"

"Me, no. Anyway, I've assigned one of our new writers to work up some stuff to wrap around your piece, but if you've got any more Cold War stories, I want to see them ASAP. Gotta run. You're the best."

Cassie acted quickly, before the phone could ring a third time, retrieving the deleted message from the previous night.

"Hi, Cassie. I wanted to make sure you got home all right." Andy coughed. "And to tell you how much fun I had."

Once upon a time everything was possible. Again.

Work in Progress

"So, sweetheart … what've you got?" Cassie chuckled. Her editor was always looking for more. "I've got an idea. It's not what you asked for, but it is a war story." "Is it good?" was all her editor really wanted to know, "And is it ready?" "Yes. And no. Gimme a break, Morris." Her editor knew that she hated to send him anything before she had a chance to polish every word.

"Look, I need it fast. Can you send me the draft?" Cassie hung up the phone without answering. Morris would have to wait until she was satisfied with the piece. Pouring herself a drink of Tullamore Dew, she looked at the work in progress.

The Mosquito Capital of New Jersey

The honeybee celebrates its thirtieth anniversary as New Jersey's official state insect, Cassie read, and yet this event passes virtually unnoticed. No parades. No banner headlines. No proclamations. Just a small gathering of aging bees meeting in a run-down lodge hall near the parkway, a keg of lo-carb mead, getting buzzed, remembering the good old days when Governor Byrne had invited them down to the statehouse for the signing of A-671.

The honeybee may hold the title, but another insect can surely lay claim to being the people's champion. And so, let us devote a moment to this other insect, the unofficial insect, the insect that sits atop the New Jersey food chain, the insect that myths are made of—the mosquito!

Imagine a simpler time here in the Garden State, a time before safety warnings, before health risks, before car seats, before cancer, a time when generations of happy children pedaled furiously down the street, inhaling deeply, enveloped by the fog of industrial-strength insecticide, the sweet narcotic of the municipal mosquito spray.

If the mosquito is the unofficial state insect, then the mosquito capital is most assuredly Jersey City. One hundred years ago, Jersey City honored its hordes of marauding mosquitoes, naming its minor league baseball team the Jersey City Skeeters. Mosquitoes were so prevalent in Jersey City that they were implicated by the Germans in the attack on Black Tom Island at the start of the First World War.

If you don't believe the story that I am about to tell you, just visit Liberty State Park and look for the Circle of Flags.

Once upon a time, Black Tom Island occupied a spot in the waters between Jersey City and New York City. In 1916, before the U.S. entered the war, Black Tom Island served as a top-secret munitions depot, storing war materiel for shipment to England. Early on the morning of July 31, the island exploded, shock waves from the explosion causing damage to the Statue of Liberty, and panic in New York as well as New Jersey. Eventually we learned that the explosion was the result of German saboteurs.

We should not be surprised that the Germans, when confronted with the evidence, denied any role in the explosion. What may come as something as a surprise to those of you who are not familiar with the story of Black Tom Island is the alternate theory of the crime offered by the Germans.

The German defense? Not us, they insisted. And who did they suggest was the real culprit? That's right, mosquitoes.

Cassie sipped her Irish whiskey and smiled, pleased with her unfinished story, anticipating her editor's all-too-predictable response.

Every Night that Week

The telephone lines hummed all week in Doah and in White Sands Beach, long conversations and brief messages traveling back and forth between Cassie and Cheyenne, Cassie and Morris, Donna and Billy, Donna and Heather, Heather and Billy, Billy and Andy, Cassie and Andy, telephone calls exploring questions of mayoral politics, Cold War incidents and oddities, concert tickets, minor league baseball, loyalties and love…

Cheyenne was feeling the excitement of her mayoral campaign. "The experts say you've got to put your own negatives out there for the voters to see. That way, you control the message."

Cassie was skeptical. "Well, did you hear the one about the traveling salesman and the developer's daughter? It definitely puts your negatives right out front."

"It's branding, Cassie. Its sound bites. And it makes the mayor look bad if he attacks me."

Morris was feeling the excitement of a special Cold War edition. "The research is turning up great story ideas. Radiation exposure and nuclear accidents. Abandoned missile silos. Fluoridation. It's all about the Russians and it all happened right here in New Jersey. I read your mosquito thing. It's cute, but you're cheating the reader. I need to feel the shock waves jumping off the page. Gimme more explosions. Call me."

Billy was psyched about the White Stripes. "C'mon, Donna. You're not gonna miss the concert for the friggin' Sand Skeeters? Be real."

Donna was tired of repeating herself. "Listen to me, Billy. It's my job. Maybe if you had a job, you'd understand."

"What I understand is I got two tickets for Friday night. What I understand is maybe I'm dating the wrong girl."

"Maybe you are."

Heather was unsympathetic. "You know, Donna, maybe Billy is right. I can't believe you're even thinking about going to work Friday night. There must be someone else who can be the mosquito."

"It's not 'the mosquito.' It's Skeeter. I'm Skeeter."

"Look, I'm your friend so I can tell you this."

"Tell me what?"

"You're effing nuts."

Heather was sympathetic. "I know what you mean, Billy. If it was me, well, you understand. Look, why don't you just call your brother. Tell him Donna can't work Friday."

When Andy answered the phone, he was startled to hear Billy's voice. It had been months since they last talked. Andy would not get sucked into another argument. "Billy, is everything okay?"

"Yeah, fine. Listen, Andy, I need a favor."

"What is it this time, Billy, money?"

"No, nothing like that. You know I'm dating the mascot, right?"

Andy cringed. "She's got a name, Billy."

"Yeah, yeah. Look, cut me a break. She wants to take off Friday, but she's afraid to ask. Do me a solid, okay?"

Andy knew better than to believe his younger brother. If Donna even suspected that Billy had called, she'd be furious. "Billy, I will do you a 'solid,' as you put it. I'll forget you ever asked me."

"You know something, big brother? After all this time, you're still an a-hole."

Andy hung up the phone before responding. "And you, little brother, still don't get it."

Every night that week, as Cassie was getting ready for bed, the phone would ring. "How was your day?" And they would talk on the phone for hours.

Cassie was amazed by the range of Andy's knowledge. She would make a comment about Cold War radiation risks and Andy would direct her to look into workers' compensation claims involving exposure to beryllium. She would ask his opinion of Cheyenne's campaign strategy and he would respond with the history and philosophy of traveling salesman jokes. And if they didn't feel like talking, still they would stay on the phone, until Cassie, unable to keep her eyes open, would say good night. Sometimes, it seemed to Andy that Cassie would fall asleep on the phone, but he didn't really mind. "Good night, Cassie." And he would put the receiver gently in its cradle.

Friday night's ball game would close out the inaugural season of Sand

Skeeter baseball. It had been a successful effort, Andy concluded, mentally reviewing the ledger. There had been the unpleasantness at the beginning when certain local groups opposed the proposal. Some of the bed-and-breakfast types had complained that the ballpark would attract the wrong type of tourist business. The birders raised concerns about migratory waterfowl. The birders, Andy realized, were an especially vicious adversary, going so far as to recruit his little brother Billy to speak out against the team. But most of the citizens of White Sands Beach embraced the Skeeters. Attendance had been better than expected. The team was turning a profit in their first full year of operation. If the Skeeters could win their final game, they would finish the season with a winning record.

It was hot and dry by mid-morning, with record temperatures predicted for game time. Everyone was busy, the grounds crew trimming grass and painting lines, vendors checking inventories, food service arranging delivery of extra bottled water, ballplayers in the weight room, or getting wrapped, or in the clubhouse playing cards, ticket sellers doing a brisk business all afternoon at the walk-up windows. Andy MacTavish was busy planning his date with Cassie O'Malley.

When Cassie pulled into the parking lot, there was still one hour until game time. It was hot and getting hotter. Andy suggested a walk on the boardwalk.

"But don't you have things you have to do at the ballpark?"

"I'm the boss. I don't do anything."

Cassie and Andy strolled arm in arm on the boardwalk, sharing a black raspberry ice cream cone, scanning offshore, watching for dolphins.

"There's one."

"Where?"

"There." Cassie pointed down the beach.

"I don't see it. Whoa. Check it out, Cassie." Andy had spotted not one, but a pod of dolphins, their fins breaking the surface, shimmering in the late afternoon sun.

Cassie debated asking Andy if they could get their fortune read, but as they approached Madame Alexina's boardwalk kiosk, the neon eyeball was dark. Instead Cassie challenged Andy to a game of Skee-Ball. She proceeded to beat Andy three games in a row, outpointing him in the third game by a score of 340 to 210.

Cassie gave Andy a kiss. "Maybe we better head back to the ballpark."

By the time they returned, the game was two innings old. The Sand Skeeters were down by a run and Skeeter was rounding second, heading for third, two young fans circling the bases in hot pursuit. Andy was pleased, but not surprised to see that Donna had put her job ahead of the rock concert. Cassie was delighted by Skeeter's antics, tripping over third base, the elaborate display of disequilibrium, everyone at the ballpark hot and sweaty and thoroughly enjoying the evening of minor league entertainment.

Three innings later, Skeeter was back for the dizzy bat race.

"Will the fan holding the ticket marked Section one-oh-eight, Row B, seat three, please come down to the infield," intoned the public address system, but no one came down to challenge Skeeter.

"Please check your tickets. Section one-oh-eight, Row B, seat three."

Andy checked his pockets. "What's this?" and he pulled out a ticket. Smiling broadly, he offered the stub to Cassie.

And so it came to pass, on a hot September night, Cassie O'Malley challenged Skeeter to the last dizzy bat race in Sand Skeeter history.

Bending over, Cassie rested her forehead on the knob of the aluminum bat, surprised by the spot of cool in the otherwise sweltering evening heat. Sneaking a peek at Skeeter, she prepared to spin. Cassie did not like to lose, not at life, not at love, not at Skee-Ball, not at dizzy bat racing.

On command, she began to spin, not too fast, not too slow, but just right to build up momentum for the race up the first base line. "You can do it," she told herself. "Just don't fall down," she counseled. As Cassie weaved toward first, she didn't see Skeeter as he staggered out to the pitcher's mound, falling in a heap, in mock exhaustion.

On cue, the team trainer ran out to the mound to check on the prostrate mascot. On cue, the trainer fanned Skeeter, waiting for his revival. On cue, the trainer waited. And waited. And waited. The crowd sensed the problem, just before the trainer looked back at the dugout, frantic now, yelling for assistance. Grabbing at the costume, he pulled off the mosquito head, but he had waited too long. Inside the costume, on a night of near-record temperatures, Skeeter was dead of heat stroke.

Five thousand fans watched in silence. In the owner's suite, Andy was speechless.

Somewhere near first base, dizzy and disoriented, Cassie tried to follow the events as they were unfolding on the infield. And on the pitcher's mound, bent over the mascot's body, the trainer desperately tried to revive

Skeeter, too shocked by the tragic accident to fully comprehend what he saw. The dead woman on the pitcher's mound was not Donna.

The Woman Who Would Be Skeeter

No one at the ballpark was able to identify the body of the dead woman who would be Skeeter. The first-aid squad responded quickly, followed shortly by the medical examiner and the local police. Medical personnel agreed with the trainer's preliminary determination of heat stroke.

The dead woman carried no identification, but the detectives were confident they would trace her car key back to an identity. No one in the ballpark knew what to do. The game, of course, was halted. Fans milled about in the stands, unsure whether they were supposed to stay, whether they were allowed to stay. Gradually the stadium emptied as the police interviewed anyone who might be helpful. Despite the announced attendance of more than 5,000 fans, the list of helpfuls was exceedingly brief. Notwithstanding her role in the dizzy bat tragedy, Cassie explained to an officer that she had little of value to contribute.

Andy was surrounded by Skeeter management and staff, by police and by fans. Young fans, in particular, were stunned by the events unfolding on the infield. Andy was desperately trying to manage the tragedy and was already fielding telephone calls from local news outlets when he spotted Cassie standing quietly on the infield grass, alone amidst the chaos. Excusing himself, Andy made his way down to Cassie.

"Are you all right?"

"I guess."

"Look, Cassie, I'm going to be here for hours. I'm sorry."

"I'll wait. Do you know who she is?"

"No."

"I'll wait."

A patrolman marched through the parking lot carrying the dead woman's car key like a dowsing stick, pressing the panic button, searching, heading up one aisle and down the next and waiting for her car to respond. Suddenly a yellow Matrix one aisle over came to life, its lights flashing as its horn began to honk. Checking in the glove box, the patrolman quickly located the vehicle registration and hurried back to inform his superiors that the dead woman's car was registered in the name of Heather Dean.

The name attached itself to the dead body like a toe tag, establishing a name, but not an identity. Andy explained again to the detective that he did not know the woman and that she most definitely was not an employee of the Sand Skeeters. But when the detective wondered where the regular Skeeter might be, Andy realized he knew more than he was ready to admit. Andy simply offered to check the personnel files for Donna's address and telephone number.

It was nearly three in the morning when Andy finally escorted the assorted officials to the exit, said good night to the employees and returned the phone messages that could not be put off. What he could not do was locate Cassie. Too tired to hunt, Andy went to the public address system. "Would Cassie O'Malley please report to the owner's box? Cassie O'Malley to the owner's box, please."

"I'm sorry, Cassie. This isn't how I imagined the evening."

"You must be exhausted, Andy."

"I guess. I'm too tired to gauge how tired I really am."

Cassie was glad she waited. "C'mon, Andy. I'll drive you home."

Andy wanted to tell Cassie it was unnecessary. He was embarrassed that she had been witness to the evening's tragic events. He searched for the words that would gracefully say no. The words he discovered, however, were "Thank you, yes."

They rode in silence to Andy's beachfront home, Cassie unsure of what to say and Andy limiting his remarks to comments such as "turn right at the stop sign" and "follow this road until it dead-ends at the water."

So Cassie drove in silence and followed the road until they arrived at the dead end. Andy's house was a modest bungalow of weathered wood and glass, a comfortable house, a private house, but with a truly spectacular view. Sitting on a narrow spit of land that jutted out into the water, Andy's home was built on a stone block retaining wall, surrounded on three sides by the Atlantic Ocean.

"Nice." Cassie hardly knew what to say.

Andy smiled. "Let me show you the inside." And he gave her a quick tour.

Inside, Andy's home was simple, yet chic, clean, yet lived in, a home for walking barefoot, tracking sand, for sinking into overstuffed sofas, reading a good murder mystery, staring at the ocean and listening to Andy's extensive collection of 45s on his mint-condition Wurlitzer jukebox.

His office was decorated in doo-wop revival, outfitted in Formica and steel, with a splash of color and retro-modern furniture, his computer neatly disguised inside a circa 1952 Dumont black-and-white floor-model television.

"I still need to make a few phone calls."

In her bare feet, in Andy's bungalow, soaking in the doo-wop and salt air, Cassie had briefly forgotten. "It's three in the morning, Andy. Are you sure it can't wait?"

"I'm sorry, Cassie, but a woman died at the game tonight, standing on the pitcher's mound, dressed like Skeeter. Why don't you get some rest?"

It was nearly fifteen years since Cassie had slept with a man. At first, when Rob died, it was a simple promise she made to herself. Then for the longest time, it was just her routine, what she did (or more to the point, what she didn't do). In the last few years, habit had morphed into a crisis of confidence. After so many years in her half-empty bed, Cassie had come to doubt that she could still please a man. But now, finally, Cassie was ready to find out. Only she still was unsure of Andy's intentions.

Andy sensed her uncertainty. "I'll try not to be too long." Andy kissed her and, for that moment, Cassie knew that Andy was fully in the moment, no dead body, no Sand Skeeters, no phone calls, no doowop, just a man and a woman and a kiss.

"Is it okay if I take a shower while you're on the phone?"

"Of course." Andy got her a bath towel and robe. "You'll need something clean to wear." And he found several t-shirts for Cassie to try.

"The hot water is tricky." Andy helped adjust the temperature and kissed her again.

Cassie smiled. "I'll wait up."

Andy went off to make his phone calls. Disrobing, Cassie marveled at how comfortable she felt, standing naked in a man's bathroom. She examined herself in the mirror and, for a change, saw nothing to critique, not the five extra pounds, not the lingering sunburn on her cheekbones, not her cuticles, or her hips.

Cassie allowed the hot water to rain down on her, picturing Andy in his office on the telephone, picturing Andy in the bedroom, on…Drying off, she tried on the t-shirts. She looked sexy, Cassie decided, in the doo-wop revival T, the logo accentuating her chest, the t-shirt long enough to wear as a nightshirt, but just barely.

Andy was still in his office, on the phone, but Cassie made sure that he noticed her as she padded down the hall, heading for bed. Covering the mouthpiece with the palm of his hand, Andy turned to Cassie. "I'll be off in a minute. You look wonderful."

Cassie marveled at how comfortable she felt, wearing nothing but a t-shirt, in Andy's bedroom, under the goose-down comforter, Andy's bed not half-empty, but suddenly, half-full. She closed her eyes and rested, waiting for Andy to join her, waiting for Andy to …

And then, warm and comfortable, cozy and sexy, and exhausted, Cassie fell asleep.

There is something about the hour before the sun comes up. For a decade and more, the pre-dawn hour had been a time for Cassie to leave her bed and explore the back roads of rural Doah Township. Now she slept, soundly, deeply, peacefully, her breathing synched to the gentle rhythm of the Atlantic surf outside the window.

When Andy finally finished making his phone calls, he put aside the mystery of death and turned his attention to the glorious mystery of life that was quietly snoring on his side of the bed. He would not wake her; she was exhausted by the events of the day. Andy MacTavish stripped down to his boxer shorts and climbed into the available side of the bed (like he was sitting in the visitors' dugout at Sand Skeeter Park). He, too, was exhausted, but Andy sat up in bed, staring at the beautiful woman asleep at his side, looking at the way her cheekbone, red from sun, rested against his pillow, the way her dirty-blond hair, unrestrained, advanced across the bed, the way her body curled under the comforter, the curve of her hip, of her chest, the way her presence revealed new color and texture in his bed linens, the way she forever changed his doo-wop revival t-shirt. While Cassie slept, Andy breathed her in, the air in his bedroom suddenly fresher, sweeter, with hints of berry and vanilla.

By the time she awoke, the tide had come in, the sun had climbed high in the sky and Andy MacTavish was unabashedly in love with Cassie O'Malley. She rolled over in bed, more asleep than awake, out of the habit of sharing a bed, bumping into Andy's manhood.

"Ummmm." Cassie reached out and took him by hand.

Cassie was afloat in the Atlantic, riding the waves, bodysurfing. Bouncing up and down in the swells, she waited patiently for her wave. At just the right moment, Cassie caught the perfect wave and rode it to shore, rode the wave hard, until it crashed against the shore and she lay spent in the warm sand.

They cuddled in Andy's bed, feeling no urge to venture beyond the boundaries of this private world they had just discovered. When the telephone rang, Andy made no move, allowing the machine to answer. "It's me. Pick up. Holy shit, Andy. Pick up."

Cassie looked at Andy, saying nothing and handing him the phone.

"Billy? Where are you?"

"Uh…Ocean City, I think."

"I thought you were going … hell, it doesn't matter. Is Donna with you?"

"We had a fight."

"Is that a no?"

"Yeah, that's a no. I haven't seen her since yesterday afternoon."

Andy knew better than to trust his little brother. "So you don't know anything about what happened last night?"

Long Board Trunks and Green-Tipped Hair

Billy knew better than to share the details of his day with his older brother Andy. He knew that Andy thought he was selfish. Andy thought he was immature. If he told Andy about the previous twenty-four hours, Andy would think he was whining. And Andy would be right.

The day had started poorly and it had started poorly early with an urgent banging on the door.

"You shoulda been there last night, Billy, you shoulda been there." Spit was standing in the doorway, all nervous energy and caffeine-rush. "We were out there last night, listening for warblers, you know, man, just minding our own business, and she showed up." Standing behind Spit, Madame Alexina tried her best to be invisible.

A hangover had rented all the rooms that morning in Billy's cerebral cortex. A no-vacancy sign hung at the entrance to his frontal lobe, but Spit dumped his luggage on Billy's aching brainstem and barged right in.

"The bird Nazi showed up. We don't belong there…we're giving legitimate birders a bad name…we're…shit, you've heard her rap. Anyway…"

Billy put a hand on Spit's shoulder. "Easy, big man. Look, let's not do this in the doorway. C'mon in."

Spit rushed by him, bouncing from foot to foot. "Thanks, Billy. I got to hit the can."

Billy used the potty break to clear his head, but when Spit returned, so did the headache. Billy summed up what he had learned so far. "So you went out last night midnight birding and someone gave you a hard time, huh? Who was it, Spit?"

Spit's bouncing had subsided. "You know the lady. The one with a broomstick up her butt. The one thinks her birdshit don't stink."

Billy knew the one. "Red hair. Looks like she was born middle-aged? Right?"

Spit was nodding, a bobble-head birder. "Yeah. Ms….damn…what's her name?"

Madame Alexina smiled. "Patterson, Spit. Her name's Mrs. Patterson."

Satisfied that he had passed along the crucial information, Spit relaxed. "You look like shit, Billy."

Billy did his best to remember what he'd been up to. "Tequila."

"Yeah. That'll do it." Spit stroked his chin. "I know what you need." And with that, he jumped up, pulling bottles and cartons, seemingly at random, from Billy's refrigerator.

"I learned this in Iraq. It's called … damn, I used to know what it was called …" Spit proceeded to mix two glasses of his Desert Storm hangover remedy—in each glass he poured an ounce of brandy, one tablespoon each of vinegar and…

"Hey, Billy, you got any Worchestirshire sauce?" Billy waved in the general direction of the kitchen. Madame Alexina looked inside the refrigerator and handed a bottle to Spit.

"Thanks." Spit added the Worcestershire, and one teaspoon each of ketchup and bitters. He mixed the glasses and then into each he carefully placed an egg yolk.

Billy was skeptical, but anything was better than the throbbing in his head. He took a sip and then, jumping in the deep end, chugged the glass.

Electricity shot from Billy's green tips, setting off explosions in his stomach and larger blasts in his head. Billy jumped upright, prepared to bolt the room (the cartoon animal, its butt on fire, on a mad dash for a bucket of water), when, just as suddenly, he fell back in the chair, slumped over the side and puked for what seemed an eternity. Madame Alexina, foretelling this result, had strategically placed a bucket on either side of the chair.

"What the hell was that?" Billy asked, weak but defiant.

"I remember now. It's called a Prairie Oyster." Spit beamed triumphantly and, recognizing a good exit line, let himself out. Madame Alexina drank down the second Prairie Oyster and followed Spit out the door.

Billy, exhausted by the encounter, sank deeper into the chair, in a wordless prayer for a lengthy intermission. In his pocket, Billy's cell phone began to vibrate.

"Yeah?"

"Hi, Billy. It's me."

Here it comes, Billy thought. Donna was about to blow off the concert in order to do her job.

"You were right, Billy. All's I do is run around dressed like a mosquito."

Billy loved it when Donna admitted he was right. Especially when he wasn't. "I'm glad you finally figured it out. So, we're on for tonight?"

For a moment, all Billy could hear was static on the phone line. "What?"

"Yeah, Billy. We're on."

Billy turned off his cell phone, fired up a joint and sank even deeper into the chair.

For the second time, Billy was startled by a knock.

"It's open."

At the door, the knocking continued.

"It's open," Billy repeated, as if that were all the effort he could muster. "C'mon in."

Still the knocking continued.

Billy pulled himself up out of the chair, stubbing out the joint and cursing. "Hold your water. I'm coming."

When Billy opened the door, he was surprised to find Mrs. Patterson standing in his doorway. He was surprised that such a small woman could so completely fill the entry. Even after Labor Day, he was surprised that anyone would wear tweed at the shore. And, mostly, he was surprised by the curve of her legs as they peeked out from under the brown wool skirt.

"Mr. MacTavish?"

"Billy."

"Mr. Billy MacTavish?"

"Mrs. Patterson, would you like to come inside?"

Inspecting the apartment from the doorway, Mrs. Patterson shook her head no. "No, thank you, Mr. MacTavish," but she took a step inside the apartment.

"Mr. MacTavish, I'll come right to the point." Mrs. Patterson spoke quickly, through clenched teeth. "I don't like you."

Billy, wearing long board trunks and green-tipped hair, with an unlit joint in his left hand and a Budweiser in his right, tried for charming.

"But you don't know me, Mrs. Patterson."

Mrs. Patterson coughed. "I don't like you and I don't like midnight birding."

Putting down the joint and sipping the Bud, Billy tried for reasonable. "With all due respect, Mrs. Patterson, we midnight birders are serious about our activities."

"And what activities are those?" Mrs. Patterson wanted to know. "Drinking, necking, trampling the nesting areas. When your brother built his ballpark, he nearly destroyed the coastal habitat. Are you trying to finish the job?"

Billy had heard enough. "I think it's time for you to leave, Mrs. Patterson."

Wordlessly, Mrs. Patterson turned and left.

Billy watched her go.

It was a busy day at Billy's front door—Jehovah's Witness, Avon lady, Young Republican. Each time Billy dispatched a guest, he poured himself a drink and sank ever deeper into the chair. Billy perked up when he heard the girls giggling just outside the door. Donna and Heather let themselves in the apartment.

Donna kissed Billy hello. Heather kissed Billy as well, more than hello. Donna held her tongue, even while Heather didn't. Donna stepped between them.

"So here's the plan, Billy."

Billy was confused. "Huh?"

"The plan, Billy. Tonight. The concert, remember?"

"Oh yeah."

Donna explained to Billy how Heather had agreed to stand in for her at the ballpark.

"Did my brother really agree to that? There's hope for him yet."

Donna explained. "Your brother doesn't know about it. I'm going in to work just like any other game day, I'll make sure he sees me, same as always so there's no questions, and then Heather and I will make the switch."

Billy was impressed. "My little evil genius."

Donna continued. "So here's the thing, Billy. I'll ride to the ballpark with Heather, help her get ready. When it's time to split, you've got to pick me up at the ballpark. Okay? I'll meet you in the parking lot. You got that?"

With that, the girls left for Sand Skeeter Stadium. Billy poured himself a drink and sank ever deeper in the chair.

An Unsuspecting Father and Son

Donna made a point of saying hello to the shy young men working the ticket windows when she arrived at the ballpark. No one paid any notice to the girl that accompanied her on this final game of the season. Soon enough, the two girls had arrived at Skeeter's dressing room and were safely inside, sitting on the sofa, Donna preparing a step-by-step instructional guide to Skeeter's game-day routine, Heather sneaking shots from a pint of peppermint schnapps.

Donna was worried that Heather was not paying attention. She worried that something could go wrong before the season drew to a close. "Heather, c'mon, this is important to me."

Heather knew that Donna took her mascot duties way too seriously. She tried her best to sound sincere. "I got it, Donna."

"Okay then. Lemme quiz you."

Heather gulped a quick shot of schnapps. "Relax, Donna. I said I got it. Look, I walk around. I wave. I pat little kids on the head. I pose for pictures. And between innings, I do those dumbass races down on the field."

Donna was compelled to defend Skeeter's honor. "They're not dumb."

Heather tried not to laugh. "Okay, I'm sorry. They're not dumb."

"They're not."

"Okay, Donna. I'm sorry."

Donna wondered whether it was too late to back out, too late to change the plan. She considered giving her concert ticket to Heather, giving Billy to Heather. She knew that her boyfriend and her best friend secretly had the hots for each other.

Donna wondered whether Billy was worth fighting for. He was cute and fun to be with. When they were alone, Billy was loving and attentive. Sometimes, in the salt marsh after dark, it was a deeply spiritual experience, almost like midnight mass. But recently, Billy had been a real jerk. Someone was in the way, Donna decided, unsure whether it was she herself, or perhaps Billy, or Heather.

Donna made her decision. "Look, Heather, I've got to meet Billy in the parking lot. Are you ready to do this? Do you need anything? Please tell me you're not gonna screw around."

Heather had everything under control. "I'm okay. I'll climb into the costume in a couple of minutes and find a little kid to terrorize."

"Hea—" but Donna recognized Heather's gotcha grin and caught herself before Heather got her all worked up over nothing.

Donna cracked open the door and, blending in with a small crowd, made her way quickly toward the stadium exit. Meanwhile Heather checked out the latest in mascot-wear. Two nearly identical Skeeters hung in the closet. Giving them both the smell test, Heather selected the costume less overdue for the dry cleaners. There were still a few minutes until she would be expected in the stands, but she thought it might be fun to get off to a quick start. Treating herself to one last snort of schnapps, the woman who would be Skeeter walked over to the concession stand and got in line behind an unsuspecting father and son.

Trying to act nonchalant while dressed as a giant mosquito, Heather patted the boy on the head before goosing the young boy's father. Dad spun around in anger, ready for a fight, when he spotted his gooser and laughed. Pulling out a camera, the man took two quick photos of Skeeter clowning around with his son. This is gonna be easy, Heather told herself, as she sauntered down the aisle, trailing a pack of young fans.

While Heather was entertaining the pre-game fans, Donna made her way out to the parking lot without being seen. Skeeter employees were busy preparing for the final game of the season and the fans only knew Donna in costume. When Donna reached the lot it was nearly empty. Most of the fans were already inside the ballpark. The parking area was small enough for Donna quickly to canvass the lot. She was disappointed, but hardly surprised, to discover that Billy was missing in action. Donna moved to the far back of the lot, eager to avoid detection. Even in the nearly empty lot, she felt exposed. Out of uniform, she felt nearly naked. Still, no one bothered her. She had just enough time to finish a nervous cigarette, when Billy finally pulled up in his 4-Runner.

"Is everything okay?" Billy wondered.

"Yeah. I think so. Heather should be fine."

Billy tried to picture Heather in the mosquito outfit. "I'd like to see Heather in the Skeeter suit."

"Dammit, Billy." Donna spat the words out, her voice getting dangerously loud. "What is it with you and Heather?"

Billy looked around the quiet lot. "Let's not do this now."

Donna challenged Billy. "Do what now?"

Billy pretended not to understand Donna's anger. "Let's just go, okay?"

Donna stood there.

"Dammit, Donna. Why does everything have to be such a big deal?"

Donna stood there, afraid to move, unwilling to respond.

Billy sat in the 4Runner.

Donna folded her arms across her chest. "I'm not going out with you tonight."

Billy took a deep breath, measured his words carefully. "I don't understand what's going on here, Donna. I don't understand what I did that pissed you off."

Donna was tired of the games. "I like you, Billy. You know that. But you have to stop being such a jerk."

Billy thought it over. "I'm going to the concert. You can get in the truck or you can stand there. It's your choice.

Donna chose to stand there. "Then go."

Donna stood, alone in the lot, and listened to the sounds of minor league baseball drifting from the ballpark. Unnoticed, Donna slipped back inside Sand Skeeter Stadium.

She briefly considered trading places with Heather, but, of course, it was far too late to make the switch. Skeeter was standing in foul territory down the third base line, flinging t-shirts into the stands. Donna ducked into the mailroom, before she was noticed by any of her friends on staff.

The mailroom was dark and deserted, unmanned in the evening, even on game day. Donna located the monitor and turned it on, a closed-circuit telecast of the ball game available in every office at the ballpark. When the cameras cut to Skeeter, she was pleased to see that Heather had warmed to the role. Donna had an out-of-body experience watching Skeeter performing down on the ball field.

When it came time for the dizzy bat race, Donna was finally able to relax in her hiding place in the mailroom. She was still angry with Billy for getting her into the situation, but at least Heather was believable as Skeeter. Donna was relieved that the masquerade was working. Other than her own guilty feelings and the damage to her relationship with Billy, nothing bad would come of her deception.

Donna watched as Skeeter's dizzy bat rival was called down onto the infield. She watched as Skeeter and the fan both began to spin. To Donna's trained eye, Skeeter was unsteady even as she began to spin. Later, Donna would remember thinking that Heather was overplaying the scene. She watched as Skeeter and the fan began to wobble down the first base line. She watched as Skeeter careened off course, veering toward the pitcher's mound. *So that's what I look like,* Donna imagined, watching Skeeter teetering on the mound. She watched as Skeeter collapsed in a heap, as the trainer came out to assist. She watched as mock concern gave way to genuine panic on the pitcher's mound. Panic spread quickly throughout the ballpark, even into the mailroom, where Donna suddenly felt the room closing in on her. Flinging open the mailroom door, Donna tried to race out onto the field, instead running smack into an unsuspecting Madame Alexina.

"Ow!" Madame Alexina rubbed her forehead. "I should have seen that coming." And she pushed Donna back inside the mailroom.

In the silence of the mailroom, the women watched in horror as the EMTs swirled around Heather's lifeless form.

Madame Alexina fixed her gaze on Donna, probing. "What's going on, Donna?"

Donna turned off the TV monitor and sat in the mailroom, softly sobbing. "Is she going to be okay?"

Madame Alexina tried to read the moment. "I don't know, Donna."

"When she collapsed…Skeeter lying there like that…like it was me down there."

"It's not your fault, Donna."

Donna wouldn't meet her gaze.

"Is it?"

So Donna explained to Madame Alexina about the concert, about the masquerade and about her fight with Billy. "All I know is," Donna concluded, "that should be me down there."

Madame Alexina was growing uncomfortable. "It was an accident, Donna."

Donna didn't feel as if it was an accident. "Maybe…I don't know…" Donna was puzzled. "It must have been an accident. Who would want to hurt Heather?"

Madame Alexina saw the event unfolding in front of her. "If someone did this deliberately, then Heather wasn't the target." Madame Alexina waited for her meaning to become clear to Donna.

"Omigod." Donna could hardly believe it. "You've got to get me out of here."

In the midst of the confusion surrounding the tragedy on the field, no one paid any attention to Madame Alexina and Donna as they walked out of Sand Skeeter Stadium, marching through the parking lot and up onto the boardwalk.

"We need to find a safe place for you to spend the night."

Sitting on a bench on the boardwalk, looking at the full moon reflecting in the surf, Donna wondered if she could trust Madame Alexina. She wondered if she really had a choice.

Madame Alexina called for backup and, within minutes, a familiar yellow cab pulled to a stop alongside the boardwalk. Donna allowed Madame Alexina to put her in the back of the cab.

"Thank you, Spit. You're sure it's safe?"

"Even I don't know where we're going," Spit said, laughing nervously, "and I live there."

Donna looked at Madame Alexina, alone in the night, standing outside the cab. "Aren't you coming, too?"

Madame Alexina shook her head no. "It's okay. You'll be safe with Spit." Leaning in through the driver's side window, Madame Alexina kissed Spit lightly on the cheek. "Don't forget to turn on your headlights."

Donna didn't feel safe with Spit. They had, from time to time, seen one another in the salt marsh, but midnight birding was all she really knew about him. That, and his Desert Storm disability claim and his questionable reputation. Spit believed himself to be a victim of exposure to toxic chemicals, which had resulted in memory loss, confusion and irritability. In his written claim, Spit alleged that the Iraqis were engaged in chemical and biological warfare—sarin, soman, tabun, cyanide, phosgene—but Spit told anyone who would listen that his exposure had been to the American stockpile.

They rode in silence, Spit navigating the narrow local roads, heading north, leaving White Sands Beach. Donna trusted Madame Alexina and she wanted to trust Spit, but she did not find it reassuring to be alone in the cab with this trained killer with a bona fide mental condition. "Spit … you can let me out here."

Spit looked around. "Here? It's not safe here." Spit paused, deep in thought, determined to puzzle out Donna's intentions. His face brightened.

"I get it. You don't think it's safe with me. Am I right?"

Donna stammered, admitting that yes, Spit was right.

"Truth is, Donna, maybe I don't feel safe with you."

This time, it was Donna who was perplexed. "Me?"

Spit explained. "Yeah, you. Look at this from my perspective. From what I understand, you're worried that maybe it wasn't an accident at the ballpark. Am I right so far?"

Donna nodded.

"And if it wasn't an accident, you're worried that it was supposed to be you dead down on the infield. Right?"

Donna looked into the mirror and nodded again.

"And if you were the target, you figure, you're still in danger." Spit was pleased with himself. "Am I right?"

Donna nodded a third time.

"But I see it different. Probably it was just a horrible accident. But maybe not. Maybe someone wanted to hurt Heather. Maybe Heather was the target all along."

Donna was confused by Spit's explanation. "But no one knew about Heather and me switching places tonight."

Spit watched Donna in the rearview mirror.

The Obstacle to Good Government

There were six weeks remaining until Election Day. Across the country, as races tightened, campaigns grew vicious and personal. Doah Township was no exception. As Cheyenne's campaign gained momentum, the mayor's attacks grew more direct, challenging her competence and questioning her motives.

The second debate promised to sharpen the political dialogue in Doah. The Municipal Building began filling at seven, an hour before the debate was scheduled to begin. By eight, the hall was filled to overflowing. In the early rounds, the candidates circled, jabbing at their opponent, looking for an opening. Ninety minutes into the debate, the audience was growing impatient. Joe Caputo, serving once again as moderator, struggled to quiet the audience at Doah's second mayoral debate.

"Mr. Mayor, the hot issue in Trenton this year is pay-to-play. Until recently, you have not shown any great interest in campaign finance reform. In fact, your party has a long history of accepting questionable campaign funds. However, you are now proposing that Doah adopt a stringent pay-to-play ordinance. Cynics have suggested that your position on pay-to-play is a not-so-subtle attack on your opponent, Ms. Harbrough. Would you like to comment?" The boy barrister sat back in his seat, pleased with his question.

Mayor Big Jim Donovan cleared his throat and looked directly into the camera, speaking to the audience of voters, watching at home on cable channel eight.

"My friends, you all know that I am not a career politician. Four years ago, when I first ran for mayor, I did not realize the enormous influence of money in local politics. Perhaps I was naïve. Perhaps I wanted to believe that here in Doah we were somehow immune to these influences. Unfortunately, I have come to realize that money is even more dangerous in local campaigns than it is in national contests. Perhaps I have come to this issue late, but I am proud to support meaningful pay-to-play legislation.

With all due respect to Ms. Harbrough, we can no longer allow developers to buy influence here in Doah and in Trenton." The mayor smiled into the camera, struggling in the heat to maintain his polished look, his suit creased, sweat pooling along the edges of his toupee.

Joe Caputo turned to Cheyenne Harbrough. An hour and a half into the debate, on a hot night in the crowded council room, and Cheyenne still radiated charm. The perspiration at her throat was reason enough for the men watching at home not to change the channel.

"The mayor wants you to believe that the obstacle to good government is dishonest contractors and developers buying influence with naïve politicians. The truth is…" Cheyenne paused for effect, leaning in to the TV camera, "there are too many politicians lining up to be bought!"

Joe Caputo had three more questions on the debate agenda, but he recognized a closing line when he heard one. "I'd like to thank our candidates for meeting tonight in the second of three scheduled debates, and I'd like to thank the voters, those of you here in the audience tonight and those of you watching at home. As citizens, the choice is ours. I hope to see you all here again in two weeks for the last of our mayoral debates. Thank you and good night."

The debate having concluded, Big Jim and Mrs. Donovan retreated to the mayor's office. Rocki Donovan tried to pump up her husband's waning confidence.

"You were good tonight, Jim, poised, confident, mayoral."

Big Jim's own assessment was less positive. "The race is tight, Rocki. Face it, she may beat me."

"Listen to me, Jim. You've been a good mayor. The voters know that. It's late. Let's go home."

Big Jim kissed his wife. "I need to go through a couple of briefing reports before morning. Go on home. I won't be but an hour or so."

Busy with the campaign, Rocki missed her husband. She hardly recognized the man sitting behind the mayor's desk. Big Jim was not the man she married. Rocki missed Jim. "Don't stay late."

Big Jim promised to get his work done and come straight home.

When Rocki said good night, Big Jim flipped on the TV in the corner of his office, one eye on "NJN News" and one eye on the briefing report.

"Do you mind if I come in?" It had been a very long time since Cheyenne Harbrough had invited herself into the mayor's office.

Unsure what to say, Big Jim waved her into the office. Little Jim did too.

"You've become a very accomplished campaigner, Cheyenne, in a very short time."

Cheyenne smiled and batted her eyes, unsure whether she was teasing the mayor or herself. "Why, Mr. Mayor, you say the sweetest things."

But the mayor was distracted by the news report. NJN was showing tape of a minor league baseball game. The mayor wondered whether he could attract a team to Doah, whether he should campaign on the idea. Watching the dizzy bat race, the mayor suddenly realized that he knew the woman on the tape. "Cheyenne, isn't that your friend Cassie?"

Cheyenne looked up at the television in time to see Skeeter collapse on the pitcher's mound.

It was six weeks until Morris planned to release the special Cold War edition of the magazine. His readers were mostly true believers, but for Morris, the magazine was just a job. It had been a long time since he felt passionate about a story, but Morris found himself growing excited about a Soviet–New Jersey story line. An old girlfriend introduced him to an importer-exporter who specialized in Soviet memorabilia. Morris had spent the day in Manhattan, buying Soviet artifacts and government documents. He felt as if he'd smashed a Soviet piñata, unleashing a shower of Cold War secrets. He bought KGB badges and booklets, oxygen masks and navigation instruments. There were maps and helmets and an array of military pins and medals. He found carrier pigeon cages, Kremlin flatware. He found blueprints and language texts and surveillance plans. There were travel plans for the ballet and the hockey team and for Khrushchev's visit to Glassboro.

Morris needed his best writer to organize the Russian treasures and turn them into a story. Dialing Cassie's phone number, the editor left a message on her machine.

"Where are you, baby? Call me."

Morris put aside the memorabilia and flipped on the television, just in time to see his favorite writer, dizzy and disoriented, standing on first, while the mascot laid motionless, dead of heat stroke according to the report, on the pitcher's mound.

After the Hunt

Spit turned off the highway, onto an unmarked, unpaved road that led down to the inlet. No other cars were evident in the dark, in the night, on the old abandoned roadway. Spit parked the ancient Rambler taxicab at the barrier where the road dead-ended at the waterline.

Donna peered into the darkness. "Where are we?"

Spit turned toward the back seat of the cab and smiled. "Home."

Donna tried without success to identify evidence of Spit's domicile. "You live here?"

But Spit didn't answer. He exited the cab, heading on foot along the rotting wooden walkway that reached out over the saltwater and marsh grass.

Donna hurried to catch up, nearly tripping on the uneven wooden planks. "Wait," she implored, her voice suddenly higher by two octaves.

Peering into the night, Donna realized that there were several ramshackle cottages built on stilts, tilting out over the water. As they approached, it was apparent that each cottage was empty. Donna felt a knot tighten in her stomach. "How many people live here?"

Spit waited for Donna to catch up before answering. "This time of year? I'm not sure. There's me and let's see…well, I guess it's just me." Spit was suddenly embarrassed. "But you should see this place in the summertime."

Donna tried to imagine the place in the middle of summer. "How many people live here in season?"

Spit was not good at mental math. "Counting me?"

Donna was already counting the hours until morning. "Yes, Spit, counting you."

Spit grinned. "One."

Spit followed the wooden walkway to another, smaller path, which led to a cottage hidden among the marsh grass. The front door was unlocked. Spit held the door for Donna, inviting her to enter his cozy four-room house. "Make yourself comfortable."

Donna looked around at the cluttered living room, an explosion of magazines in piles on the floor and on the sofa—*Rolling Stone, Mother Jones, High Times, Natural History,* the *New Republic* and *Juggs*—magazines and jigsaw puzzles, boxes and boxes of puzzles, and one enormous puzzle, easily six feet in length, half-finished and sitting out on a plywood board perched on two unpainted sawhorses, magazines, and jigsaws, and pizza— empty pizza boxes stacked high along the wall, a leaning tower of pizza tilting toward the ocean—magazines and jigsaws and pizza, and cigarette butts, hundreds of butts, in dozens of ashtrays, and Donna didn't know what to say. "It's…" and she searched for the right word, "…nice."

"I don't get many visitors." Spit stared at his shoes. "Let me show you the guest room."

Donna was relieved to see that her room was habitable: a sleep sofa, old but clean, a seventeen-inch TV, an Indian throw rug on the floor, and another hanging from the wall, a room that she could call home for the night. "Thank you, Spit… I'm pretty tired. I think I'd like to get some sleep."

But Donna was unable to sleep, lying awake in Spit's guest room, thinking about Heather. She pictured Heather lying motionless on the pitcher's mound dressed as Skeeter. Was she going to be okay? And thinking about Madame Alexina's warning. Did someone want her dead? Donna pulled the blanket up around her shoulders, huddling against the sudden chill in the room. The weather was changing. Donna lay awake in bed, listening to the quiet patter of rain drops overhead, finally allowing herself to fall asleep on the sleep sofa, in the guest room, in Spit's isolated cabin, a long walk off a short pier, an unmarked outpost somewhere on the New Jersey coastline.

Near morning, Donna was jolted from sleep by an extraordinary thunderclap. The sky was electrified and rain beat down in torrents on the roof. She was almost relieved to pull herself out of the sleep sofa. Walking into the living room, Donna was surprised to find that Spit had spent the night straightening the clutter: magazines now neatly sorted and stacked, ashtrays ash-free, and a large green trash can, in the corner, catching rainwater as it leaked in through the roof. Spit himself was seated at the jigsaw, staring intently, motionless, breathing lightly, and every so often adding another piece to the gradually developing puzzle. Without looking up, Spit greeted his houseguest, grunting, "Mornin'."

Looking out the window at the wall of water, Donna had to ask, "Is it always this bad?"

Spit laughed. "Only when we get a storm."

Donna found it hard to imagine that anyone lived this way. "How do you manage?"

Spit gestured at the jigsaw. "Pull up a chair and join me."

The rain came down all day, depth charges, a full-out assault, and Donna and Spit spent the day underwater, rigged for silent running, slowly adding to the jigsaw as it spread out across the plywood.

The following day, the rain stopped, but not before the wooden walkway connecting Spit's cabin to the rest of New Jersey, lay deeply, dangerously, submerged. Late in the afternoon, placing the final piece of the puzzle, Spit turned to Donna, smiling broadly, "Done!"

Donna stood up and stretched, her body sore from two days in the metal folding chair. Looking down at the puzzle, Donna focused for the first time, not on the detail of single puzzle pieces, but on the finished panorama. Titled "After the hunt," Donna found the picture unsettling, some half-dozen pterodactyls flying in circles overhead, while down below on the prehistoric plain, hundreds of microceratops lay dead, and in the midst of the herd the most disturbing image of all…one dead microceratops clad in chili pepper boxer shorts.

Clean Undies

Dressed in Andy's thick terrycloth robe, sitting on the enclosed deck, looking out over the water, the tide coming in, Cassie could hardly believe she had stayed at Andy's oceanfront home for two days, listening to doo-wop and making whoopee. The dead woman at the ballpark had served as an accelerant, fanning the flames of their lust. It surprised Cassie to realize she was growing confident of the relationship, that she was worried only by the pace of love's progress.

Andy stepped out on the deck, dressed for work. "I've got to spend a coupla hours at the ballpark today."

"Don't be long, okay?" Cassie detected a note of resentment in her voice, jealous of the Sand Skeeters for laying claim on Andy's time.

Andy explained. "I need to meet with my attorney, and then briefly with my banker. You understand…the dead woman."

Alone at Andy's home, Cassie seized the opportunity to do laundry. When she left Doah, heading for her date with Andy MacTavish, she had not packed for an extended stay. She had not packed at all. Andy's terry robe was comfortable and, according to Andy, sexy. Still, she longed for clean undies. With the rinse cycle underway, Cassie returned to the deck, with a cup of hot coffee and the morning paper. She read the paper out of habit, thoughts of Andy MacTavish crowding out the hard news and features. Cassie had to read the headline twice before it registered—"NJDEP Issues Dead Deer Findings."

Suddenly Cassie understood how the Sand Skeeters could pull Andy from his home, even in the throes of their new love. Cassie felt the same tug when she read the news story. For Andy, it was his minor league baseball team. For Cassie it was the mysterious dead deer of Doah Township that demanded her attention. Love could wait. Lust could wait. Even laundry, beeping in the hall, would have to wait. The dead deer were back in the news.

Cassie had written a series of magazine articles about the dead deer of Doah Township. She had documented the circumstances surrounding many of the largest sightings and, in some circles, was considered to be an expert on the phenomenon. The New Jersey Department of Environmental Protection, Division of Fish and Wildlife, however, was not located within such a circle. The NJDEP did not believe the dead deer phenomenon to be mysterious or the cause of death to be paranormal. Cassie was yelling at the newspaper by the time she finished reading the account.

She picked up the phone and dialed her editor's number.

"Morris!" she yelled into the phone when she heard the answering machine. "Pick up, dammit."

"I'm here, sweetie. What is it?" Morris sounded tired.

"You know what it is?"

Morris stifled a laugh. "Oh yeah, the DEP."

Cassie was not amused. "You're damn right … the DEP. Get me the full damn report."

Morris, anticipating the call from his star writer, had already located the full report online. "I'll do the best I can, sweetie. Maybe in a day or two …"

Cassie was shouting again. "Cut the crap, Morris. You already have a copy, don't you?"

"Let me see what I can do, Cassie. In a coupla hours. Where are you, anyway?"

Cassie knew that Morris would retreat into a funk if she told him about Andy MacTavish. Not that he had any right to, Cassie reminded herself, but still, there it was. "I'll be home later today. I want to find the damn report on my computer by the time I get there."

Until she saw the newspaper, Cassie had been on a two-day vacation from her own life. Now she needed to return home. And she needed Andy to understand. During the last two days, she and Andy had not had a single conversation about her staying … or about her leaving.

Cassie checked her clothes, damp and tumbling happily in the dryer, oblivious to Cassie's changing mood. They were dry enough, she decided, and pulled them from the machine, dressing for the drive home to Doah.

Cassie set out first for the ballpark, rehearsing her explanation in the car, constructing the explanation as if it were one of her stories, agonizing over every word. By the time she pulled into the parking lot, Cassie knew what she wanted to say. But approaching Andy's office, she heard angry words being exchanged. Peeking into the office suite, Cassie was struck by the ramrod-stiff posture of the woman in Andy's inner office, by the tweed business suit that fit her like an exoskeleton.

Wanting nothing more than to kiss Andy goodbye, Cassie waited in the outer office, the combination of dead deer and doo-wop causing her head to ache. Locating the controls to Andy's sound system, she reset his presets, switching the radio from oldies to jazz. Wayne Shorter on soprano sax. Andy winced when he walked into the office.

"Cassie, is everything okay?" Andy had not expected to find Cassie at the ballpark.

Cassie kissed him on the forehead. "You look tired."

Andy shrugged. "I've had better days."

"The dead woman?"

Andy nodded. "Yeah. The dead woman."

Cassie waited, letting Andy figure out how much he wanted to tell her. "For now, everyone seems willing to call it an accident. Except …"

Cassie already knew what Andy was going to say. Still, she let him finish.

"Except that Donna is still missing."

Cassie and Andy sat in the office, Nicholas Payton on trumpet, Cyrus Chestnut sitting in at the piano. Cassie remembered what she had come to the ballpark to say.

"I have to go home, Andy." She spoke quickly, trying not to think about the words.

There was so much Andy wanted to say, but he barely knew where to begin. "When are you leaving?"

Cassie couldn't make eye contact. "Today. Now." Andy swallowed hard. "Can I call you tonight?" "You just better." Cassie smiled. Andy saw his future reflected in Cassie's smile. "I love you, Cassie O'Malley." "And I love you, Andy MacTavish."

A Renewable Natural Resource

Driving home to Doah, Cassie felt good to be back on the familiar country roads, Dizzy Gillespie riding shotgun, the pygmy pines, the cranberry bogs, the same familiar signs for small appliance repair, for barbecue, for Cheyenne Harbrough, independent candidate for mayor.

Cassie sucked in the familiar Pine Barrens air. Somehow, she had expected that everything would be different, or maybe everything really was different; Cassie wasn't certain anymore. The car rang out with a dizzying display of bebop, but Cassie's head overflowed with the a cappella harmonies of doo-wop. She thought about dead deer and dizzy bats, about mayoral campaigns and minor league mascots, but mostly she thought about Andy MacTavish. Cassie pushed the Mustang hard, churning up the miles, heading home.

Booting up her computer, Cassie was pleased to find an E-mail from Morris: no message, just a link to the DEP report. Waiting for the document to download, she pulled on her ancient black sweats and poured herself a Jameson and water. The full report was more than fifty pages, filled with pie charts and trend lines, with bar graphs and data tables, cholesterol clogging the arteries of her default browser. Cassie sipped her whiskey and scrolled through the computer file, until she found the summary:

Deer are a renewable natural resource, Cassie read, of great importance to the state of New Jersey and its residents. The New Jersey Department of Environmental Protection, through the Division of Fish and Wildlife, is committed to its Deer Management Program. The goal of the program, according to the report, is to maintain the state's deer population in harmony with the needs and desires of the citizenry.

Between, April 2001 and October 2003, numerous complaints were received by the New Jersey Department of Environmental Protection regarding deer fatalities in the Pine Barrens. As habitats shrink, it is not uncommon to find deer carcasses on New Jersey roadways. However, these complaints were atypical, and it soon became apparent that a comprehensive review of the dead deer phenomenon, as it came to be known, was indicated. The mayor of Doah Township, the Honorable James T. Donovan, appointed a blue ribbon panel to investigate. When the blue ribbon panel was unable to unravel the mystery, the mayor requested the involvement of the DEP. The present report, according to the DEP, is the result of that involvement. In preparing the report, the DEP set out to address three specific issues:

1. The unusually large number of sightings as well as the unusually large size of specific sightings;
2. The sudden appearance of deer carcasses; and
3. The reports of puncture wounds to the deer's necks.

It has generally been reported that there were an unusually high number of deer carcasses found in the Pine Barrens, specifically in Doah Township, between April 2001 and October 2003. The DEP reviewed deer fatalities for the past ten years. We have considered average annual mortality and morbidity statistics. We have scatter plotted the data, with special emphasis on outliers. We have computed the analysis of variance and have compared actual data to the levels anticipated by trend analysis and we have come to the inescapable conclusion that the phenomenon is not statistically remarkable. That is, the number of dead deer reported, although atypical, falls within acceptable mathematic parameters.

Next the DEP examined claims that the deer carcasses were materializing suddenly on otherwise empty roadways. Our review indicates that these sightings typically occurred on small back roads before sunrise. Several points seem to be of importance here. The roads in question are in remote sections of the Pine Barrens and are lightly traveled, especially at night. It is probable that the drivers who made the various sightings were the first vehicles to pass by these locations for several hours, and in some cases, for days. Furthermore, visibility before dawn on these back roads is limited at best. Although the deer carcasses may have appeared suddenly to the drivers who were involved, there is no basis to jump to the conclusion that the carcasses themselves materialized suddenly on the roadway.

Finally, the DEP examined the claim that the deer carcasses were all marked with mysterious puncture wounds to the neck. This is the most troubling element of the rash of sightings, for this observation, if true, raises the specter of some sinister cause of death. After thousands of hours of *research, the DEP cannot identify even one sighting in which independent corroboration of this claim could be established to a scientific certitude. It seems that this claim can be traced back to a series of stories that appeared in a certain magazine with a track record of questionable reportage.*

In summary, the DEP finds no legitimacy to the outlandish claims which have surrounded the dead deer of Doah Township. Previous efforts to solve the mystery have failed, largely because those efforts were built on a faulty premise. The faulty premise was that the deer fatalities were not explainable as natural events. This faulty premise, fueled by an irresponsible media, led to efforts to posit the impossible and to prove the improvable. However, the conclusions now reached by the DEP are not open to debate or interpretation. There is no mystery (according to the Department of Environmental Protection). There is only dead deer.

Cassie poured herself a second Jameson and water, and dialed the telephone. "Morris," she yelled into the receiver. "I want to get those assholes at the DEP!" Morris chuckled. "You read the report?" "Don't you be laughing, Morris. This is serious." Morris assumed his serious face. "Okay, Cassie. What do you want to do?" Cassie had it all figured out. "A couple of thousand words about the DEP should do the trick." Morris knew it was a long shot, but he tried anyway. "No."

"What do you mean, 'no'?" Cassie was shouting again. "They as much as said I made up the whole dead deer phenomenon. My reputation …"

"… will be fine, Cassie. You know what our readers will say. 'Government cover-up' is what they'll say. You'll be a hero."

Cassie wasn't listening. "I can't let the DEP report sit out there as the last word. Our readers rely on us for the real story. They read us because, in an unimaginably bizarre universe, we give them answers."

"Cassie, sweetie … I can't believe I have to tell you this. Our readers don't rely on us for answers. They read us for the questions."

Cassie was not ready to drop the subject. "But …"

Morris was adamant. "Let it go, Cassie. Say goodbye to the dead deer. It's time to move on to new stories."

"But our readers want …"

Morris knew exactly what their readers wanted. "They want the same as me. They want us to finish the next issue."

Russian Vodka and Beluga Caviar

Cassie poured herself a Jameson and considered her options. She understood that some people dismissed her stories and the magazine for which she wrote as disreputable. She earned her living by writing about improbable events.

Cassie took great pride in the research base for her outlandish claims. She didn't make up her stories; she didn't have to. Instead, Cassie juxtaposed unlikely events to create an alternate reality. She never made the claim that her stories were true, only that they might be true. Now the Department of Environmental Protection had accused her of fabricating the dead deer story. The DEP had crossed the line. Cassie wondered whether it might not be possible to satisfy her editor and still get even with the DEP.

Cassie dug deeply into her files, retrieving seemingly unrelated news items, piecing them together like a jigsaw puzzle. She found stories about mysterious tunnels underneath the state capitol in Trenton. She read news items about Cold War bomb scares. She stumbled on a state budget report outlining a series of unexpected state purchase requisitions. She sipped her whiskey and began to construct an alternate reality. And then she began to type.

Soviet Spy Ring Infiltrates NJDEP?

At the height of the Cold War, ordinary Americans from coast to coast were building bomb shelters. Determined to preserve our way of life, underground if necessary, families were laying in stores and preparing for the apocalypse. Young children went to school and practiced for an attack, kneeling in the halls, head down (thereby protected from nuclear radiation). Young mothers went to the market and bought extra toilet paper. Young fathers worked overtime to pay for their backyard bomb shelters. Quietly, government agencies did the same, justifying their place in a post-apocalyptic America (the surface world might be uninhabitable for tens of thousands of years; still, America would need its interstate highway system).

Faithful readers will know about the unexplained network of tunnels that has been found beneath the state capitol in Trenton. We now have reason to believe that one or more of those tunnels led to a secret government bomb shelter. No state agency will admit to operating a bomb shelter. There is no official record of such a shelter. But we have reviewed New Jersey budget and expense reports line by line, year by year. In 1960, with Soviet-American tension at its peak, the New Jersey Department of Environmental Protection was making highly unusual bulk purchases—canned beans and vegetables, beef jerky, iodine, toilet paper, bottled water … The list goes on.

Is it not possible that a highly secret state government bomb shelter was being provisioned, the expenditures hidden as completely as the shelter itself, deep within the NJDEP budget? If only the story ended there with a top-secret bomb shelter for state bureaucrats.

Recently we discovered several boxes that we believe may have come from the shelter's stockpiled supplies. We found dehydrated meals, first-aid kits, flashlights and paperback books. We found cans of lima beans, pinto beans, peas and carrots and fruit cocktail. We found transistor radios and portable generators. But as we unpacked the boxes, we also found Russian vodka and beluga caviar. We found Soviet military supplies—pea coats and hats, pistols, knives and codebooks. We have had these artifacts examined by experts who tell us that these objects are authentic.

We cannot as yet claim with a scientific certitude that these objects were found in a bomb shelter located under the state capitol. Nor can we assert as a matter of fact that the New Jersey Department of Environmental Protection operated this bomb shelter. Certainly we cannot as yet prove that a Soviet spy ring infiltrated the NJDEP.

But we believe it is possible. We believe there is sufficient evidence to call for an official inquiry. We believe it is our responsibility as patriotic Americans to ask the tough questions. We have our concerns, but we want to be fair. We will give the NJDEP every opportunity to respond. And we will let our readers draw their own conclusions.

Cassie finished her whiskey, typed in her editor's address and hit send. She pushed her chair back from the computer screen and smiled.

A Zen Thing

Andy MacTavish marveled at people who saw subtlety in the workings of the universe. Andy lived in a digital world, a world of stark choices and powerful consequences, a world of ones and zeroes, of absolute zero.

It had been an outstanding first season of Sand Skeeter baseball, he told himself, and then a young woman died on the pitcher's mound and it wasn't such a great season anymore. It had been a romantic two days with Cassie O'Malley, and then she was gone, leaving a hole where his life had been. When Andy said goodbye to Cassie, he took comfort, at least, in the knowledge that his day had bottomed out. And then he answered the telephone.

"Mr. MacTavish?" Andy didn't recognize the woman's voice.

"Yes?"

"This is the morgue." There was an uncomfortable silence on the line. Finally the woman continued. "I believe you are aware that Ms. Dean's death has been ruled an accident … heat stroke." Andy's attorney had confirmed the finding during their meeting that morning at the ballpark.

"Yes." "We are making arrangements to release the body to the family later today."

Andy had no idea where the conversation was heading. "Yes?"

"We'd like you to come get your mascot costume."

Andy tried not to think about the dead woman as he drove to the morgue. He tried not to think about the dead woman as he pulled into the lot, parking alongside the grieving family. He tried not to think about the dead woman as he marched into the morgue to retrieve his costume and again, leaving the morgue, as he loaded the costume into a duffel bag and loaded the duffel into the trunk of his Lexus. He tried not to think about the dead woman as he drove back to his oceanfront home. Of course, he explained later that night on the phone with Cassie, he could think of nothing but the dead woman the entire time.

"I can't think about Skeeter anymore without seeing the dead woman.

And as hard as I try, I can't not think about Skeeter."

"You can't not think about Skeeter," Cassie explained, "by trying to not think about her. It's a Zen thing. You have to stop trying and then you can stop thinking."

Andy took a moment to untangle Cassie's grammar. "I'll try. I mean I'll try not to try … I mean I'll not try to not try … oh hell, you know what I mean." Andy tried to stop trying; still all he could see was the dead woman on the pitcher's mound. "I don't know if I can get past this."

Cassie had an idea and trusted that Andy might be ready to hear it. "Maybe you need to retire the mascot. Can you really imagine the fans frolicking with Skeeter next season?"

Andy had been asking himself the same question all day. "Maybe you're right."

"Of course I'm right." Cassie laughed. "I'm always right."

Andy chuckled. "Always?"

Cassie left no room for doubt. "Get used to it."

That night Cassie dreamt of her late husband Rob. In her dream, Cassie and Rob were twenty. In her dreams, they were always twenty.

It was sunny and warm, a beautiful spring evening, and they were at the ballpark. Sitting in the bleachers, watching the game, sitting among thousands of screaming fans, they were strangely, silently, alone. Rob wanted to talk, but Cassie turned away. She would not speak to Rob; she was still mad at him for dying.

Finally Cassie relented, turning to look at Rob, to look beyond the terror frozen in his sad blue eyes. "It's not fair."

Rob nodded in agreement. "Life's not fair, Cassie."

Why didn't he understand? "No, Rob, not life. Death. It's death that's not fair."

Rob knew better. "No, Cassie. You're wrong. Death is the one fair thing." Rob wished he could do something to diminish her pain. "Can I get you a hot dog?"

Cassie watched Rob as he headed off for the concession stand, following him with her eyes until he gradually disappeared in the crowd. She watched for his return, eternity in the form of the seventh-inning stretch.

But Rob did not return, not before the end of the seventh-inning stretch, not before the end of the ball game. Rob did not return and Cassie did not move on. She watched as the bleachers emptied and still she sat there waiting for Rob to reappear. Eventually Andy MacTavish walked up to Cassie and handed her a note. Cassie could not bring herself to read the note. "Read it to me, please," she begged.

Carefully, Andy unfolded the note and read, "They ran out of hot dogs. I'm sorry." Andy folded the note and handed it to Cassie, repeating again, "I'm sorry."

That night Andy dreamt of business and baseball, of boardwalks and ballparks, of bankers, barristers and birders. His dream was all jumbled, birders taking batting practice, bankers in blue serge suits, in the salt marsh, in the moonlight, listening for the plaintive doo-wop of the migratory water fowl, and everywhere there was one dead mascot, in the salt marsh, on the boardwalk, in the ballpark. No matter where his dream jumped next, the dead mascot would be there, waiting for him, dead mascot walking, night of the living dead mascot.

By morning, Andy had made his decision. The team would hold a contest in the off-season. He would ask his fans to choose a new name for the baseball team and with the new name, a new mascot and a new beginning. It was time to say goodbye to Skeeter. Andy retrieved the duffel bag from the trunk of his Lexus. In his boxer shorts and t-shirt, Andy carried the duffel bag to the rock wall overlooking the chill Atlantic surf.

Without trying, Andy remembered the good times … Skeeter greeting fans on game days, signing autographs, playing catch with the kids, making public appearances at shopping malls and car dealerships, the fans buzzing with excitement for the team's unlikely goodwill ambassador, a mosquito.

Andy unzipped the duffel bag, carefully withdrawing the costume. "Goodbye, little feller." Andy was relieved that no one was there as he wiped a tear from the corner of his eye.

And with that, Andy tossed the costume over the rock wall. He watched as Skeeter rode the waves, gradually washing out to sea, slowly sinking in the offshore surf. Andy watched as the costume gradually disappeared and then he watched the ocean, fixing on the spot where Skeeter succumbed to the inevitable. Andy turned and walked back inside his oceanfront home.

Andy lived in a digital world, a world of stark choices and powerful consequences. In order that minor league baseball might survive in White Sands Beach, Skeeter would not be returning for a second season.

The Fatal Combination

Perhaps it was nothing more than the new waitress, but Cassie felt like a stranger at the Eggery. She put down her menu and stared across the table at Cheyenne. "Has it really only been a week?"

Cheyenne tried to remember the last time she saw Cassie. "I guess. You know, I saw you on TV."

Cassie tried without success to flag down the waitress, still waiting for her first cup of coffee. TV?"

Cheyenne nodded. "You were on the news. Well, not you really … the mascot … the dizzy bat race."

"You want to—grr—order breakfast, yes?"

Startled by the unexpected growl, Cassie looked up. The first thing she noticed about the waitress was her eyes. They bounced around on her face like ships pulled loose from their moorings. "A short stack of blueberry pancakes and a cup of coffee."

Cheyenne examined the fortyish woman waiting to take her order, the pain of standing apparent on her overly made-up face. She felt sorry for the prematurely gray lady with the crazy eyes and aching feet. "And I'd like a fried egg sandwich and coffee."

"I'll—grr—be right back with the coffee." And with that, the waitress turned and walked off.

Cassie watched her all the way back into the kitchen. "That was odd."

Cheyenne was more accepting of the waitress's growl. "I wonder if she's registered to vote."

Cassie had nearly forgotten. "Geez, Cheyenne, that's right. What's the latest on the campaign?"

Cheyenne grinned. "They say it's dead even." Cassie was impressed. "Yeah?"

"Yeah. They say it's gonna come down to the last debate."

"No matter how it turns out, Chey, I want you to know that I'm really proud of you."

Cheyenne was proud of her campaign, but that's not why she had agreed to meet Cassie for breakfast. A mayoral election was routine. It happened in Doah every two years, but it had been more than a decade since there'd been a man in Cassie's life. "Thanks, Cassie, but what I really want to know is, what's going on with you and Andy?"

The waitress reappeared with their coffee. Cassie waited while she poured them each a cup. "Your food—grr—will be right out."

Cassie took a deep draft of coffee before proceeding. "I think I'm in love."

"That's wonderful, Cassie." Cheyenne paused. "It is wonderful, right?"

Cassie grinned. "Yes, Chey, it's wonderful."

The two ladies picked at their breakfasts and talked, old friends catching up on new love, until finally the conversation made its way back to the baseball game.

"Anyway," Cheyenne wanted to know, "what the hell happened during the dizzy bat race?"

"She collapsed … heat stroke. Apparently it's not a good idea to drink large quantities of peppermint schnapps before zipping yourself into a mosquito suit and spinning around in circles on a night of record high temperatures."

Cheyenne considered the fatal combination. "You'd think she'd know that after a full season as mascot."

Cassie explained. "That's the strange part. The girl who died wasn't the regular mascot."

Cheyenne thought everything about the dead woman on the pitcher's mound was strange. "What happened to the regular mascot?"

"I don't know what happened to Donna." Andy MacTavish wondered whether his attorney believed him. "I wish I did, but I don't."

Mr. Garibaldi was an extraordinarily large man with unusually small feet. Years of litigation experience and a wardrobe of hand-tailored three-piece suits gave the attorney a command of the space that he inhabited, even when he was squeezed into a narrow booth at Cubby's for a breakfast meeting with his most successful client.

Donna's disappearance had made Andy uneasy, but he failed to see that he bore any responsibility. "Am I in any trouble here?"

"Criminally, no, I don't think so. The police are satisfied that Ms. Dean's death was accidental."

The corpulent attorney paused to rearrange himself in the cramped breakfast booth. "Civil litigation is another matter entirely. The family will surely want to know why their daughter was filling in for your regular mascot."

Andy was nodding as his attorney spoke. "Me too. One girl dead, another girl missing … it's not the best publicity for the Sand Skeeters … not good for business … not our image …" Andy lapsed into silence.

Mr. Garibaldi cringed. "No. I would think not. That's why it's so important that we find Ms. Donna Carter. Isn't she your kid brother's girlfriend?"

"No, I mean we used to date sometimes, but I broke up with her." Billy was naked, lying in bed, spending a few postcoital minutes getting to know the girl he had spent the night with, before easing her out of the apartment. He looked her straight in the eye as he answered, so that she might read his lips.

Billy took stock. She was a skinny girl, not really his type, more angles than curves, her red hair cut short, and her face freckled. She was not a pretty girl, he decided, but still Billy found her appearance pleasing. Her name was Sheila, he remembered, or Shirley.

Cheryl purred, her tone thick with sex and conductive hearing loss. "Either way, Billy. It's okay, you know?" As if to demonstrate just how okay, she took his hand and placed it between her legs. "Let's do it again, okay?"

Billy knew it would be more difficult to get her out of his apartment, if he couldn't get her out of his bed. It was a classic example of Newtonian physics. A body in motion tends to stay in motion. A body at rest … Billy tried to calculate the pressure that would be needed to bid farewell to Sheila … or Shirley.

His hand between her legs, Billy tried counting with his fingers. Cheryl squirmed, marveling at the mathematical precision of his touch. She did not share Billy's grasp of Newtonian physics, but she was not without talents of her own. Her hand resting lightly between Billy's legs, Cheryl practiced finger spelling, demonstrating for Billy why sign language is truly the language of love.

Still, there came a moment later that morning, Cheryl in her panties and t-shirt, brewing coffee in the kitchen, that Billy again debated how to get her out of his apartment. He could be brutally honest, but it seemed unfair, even to Billy, to force her to lip-read rejection. Unfair and, as it happens, unnecessary. Cheryl pulled on her blue jeans, poured herself a cup of coffee and turned to ask Billy a question.

"Do you think you could give me a ride home?"

"I don't think I can do that." Spit put down his coffee, waiting for Donna's reaction.

Stepping outside, Donna surveyed the receding floodwaters. Tidal pools dotted the landscape, but there had been no new rain for two days. The sedge grass was peeking out above the water line, and the path to the mainland had mostly resurfaced. "It looks safe enough to me."

Spit had made a promise to Madame Alexina to keep Donna safe. He knew that the submerged sections of the path would be treacherous. And neither of them knew what dangers awaited Donna's return to the mainland. "Soon maybe, but not yet. Give it time."

Donna exploded. "Time! I've been cooped up two days already. If I look at another jigsaw puzzle, I'll ..." Donna sputtered to a halt, before her words cut any deeper.

"I'm sorry, Spit. I didn't mean ... you know what I mean ..."

Spit forced himself to smile. "Yeah ... it's okay. I guess this place is kinda hard on you, huh?"

Donna laughed. "It is sorta strange out here. Like I'm Mary Ann and this is Gilligan's Island."

Spit relaxed, smiling for real now. "And that would make me who? The Professor? Could I be the Professor? I always wanted to be the Professor."

"Okay, Professor," Donna inquired, "what's your plan for getting me off Gilligan's Island?"

"My plan?" But Spit had a plan and he shared it with Donna. "I'm gonna wait for Madame Alexina."

Tin Can Aliens with Their Cardboard Death Rays

The campaign rally had already started when Cassie pulled her car up to the entrance to Wehnke's Woods. The tiny parking area was filled beyond capacity; cars spilled out onto the road, parking on the shoulder on both sides of the narrow roadway. Cassie waited for a spot on the shoulder, pulling off the road far enough for traffic to safely pass. Locking her car, Cassie walked along the footpath to the clearing in the woods. Cheyenne was standing on a makeshift platform, speaking to a crowd of some fifty supporters and perhaps as many as a dozen undecided voters.

"My friends," and looking out at the crowd Cheyenne knew they were her friends, "I want to thank you for coming out today to this lovely spot to discuss the future of Doah Township."

The crowd murmured in approval.

"Big Jim wants you to believe that development will run amok if I am elected mayor." Holding out her arm, Cheyenne invited the crowd to consider the vista, a spokes-model for open space. "Does this look like development run amok?"

From the crowd, Cassie heard a chorus of "No," and a chant, "Cheyenne for Mayor."

Cheyenne allowed the chant to build for a moment before continuing with her speech.

"Some of you are probably aware that my company donated this lovely spot, this undeveloped land, to the township. There was a time when the mayor and I saw eye to eye on the subject of responsible development. There was a time when the mayor understood that development and open space were not in conflict. There was a time when the mayor believed that responsible development contributed to quality of life."

Cassie marveled at the power and grace of Cheyenne's delivery.

"There was a time when the mayor believed that developers and local governing bodies could partner to enhance that quality of life." Cheyenne paused for effect.

"But that was before the mayor realized he might lose the election." Cheyenne played the crowd, allowing the cheers to build before continuing to make her case.

Gesturing vaguely toward the woods, Cheyenne again adopted her best spokes-model pose. "Look out on the beauty of these woods. When you hear Big Jim's friends attack me because I'm a developer, remember this spot. If Big Jim wants to make this race about development, so be it."

The crowd again began to chant, "Cheyenne for Mayor."

As Cheyenne returned to her stump speech, Cassie was distracted by the appearance of a crew from the public works department unloading equipment from the back of a municipal truck parked at the edge of the woods. Cassie watched with interest, but at such a distance, she could not be certain what the crew was up to. As far as she could tell, no one else in the crowd was bothered by the work crew. Cassie continued watching as the crew made its way toward the rally. At close range now, Cassie recognized their activity, wondering why the public works department was taking soil samples in Wehnke's Woods.

No one else seemed to be paying attention to the activity of the work crew until they began to hang yellow "Do Not Cross" tape among the trees. Cheyenne continued to talk about her plans and her priorities, but when the work crew began marking the area with biohazard signage, her audience began pointing and shouting, supporters and undecided voters alike rushing off to find their automobiles. Everyone but Cheyenne, Cassie and the work crew itself bade a hasty retreat from the suddenly toxic campaign rally.

Cassie confronted the crew. "What the hell is going on here?" But no one answered.

Cheyenne, visibly shaken by the abrupt end of her rally, stepped down from the makeshift platform. "Who's in charge here?"

The men on the work crew scuffed their boots in the dirt, waiting for their supervisor to respond. Finally he decided to explain. "I'm sorry, ma'am, but we have reason to believe that the soil is contaminated."

Cheyenne forced herself not to scream, responding instead in measured tones. "This is bullshit."

The supervisor again apologized. "I'm sorry, ma'am ... public safety." With that, the supervisor turned to leave, walking quickly back to the truck, his crew following like ducklings all in a row.

The woods had emptied save for Cassie and Cheyenne. Cassie felt sorry for her best friend and would-be mayor. "C'mon, Chey, let's get out of here. We can go to my condo. I'll get us a pizza."

Cheyenne surveyed the clearing, as though she might still find a reason to continue the rally.

Cassie nudged Cheyenne. "C'mon, Chey. I'll make some phone calls."

Cheyenne made no move to leave. "But I'm not done yet."

"I'm sorry, Chey. We'll get to the bottom of this." And with that, the two ladies turned and walked back to their cars.

Flipping channels, Cheyenne found a low-budget, sci-fi adventure flick and watched for a moment before flipping channels. She watched as tin-can aliens with cardboard death rays launched an attack on Planet Earth, and nothing stood between them and the domination of all humankind but a too-earnest nerd scientist and his ingénue assistant in her high heels, torn skirt and imitation pearls.

Cassie was standing at the open refrigerator, getting a beer to wash down the slice of pepperoni pizza, when she stopped dead in her tracks, halfway to a Heineken, stopped by the image on her television. "They weren't wearing any protective gear, Chey."

Cheyenne was surprised by Cassie's criticism of the movie. "C'mon, Cassie, you've got to watch the movie on its own terms."

Cassie tried to explain. "Not the movie, Chey. Today. In the woods. They weren't wearing gloves, or masks, or anything."

Cheyenne waited for Cassie to continue.

"If the public works crew believed that there were biohazards in the soil, don't you think they'd be more careful about their own exposure?"

Cheyenne wondered how far the mayor was willing to go to hold on to his position in town. "What happened out there? Do you think the mayor …"

Cassie didn't wait for Cheyenne to finish the question. "Of course it was the mayor." Cassie thought for a moment. "It's time to take the gloves off, Chey. Time to take him down."

Dizzy Bat, Inc.

Andy MacTavish loved coming to the ballpark in the off-season, walking through the deserted ballpark like walking on the beach in winter, a universe of one, the skeleton staff only serving to draw attention to the general emptiness in the ballpark, alone in the chill morning air, barren and desolate, with faint memories of hot summer days and the veiled promise of more to come. Andy walked past the deserted concession stands: no hot dogs today, no soda, just the sweet smell of phantom peanuts wafting through the stands. He walked through the field-level seats, empty, and out onto the field. Andy walked the outfield, stopping in right, pretending to play the carom off the wall, fielding the ball cleanly, whirling and throwing, out at second. He walked the infield, careful to avoid the pitcher's mound and the memories lurking in the raised circle of dirt. Andy walked off the field, through the dugout and the empty locker room, and on into the empty team office. Andy was surprised, in the empty stadium, to find the birder, Mrs. Patterson, in her wool plaid business separates, waiting for him at the office door.

"Excuse me, Mr. MacTavish?"

"Mrs. Patterson, isn't it? I'm sorry; did we have an appointment today?"

Mrs. Patterson smiled. "This will just take a moment of your time. I'm here as a courtesy, Mr. MacTavish."

Andy understood immediately that no matter how courteous Mrs. Patterson's demeanor, her visit was in no way one of courtesy. "In that case, please come in."

Mrs. Patterson entered the office, sitting down, her back ramrod-straight. No one in White Sands Beach, not even the Coast Guard cadets, had posture stiff as Mrs. Patterson. Still, Andy noted, she looked comfortable.

"I'll try to be brief, Mr. MacTavish. It's no secret that my group and I were opposed to the construction of a ballpark in this location."

"With all due respect, Mrs. Patterson, I believe we have agreed to disagree on that issue."

Mrs. Patterson, however, was not done disagreeing. "With all due respect, Mr. MacTavish, we have not agreed with you about anything. And now, in light of your recent difficulties, we are renewing our call to prohibit minor league baseball in this location."

Andy knew it was pointless to argue. "Surely you didn't come here today just to tell me that you still object to my baseball team."

Mrs. Patterson bristled. "Do not misunderstand me, sir. I am not opposed to your baseball team. I am opposed to the location for your team. Put your little team in Camden or in Wildwood. Put your team in Mt. Holly or in Asbury Park. I do not care. As I have already indicated, sir, I am here as a courtesy to advise you that my group will be holding a press conference to bring greater attention to the dangers associated with locating your enterprise here." With that, Mrs. Patterson pulled herself up even straighter, a drill sergeant in glen plaid, and marched out of Andy's office.

Andy wondered whether he had underestimated the ability of the birders to do damage to his business. Certainly they had been a problem when he first announced his plans to put a team in White Sands Beach. Construction had run over-schedule and over-budget when the birders had successfully managed to hold up the issuance of permits. But once the stadium was complete, the birders had largely faded from sight, an annoyance at times, but not a threat.

Andy dismissed the birders from consideration, turning his attention to the mail piling up in his inbox. There was the usual fan mail from preadolescent boys. The team turned a profit based on the loyalty of these young boys in their Sand Skeeter jerseys, but there were days that the mountain of fan mail reminded Andy of trash piling up in toxic landfills. Andy set aside the fan mail for cheerier correspondence. Heather Dean's unfortunate demise had set off a legal chain letter, as attorneys representing every imaginable interest checked in with their condolences and their threats. Andy especially enjoyed the letter from their supplier of novelty bats and balls, on sale in the Sand Skeeter gift shop.

Dear Mr. MacTavish, (Andy read)

On behalf of the owners of Dizzy Bat, Inc., their employees and families, I would like to express my sincerest condolences on your recent mascot tragedy. I understand that the woman's passing has been ruled accidental. We have, however, learned the hard way that injured parties often seek to assign blame for tragic accidents.

It is for that reason that I must advise you that Dizzy Bat, Inc. accepts no responsibility if our product is used without regard for the instructions, limitations and warnings which are included with every product shipment. You will note that Dizzy Bat, Inc. clearly advises that its product is not suitable for use as a spinning device without proper training and supervision. On behalf of Dizzy Bat, Inc., I am requesting that you forward a copy of the training protocol used by the Sand Skeeter Baseball Club to insure that all participants in any dizzy bat entertainment are fully trained in the proper safety techniques. If you utilize the safety program offered by Dizzy Bat, you can simply sign and return the enclosed affidavit attesting to the fact that Ms. Dean completed the approved forty-hour dizzy bat safety training program prior to being permitted by the Sand Skeeter Baseball Club to participate in the aforementioned dizzy bat entertainment.

I trust that it will not be necessary for Dizzy Bat, Inc. to take any further action to protect our interests as a result of this unfortunate accident. I thank you for your prompt attention to this matter. Again, my sincerest condolences on this most unfortunate tragedy.

Sincerely, Saviano, Esq.

Chuckling at the thought of his own attorney reading Mr. Saviano's letter, Andy took the correspondence from Dizzy Bat, Inc. and added it to the rapidly growing list of items earmarked for Mr. Garibaldi's action. Andy took solace in the knowledge that Mr. Garibaldi was about to earn his retainer.

Andy returned to the pile of unread mail, finding yet another letter vying for his immediate attention. In light of the unfortunate events that marked the finale of the inaugural season of Sand Skeeter baseball, the limited partners were requesting a meeting.

Like any successful businessman, Andy used other people's money to share the risk in exchange for a limited piece of the profits and an even more limited voice in the business decisions. It had been a mutually satisfactory arrangement, up until the moment Ms. Dean passed away on the pitcher's mound. Andy allowed himself to ponder what karmic atrocity could account for the sudden change in his fate before he snapped back into business mode, calculating how these new business circumstances could be used to his best advantage. Andy was interrupted in his calculations by a knock on his office door.

Andy made it a point to know all of the officers in the White Sands Police Department. It was good business, he knew, to support the local PBA. Still, he did not recognize this young black woman standing in his doorway. "Yes, ma'am. What can I do for you?" Walking to the doorway in greeting, Andy added, "We can talk inside."

The detective followed him back into the private office. "I'm investigating the disappearance of Donna Carter." She watched Andy closely, looking for the gesture that would tell her whether Andy's surprise was genuine.

Andy spoke slowly, evenly. "I didn't realize that Ms. Carter's absence was a police matter."

"At this point, we are treating her disappearance as a missing persons case."

Andy remembered a recent conversation with his attorney. "At this point?"

The detective chose not to respond to Andy's obvious question. "When was the last time you saw Ms. Carter?"

Andy MacTavish explained the team's schedule during the final week of the season. The mascot did not travel with the team to away games. With three away games leading up to the final home game, it had been a full week prior to Ms. Dean's unfortunate accident since Andy had seen Donna Carter.

It seemed to Andy that the detective was not convinced. "And you have no further knowledge regarding her whereabouts?"

Andy was quick to respond. "No."

"Well, anyway, thank you for your time, Mr. MacTavish."

"Thank you, Detective …" Andy paused, realizing that she still had not told him her name.

The detective turned to leave. When she reached the door, she paused for a moment, looking back at Andy MacTavish. "Oh, by the way, Mr. MacTavish, if you speak to your brother Billy, please let him know that Detective Sububie would like to talk to him about Ms. Carter." And with that, the newest member of the White Sands detective squad walked out the door, leaving Andy alone in an empty office, in an empty ballpark, in an empty beach town, alone with the rhythms of the off-season in White Sands Beach.

Andy dialed the telephone, unsure of what he wanted to say.

"You have reached the voice mail of Cassie O'Malley. Please leave a message at the beep." *Beep.*

"Uh, Cassie … it's me … Andy. Call me … no, wait, I mean … I miss you, Cassie. Somehow my house … I mean … anyway, I need your help with something … no, that doesn't sound right … I mean, I'm not calling because I need your help … well, actually, I do need your help, but I mean … I guess what I mean is … when can I see you again? Geez, this must sound pathetic, huh? Anyway, call me, okay?"

At the other end of the telephone line, in her condo in Doah, Cassie listened to Andy struggling to leave a message. In the background, Cheyenne Harbrough was screaming at the television. The too-earnest nerd scientist was desperately trying to reach his ingénue assistant to warn her of the impending danger. But the ingénue assistant was too busy to answer the phone and Cheyenne was screaming at the ingénue to "pick up the telephone," but the actress wasn't taking Cheyenne's advice. Neither was Cassie.

Cheyenne was disappointed by the ingénue assistant. Cheyenne was disappointed by Cassie. "Why didn't you pick up the phone?"

Purgatory

Time had never passed more slowly, Donna decided, than it had during the three days alone with Spit, waiting for the floodwaters to recede.

"That's the charm of the neighborhood," Spit explained, "and the challenge."

Donna laughed good-naturedly at Spit's explanation. "Doesn't a neighborhood imply neighbors?"

Spit gave Donna's objection serious consideration. "I guess neighborhood is the wrong word for this place, huh? What would you call it, Donna?"

Donna had a ready response. "Purgatory, Spit. This place is purgatory."

"You may be right, Donna, but take a look. I think your wait is just about over."

Donna looked. The floodwaters had finally retreated, the raised wooden path back to the mainland reasonably safe and dry. Even as they spoke, Donna recognized Madame Alexina making her way easily toward Spit's cottage.

"Omigod, Spit, you're right." Donna had never been so elated by the promise of psychic assistance. "I'm going home." Donna wanted to run inside and pack, but she had arrived at purgatory without baggage and would leave that way as well.

Spit loved it when a plan came together. "Let's wait and see what Madame Alexina has to say."

By the time Madame Alexina reached the house, Donna was hopping up and down on the deck, giddy with anticipation. "Wheeee. I'm going home!"

But Madame Alexina counseled caution. "We still don't know what really happened to Heather."

Donna wasn't listening. "Look, at the ballpark when Heather collapsed, I'll admit I was pretty freaked out, but c'mon, whatever happened to

Heather was an accident, wasn't it?"

Madame Alexina brought Donna up-to-date on the investigation. "The police have ruled Heather's death an accident, a case of heat stroke, the effects magnified by the alcohol and the costume."

Donna was already running up the path when Madame Alexina called her back. "But I have also heard that the police regret that they closed the case so quickly. Something has come up, I don't know what, that has the police getting ready to reopen the investigation."

Spit sided with Madame Alexina. "Besides, do you really want to trust your life to the police?"

Donna desperately wanted to go home, but something about Madame Alexina's counsel gave her pause. "But what about Billy? He must be going crazy by now. At least, I have to talk to Billy."

Madame Alexina envied Donna's young love. "I know how you feel, Donna, really I do. But the truth is, it could be dangerous if Billy knew where you were."

Donna jumped to Billy's defense. "C'mon, we're talking Billy here. Why would it be dangerous to see Billy?"

Her years of performing psychic readings had taught Madame Alexina to deflect the tough questions with another question. "Why do *you* think it could be dangerous?"

When Donna chose not to respond, Madame Alexina made a suggestion. "Let's go inside and sit down. Perhaps I could do a reading." With that, Madame Alexina entered the cottage, Spit just behind her. Nothing was stopping Donna from walking up the path and heading back to the mainland. Still, she told herself, it would be silly to disregard Madame Alexina's warning. Besides, after the reading, she could still make the decision to leave. Donna walked back inside Spit's stilt house.

Madame Alexina was rummaging through her enormous handbag, shaking her head and muttering. "Damn, I must have left them in my other bag." Turning to Spit, she added, "Do you still have that deck of Tarot cards I gave you?"

Spit looked away, avoiding her gaze until he came up with an idea, asking, "Could you use my baseball cards instead?"

Madame Alexina prided herself on her flexibility. "I'll improvise."

Spit kept his collection of baseball cards in an old shoebox. Madame Alexina spent the better part of an hour going through the box, feeling the vibrations in each card and checking the lifetime stats of the ballplayers before settling on some fifty-six cards.

"These will do for the minor arcana." Madame Alexina turned toward Spit in challenge. "These are your common cards, Spit. I need your good cards for the major arcana."

Spit briefly considered holding out, but he knew that Madame Alexina would only wear him down. He retrieved a smaller box from deep in his closet. Madame Alexina removed each card from its protective sleeve, rubbed the cards, even bent a few in half and sniffed the edges of the superstars before assembling the twenty-two cards that would represent the major arcana.

Madame Alexina shuffled the deck expertly and dealt the cards expertly into piles between herself and Donna. ("In a former life," she confided, "I was a dealer in Atlantic City.") In what seemed to Donna to be a random pattern, Madame Alexina selected several cards and turned them face up—Derek Jeter, Ken Griffey Jr., Josh Beckett, Jason Kendall. Each time she exposed a card she grunted and buried the card deep in the deck. She repeated this routine four or five times without saying a word. Finally she announced that the cards were ready. Donna was too nervous by then to respond; she kept her eyes focused on Madame Alexina's hands and on the baseball cards that would reveal her future.

Madame Alexina reshuffled the deck. "Normally I would do a general reading, to set the tone, before attempting to answer a specific question." She paused. "Under the circumstances, I think we can all agree to bypass the general reading and get right to the question at hand."

Spit and Donna nodded in unison.

Madame Alexina was pleased. "Good. Let's begin." With that she cut the deck and placed five cards out on the table, explaining her actions as she proceeded with the reading.

"There are many different ways that the cards can be arranged, even more ways they might be interpreted. Over time, each spiritualist develops an affinity for the arrangement that is uniquely suited for his or her individual talents."

Madame Alexina fanned out the five cards in an arc on the table. "Over time, I have found this design to be especially revealing."

Madame Alexina peered directly at Donna. "Now tell me, Donna, what would you like to ask the cards?"

Donna didn't know whether to laugh or cry, to scream or just to get up and leave. "Ask the cards if it's safe for me to go home."

Madame Alexina turned the first of the five cards face up. "Gary Sheffield," she read aloud, "Florida Marlins." Turning her attention to Spit, she said, "Tell me something about Gary Sheffield."

Spit thought for a moment. "Well, for one thing, I didn't realize he used to play for the Marlins." Spit explained, "He's the right fielder for the New York Yankees. A huge offensive weapon. Clutch."

Madame Alexina quietly soaked in Gary Sheffield's aura. "Some people don't think the first card is terribly important, but in some ways it is the key to the success of the reading. You can't possibly expect to get the right answer unless you ask the right question. The purpose of the first card is to help us to understand that question."

Donna wasn't sure if she was supposed to say anything, if she was allowed to say anything. "So what does Gary Sheffield mean to you?"

"I might just as easily ask what Gary Sheffield means to you." Madame Alexina paused, before continuing with her reading. "Gary Sheffield is the ten of swords. He tells me that you must treat your question with the respect that it deserves. You are asking the right question, but you fail to recognize how incredibly serious the question is. You wish to minimize the danger, but Gary Sheffield tells me that things truly are as bad as they appear. And so we must approach the question with a seriousness of purpose, for the consequences of a wrong answer could be devastating.

"The second card will help us understand what's important in the background." Madame Alexina challenged Donna with her eyes and she turned over the second card … Billy Ripken. Madame Alexina turned again to Spit. "I thought his name was Cal Ripken."

Spit looked confused. "So did I."

Madame Alexina examined the card more closely, reading aloud. "William Oliver Ripken … Baltimore Orioles …1987 … teamed up with his brother Cal, Jr., and his father Cal, Sr. It doesn't take a psychic to interpret this card. Anyone?"

Spit raised his hand as if he were back in high school. It was rare that Spit knew the answer and he waved his arm excitedly. "Ooooh, pick me."

"Spit?"

Spit was beaming. "Family, right?"

Madame Alexina grinned. "Maybe." Shifting her attention, she added, "Donna, what do you think?"

"I don't think so."

Spit's face dropped. "I was sure I had that one right."

Madame Alexina, too, thought Spit might be right, so she decided to probe more deeply. "Tell me a little bit about your family."

"I don't have family." Donna was almost belligerent in her response. "I left home when I was fourteen. It's been eight years since I've seen them."

Madame Alexina recognized that Donna wasn't ready to talk about her family. "Tell you what, let's just take a look at the third card."

Madame Alexina flipped over the next baseball card … Mickey Mantle.

The Mick's presence at the reading excited Spit. "Holy shit … I didn't even know I owned a Mantle." Spit's interest in the reading was renewed by the Yankee superstar. "What can you tell from the Mick's card?"

Madame Alexina thought for a moment. "Well … either Donna is a switch-hitting farm boy with bad knees, or she's a dreamer … her head in the clouds … when it's not in the bottle."

Donna felt a sudden yearning for a shot of peppermint schnapps. "Am I allowed to have a drink?" Donna saw the look on Madame Alexina's face and quickly added, "Maybe later."

Madame Alexina turned over the fourth card, revealing Osbourne Earl Smith, all-star shortstop, St. Louis Cardinals. She examined the card closely, letting Ozzie work his magic. "The world is a place of extraordinary forces, forces pushing us to find our center and at the same time pulling us into temptation. The trick is to find a way to balance these forces."

Donna was puzzled. "Do you mean moderation in all things?"

Madame Alexina snorted at the mention of moderation. "If I meant moderation, I would say moderation. Balance, Donna, the key is balance."

"I don't understand."

"Okay, think of it this way. Imagine a seesaw, you know what I mean, right?"

Donna nodded and Madame Alexina continued.

"Okay then, the key to balancing the scale isn't to limit yourself to small weights. The key to balancing the seesaw is equal, but opposite, weights."

"Equal, but opposite?"

"Yes, Donna. The key to balance is to embrace the opposite."

Donna was beginning to understand. "So I have to find my opposite, to balance me on the seesaw."

Madame Alexina smiled. "Almost, Donna. But you're not sitting on one end of the seesaw. You are the seesaw. Be the seesaw, Donna."

Spit gasped. "Wow, you're good."

Madame Alexina laughed heartily. "And I still have one card left."

Madame Alexina revealed the final card ... Blue Moon Odom. She stared at the card, saying nothing.

Donna waited for Madame Alexina to resume the reading, but Madame Alexina sat there, tension growing in the silence, like bacteria.

Suddenly Madame Alexina announced, "The Moon," before slipping back into silence. When Madame Alexina continued, she chose her words with care.

The Far End of the Boardwalk

"Why didn't you pick up the phone?" Long after Cheyenne had said her goodbyes, her words hung in the air like a blimp, taking aerial shots of Cassie's condo.

Cassie spent the afternoon ducking reflexively each time the question passed overhead. *Why didn't she pick up the phone,* she wondered. She tried to work on a new story, but the question floating overhead continued to get in the way, bumping up against her computer screen. She spent the afternoon and evening trying on excuses, but none of them were a good fit. She missed Andy already, perhaps more than she was willing to admit.

That night, Cassie fell asleep thinking about the dirigible in her bedroom. That night she dreamt of the dirigible exploding in her bedroom. Oh, the telephony.

Cassie awoke at 3:30, a dull ache above her left eye, part sinus headache, part heartache. A hot shower took care of the headache. Cassie understood what she needed to do to take care of the heartache. Throwing her essentials in an overnight bag, Cassie selected a few of her favorite CDs for the drive. Settling in behind the wheel of her rebuilt '67 Ford Mustang, Cassie bypassed the parkway, meandering along back roads through the Pine Barrens, Count Basie on the piano, setting the mood for her pre-dawn drive.

It had been more than a year since Cassie, or anyone else, had reported a mysterious dead deer sighting. Still Cassie found herself scanning the roadway, peering into the pine forest for evidence of the elusive Jersey Devil. Briefly, Cassie considered the DEP's attack on her integrity. Had she exaggerated her findings? She accepted that some might find her explanation far-fetched, but her account of the events she knew to be accurate. Cassie was satisfied with her reportage. While Cassie considered the question, Count Basie slid in some stride piano, echoes of Fats Waller reverberating in the Mustang.

By the time Count Basie was finished, the aroma of cranberry bogs and pine needles gave way to sand and salt air. Moments later, Cassie found herself pulling into Andy's driveway. She looked at her wristwatch. The time blinked 5:00 a.m.

Cassie felt silly sitting behind the wheel of her Mustang, but she could not bring herself to knock on the door at that hour. It would make her, she decided, look desperate. Cassie was determined to wait for sunup.

At eight that morning, stepping outside to get the morning paper, Andy MacTavish discovered Cassie O'Malley fast asleep in his driveway. Opening the car door, Andy kissed her lightly on the cheek. Cassie looked up at Andy. "I got your phone message."

Andy smiled. "You've got style, Ms. O'Malley."

"I was worried maybe it was a little pushy, showing up on your doorstep without calling."

"I'm glad you're here, Cassie."

"I love you, Andy MacTavish." Cassie paused. "But I need more than love. I need a cup of coffee."

Andy smiled. "Let's go inside. I just put up a pot."

Sitting on the deck overlooking the Atlantic Ocean, a mug of steamy hot Arabica warming her hands and her heart, Cassie understood why she had been scared to pick up the phone. "I love it here, Andy."

There was so much that Andy wanted to say. It was hard to know where to start. "Have you ever been to the zoo?"

"Huh?"

"The zoo. I was thinking maybe we should go to the zoo today."

Cassie was confused. "When you found me in the driveway this morning, you weren't … I mean … really … the zoo?"

Andy began tidying up the coffee cups. "You'll see. It'll be fun."

Strolling through the county zoo with Andy as her tour guide, Cassie allowed the day to unfold before her. They watched as prairie dogs peeked out from their underground tunnels, as otters swam lazily in the cement pond. They admired, from a distance, the Bengal tiger and, from behind glass, the Burmese python. They lamented the solitary bison, and its cloud of insect admirers. They spotted leopards, zebras and giraffes, camels, cougars and capybara. The prairie dogs and the otters, the Bengal tiger and the Burmese python, the bison and its cloud of insect admirers, the leopards, zebras and giraffes, the camels, cougars and the capybara all watched as

Andy and Cassie strolled through the county zoo, holding hands, pointing and laughing and pausing every few hundred feet to remind themselves of their good fortune, and kiss.

"That was fun."

Andy wasn't certain whether Cassie was referring to the zoo or to the kiss, but he was certain it really didn't matter. "Are you tired?"

"What did you have in mind?"

And so, when they exited the county zoo, Andy took them to the boardwalk, to the rides, to the carousel. Cassie felt like she'd already caught the brass ring, but she rode with Andy, again and again, the universe spreading out around them as they rode their brightly painted wooden steeds.

Each time they made a revolution, Cassie noticed another food stand on the boardwalk. "Can we get something to eat?"

Andy suddenly realized they had not eaten all day. "Of course, Cassie. What do you want?"

Cassie was ready with a most unusual response. "You know what I always wanted to do when I was a kid? I always wanted to see if I could eat one of everything. What do you say, Andy? We'll start at one end of the boardwalk and eat our way down to the other end, stopping at every food stand along the way. Are you game?"

Andy laughed. "Are you serious? You wanna eat all that crap? I bet you don't make it past the second food stand."

"You don't know me very well, Andy MacTavish. You just try and keep up with me."

With that, Cassie set out on her quest to eat at every food stand on the boardwalk, a skeptical Andy scrambling to catch up. They started with a slice of pizza (Cassie adding onions and peppers to her slice) and washed it down with a Dr Pepper.

"Give up yet?" Andy teased Cassie as she emitted a most unladylike burp.

"You better just worry about yourself, Andy. How about we try one of those foot-long hot dogs?"

They each had a foot-long topped with mustard and sauerkraut. Andy was giggling with delight, mustard flying off the end of the frank, miraculously missing them both.

Cassie showed no signs of slowing down. "Not bad," Andy admitted as she polished off the last bite of frank. "You know what I'm in the mood for?" Andy asked, hoping he could bring their effort to a quick conclusion. "How about we try the cotton candy?"

Their snack was turning competitive. Extreme eating. Cotton candy. Saltwater taffy. Pistachios. Clam chowder (first Manhattan and then New England). Onion rings.

By now the boardwalk was beginning to buzz as word spread regarding their adventure. A small crowd began to follow the couple, rooting for their favorite, editorializing on their selections and making side bets regarding the possible outcomes.

Sausage and pepper on a torpedo roll. Corn on the cob. Fried clams. Italian ices. "Genuine" Philadelphia cheese steak. Orange Julius.

Andy was in serious gastric distress, but Cassie only seemed to gain strength with each order. Andy was impressed. This was a woman of diverse talents, he told himself.

French fries. Zeppoli. Custard cones. Steamers. Chocolate fudge. Pretzels.

They reached the far end of the boardwalk, Andy grateful to have come to the end.

"Are you quitting, Andy? Give me a minute for a pee break and I'll start back the other way."

"To make things a little more interesting," Cassie suggested upon returning from the ladies' room, "why don't we try some of the amusements as we eat our way back?"

Andy tried to keep up, finally accepting defeat halfway back, between the roller coaster and the whip, and halfway through a bucket of fried chicken.

In the car, riding back to Andy's oceanfront home, Cassie realized that Andy had yet to explain the purpose of his telephone call. "It sounded like you were in some kind of trouble."

Rumor, Gossip and Story Ideas

"I had a visit yesterday from the police." Andy and Cassie were sitting on the couch in his family room, watching TV, recovering from their bout of extreme eating.

Cassie changed the channel, looking for an old movie. "About the dead girl Heather?"

Andy did his best to explain. "No, I don't think so. They were asking me about Donna."

Cassie had almost forgotten about Donna. "You mean she hasn't turned up yet?"

"No." Andy was worried. "I'm worried."

Cassie tried to downplay the situation. "I'm sure she's fine, Andy."

"I hope you're right, Cassie."

Cassie waited, giving Andy time to figure out what he wanted to say. "I need you to help me find her, Cassie."

Cassie continued to work her way through Andy's cable TV menu. "Let the police do their job, Andy. They'll find her."

"I need you to help me find her before the police do."

For the first time, Cassie grew concerned. "Tell me you're not involved in this somehow, Andy."

"I'm not involved in this."

The pain Cassie felt in her gut was not from overeating. "I mean it, Andy. Tell me again."

Andy met Cassie's gaze. "I mean it, Cassie. I'm not involved."

Again, Cassie sensed she needed to give Andy more time.

"Only I think maybe my kid brother Billy is."

Cassie turned off the television. "What does your brother have to do with all of this?"

"Do you need anything?" Andy stood up and walked into the kitchen. Retrieving a bottle of water from the refrigerator, Andy explained. "Billy and Donna were dating."

Cassie was reminded of how much she didn't yet know about the life of Andy MacTavish. "That doesn't mean he was involved, Andy ... unless ... unless there's something more you're about to tell me."

"Billy and I don't talk much, but he called me a couple of days before the end of the season, to ask a favor." Andy explained how Billy had asked that he give Donna the last night of the season off so that Billy and Donna could go to a concert in Philly.

There were too many years of bad blood between Andy and Billy for Cassie to fully understand the hostile subtext, but the point was obvious. Cassie understood what concerned Andy: that Donna had skipped the ball game to keep a date with his brother and now, a week later, Donna still had failed to reappear. Cassie understood why Andy would suspect that his brother was involved, but when she said as much, Andy explained that there was still more to the story.

"The morning after Heather died, Billy told me that he and Donna had a fight."

"What happened?"

"Billy talked Donna into skipping the ball game. It was Billy who engineered having Heather cover for her, but the night of the game, when he picked Donna up, he says that they got into a fight. Billy says that Donna refused to go to the concert with him after all and Billy, being Billy, says that he went to the concert without her."

Andy stopped to catch his breath. "I never know how much of Billy's stories to believe, but even if I accept everything he told me as gospel, he was still the last person to see Donna before she went missing."

Cassie considered the story carefully before asking, "How much of this have you shared with the police?"

Andy examined his hands. "None of it."

Cassie made a decision. "Okay, here's the deal. I can help you look for Donna, but we better find her fast, before the police realize that you've been withholding information."

Andy remembered the detective's parting comment, as she was leaving Andy's office at the ballpark. "It may be too late for that already."

Cassie debated her next move, knowing it might be awkward. "I'm gonna call the magazine."

"Do you ..." Andy thought better of the question he was about to ask. "I'll be right back." Andy walked down the hall to his office, leaving Cassie to speak privately with her editor.

"Morris, it's me."

"Cassie, sweetheart. Where are you?"

"White Sands Beach."

"The beach? What are you doing at the beach? Following a story, I hope."

Cassie took a deep breath, knowing the answer would hurt her editor. "I met a man."

Cassie listened for his pain on the silent phone line. "That's wonderful, Cassie," but the silence had lingered a half-beat too long for Morris to hide his disappointment. "Who is he?"

"Andy MacTavish." Cassie didn't wait for her editor's reaction. "Listen, Morris. I need your help with something. You remember the dizzy bat race?"

"What's wrong, Cassie?"

"The girl's still missing."

Morris was confused. "I thought the girl was dead."

"No, Morris, the other girl." Cassie reminded Morris of the details of the dizzy bat tragedy. "What are you hearing at the magazine?"

Morris had developed an effective network of sources feeding him rumor, gossip and story ideas, but he had heard nothing about the missing girl.

It seemed odd to Cassie that Morris had no lead for her to follow. "You'll let me know if you hear something?"

"Of course." Morris hated himself for what he was about to ask. "By the way, is this for the magazine, or for Mr. MacTavish?"

Cassie hated herself for letting Morris hold on to a false hope for all these years. "It's for me, Morris."

"I'm sorry, Cassie. I was being petty." Morris tried his best to sound upbeat. "Where can I call you, sweetheart?"

Cassie wasn't ready to give him Andy's number. "My cell."

Morris knew that she never bothered to check her cell phone. "Your cell?"

Cassie laughed. "I know, Morris. I'll try. Look, I'll call you in a couple of days. Okay?"

"I'll see what I can find."

"You're the best, Morris."

Morris knew he was, at best, second best. "Yeah, okay."

Cassie had barely hung up the phone before it began to ring. She stood there looking at the ringing telephone.

Andy, returning from his office, grabbed the receiver.

"I hope it's not too late for me to call." Andy knew that his attorney was just being polite.

"What is it, Mr. Garibaldi?"

"Andy, are you watching TV?"

Andy was puzzled. "No."

"Turn on the television, Andy. Channel sixty-two."

The Unasked Question

When Madame Alexina proposed to read the Tarot, Donna tolerated the reading as a means to gain Madame Alexina's cooperation and her own ultimate release from purgatory. With each card, however, she had been sucked further into Madame Alexina's world of prophecy and omen. The universe had narrowed until all that Donna could see were the baseball cards that lay exposed before her.

At some point, between cards three and four, between Mickey Mantle and Ozzie Smith, night fell like a pop fly dropping between short and center field. Donna found it hard to believe that she had spent the entire day watching Madame Alexina read the future in Spit's old baseball cards. It didn't seem possible that a full day had elapsed. And yet, at the same time, Donna felt as though she had spent her entire life seated there at Spit's card table. She looked out the window at the deepening night.

"The moon signifies darkness," Madame Alexina explained. "Unless it signifies a light in the darkness. The moon reveals a path in our darkest hour or it serves to warn us to choose our path wisely, for the dangers are enormous should we lose our way. The moon reveals to us our fellow travelers and challenges us to distinguish friend from foe."

Madame Alexina chose her words with care. "The moon is a powerful card, not to be trifled with. It holds its meaning close, daring us to act, mocking us. The moon is deception."

"So what do you think it means in my case?" Donna blurted out her question.

"For that, I must go see my own spiritual advisor. I am sorry, but I must take my leave." Madame Alexina announced her impending departure, but made no effort to stand.

"But …" Donna wanted an explanation.

Madame Alexina would only say, "My corporeal form will be here with you the entire time, but my astral body must travel an extraordinary distance if I am to interpret the final card correctly."

"But …" and this time Donna would not be cut off. "What am I supposed to do in the meantime?"

"In the meantime, you wait with Spit. You wait for my return."

Madame Alexina lapsed into silence, slumped in her chair, her physical body an empty vessel.

Donna looked at Spit. "What do we do now?"

Spit shrugged. "I guess we wait."

Donna stood up, pacing in the small room, trapped in a cage with a chemically imbalanced cabbie and his astral fare.

"How do you live like this?"

"Me?" Spit was startled by Donna's question. "I never gave it much thought."

"Never?"

Spit was philosophical. "I try not to think too much. It just makes my head hurt. You know," Spit offered by way of explanation, "I wasn't always like this."

"Like what, Spit?"

"Please, I know I'm not the brightest bulb in the deck. I used to be a Young Republican. Worshipped President Reagan. Nancy too. Just say no. When George Bush invaded Iraq—not Dubya, his father—I volunteered to go. Figured we could take out the A-rabs and cement a generation of Republican rule and be righteous all at the same time."

Donna's perspective on life in south Jersey was decidedly apolitical. "You mean George Bush had a father?" She realized the question had not come out right. "You mean George Bush's father was named George Bush? And he was president? And he invaded Iraq too? That's just weird."

Spit agreed with Donna's assessment. "Tell me about it."

Donna suddenly wanted to hear more from this most unlikely teacher. "What was it like in Iraq?"

Spit had spent years trying to forget Desert Storm. Now he did his best to remember. The sand. The blood. The dead. The pride in a job well done. "I just wish we'd been allowed to finish what we started. When I hear about these young kids today, more killing and more dying … You know, when Madame Alexina turned over the Billy Ripken card, I was convinced the card was trying to tell us something important about your family."

Donna was beginning to think that Spit might be the one who would understand. "To tell you the truth, Spit …"

"The moon signifies darkness."

Donna jumped at the sound of Madame Alexina's throaty whisper announcing her return from the astral plane. "Huh?"

Madame Alexina was ready to complete the reading. "We have to look at the moon in relation to each of the four other cards … Gary Sheffield, Billy Ripken, Mickey Mantle, Ozzie Smith. Individual cards may be subject to interpretation, but each set of five cards is unique, revealing a unique message. Deciphering that message is the province of a willing seeker and an accomplished guide."

Madame Alexina's next words cut deeply. "Are you a willing seeker of the truth?"

Donna nodded. "I am."

"We began this morning looking to answer the question, 'Is it safe for you to go home?' I tried to explain to you that the value of a reading depends on our willingness to ask the right question. I suggest that we have not yet asked that right question. The cards should not tell us what we want to know, but what we need to know. In this case, the cards reveal their answer in the form of the unasked question. Who is trying to kill you, Donna?"

An Extended Stay at Casa Spit

"What do you think?" Donna realized she was beginning to see Spit as a credible advisor.

"You're welcome to stay here as long as you like."

The Tarot had put Donna's central nervous system on full alert. She could smell the danger wafting over from the mainland. Still she was not ready for an extended stay at Casa Spit. "That's really sweet of you, but I don't think I can do that."

Spit was not satisfied by her response. "It could be dangerous for you out there."

"Spit's right. I think you should accept his offer ... At least for another few days." Stopping mid-sentence to catch her breath, Madame Alexina nudged her way back into the conversation.

Madame Alexina had nearly forgotten how much energy astral travel burned. In truth, she rarely traveled at all anymore, preferring instead to hover. There had been a time in her youth when Madame Alexina had traversed continents in astral form, but as she grew older, she discovered the danger of losing her bearings, making a wrong turn as it were and risking a permanent divorce from her corporeal form. And so, as she aged, she chose to pull in on her boundaries, keeping one astral eye on her point of origin and the other on her intended target. Whenever possible, she simply hovered at a great height directly above her own inert form, scanning the horizon for psychic clues.

On this occasion, she had traveled many miles and had done so after a full day of reading, without a proper deck, seeking meaning in Spit's collection of baseball cards. Quite simply, the effort had knocked her on her proverbial astral.

"I'm going home to get some proper rest," announced Madame Alexina. "Donna, you are an adult and responsible for your own behavior. I cannot force you to stay behind, but the cards have spoken. If the reading doesn't convince you, there's nothing more that I can do."

Donna looked at Spit and shrugged before announcing her decision. "I'll be okay here."

Madame Alexina was pleased with Donna's decision. "I didn't want this to influence your decision, but the police are beginning to ask questions about Billy. Tomorrow I will look in on him from a safe distance and see what I can learn."

With that, Madame Alexina walked out, closing the door behind her.

"I'm scared, Spit."

Spit suddenly felt sorry for the frightened young girl hiding out in his isolated cottage. "I wish I could make the danger go away, Donna, I really do, but I guess all we can do right now is wait it out."

"Madame Alexina said that the police are looking at Billy. Do you think that Billy … ?" Donna didn't even want to finish the question.

"I told you, Donna; I try not to think. It makes life easier."

"Is that why you live out here, Spit? To make life easier?"

"I like it out here. The cottage used to belong to my grandma. I spent summers with her, eeling."

"Eeling?"

"You know, catching eels."

Donna tried to picture the pre-Iraq Spit. She would not have liked the earnest Young Republican, but she wished, for Spit's sake, that he had survived Desert Storm.

"I haven't thought about this in a very long time, but when I was a little girl, my father used to take me fishing."

Spit remembered the Billy Ripken card. "Your father?"

Donna took a deep breath. "My father moved out when I was five."

Spit didn't know what to say. "That must have been hard."

"Yeah. I loved my dad. When he left …"

Spit's head was beginning to hurt. "So your dad was a fisherman?"

Donna remembered how her dad would put dough balls on her fishing line and stand on the bank feigning interest while she dangled her pole in the town pond. "No. Not really. But I do think he liked the peace and quiet."

"What about your mother?"

"Like I said, my dad liked the peace and quiet."

Spit's head was throbbing. "Your parents used to fight?"

"Yeah." When Donna remembered the yelling, she was forever the five-year-old with pigtails, hiding in the closet, trying to muffle the soundtrack of her parents' failed marriage. "My mother was always yelling at him … and then, after he left, she yelled at me instead."

"I'm sorry." Spit's head was about to detonate. "Can we finish this conversation in the morning?"

"Of course. Do you mind if I ask you one question, Spit?"

Spit pressed the heels of each hand into his temples, hoping to relieve the pressure. "As long as I don't have to think too hard."

"Do you really like living out here?"

Spit was relieved. "Yeah, I really like it out here."

"Will you teach me?"

"Huh?"

"I want you to teach me how to like it out here."

"There's no secret to living out here. Just think about the alternative."

"I don't understand."

"What's society like?" Spit asked, and answered. "Too many people, living too close, moving too fast, spending too much. And what has it brought us beside stress and debt? Cancer, cholesterol, cardiac arrest, George Bush, George W. Bush, heaven help us, Jeb Bush. No, thank you. I like it here." Spit thought for a moment and decided his answer needed emphasis. "I like it just fine."

Donna tried to see life through Spit's eyes. "Okay, but instead of all that, out here there's just … nothing. What do you do all day?"

"When I'm hungry, I eat. When I'm tired, I sleep."

Donna struggled to make sense of Spit's approach to life. "It just seems like there's a lot of waiting around for something to happen."

Spit smiled. "Sort of. I like to think of it as waiting around for nothing to happen."

Donna couldn't shake the feeling that there was a secret to this life, lurking just beyond her grasp. "Don't you get bored?"

Spit generally avoided such introspection. Still, he was enjoying the exercise. "There's a rhythm out here—the moon, the tides, the seasons—you have to reset your biological clock, get in sync with … I don't know, let's call it the infinite."

Donna furrowed her brow, as though it might help her understand. "I'm trying, Spit, but …"

"Spend the night on the pontoon boat."

Donna pictured the secret to life, moving further out of reach, taunting her from afar. "What are you talking about, Spit?"

Spit was trying to be patient. "Listen, I'm tired. If you want to understand, spend the night alone on the water. You can take the pontoon boat out just beyond the channel markers. Spend the night looking at the stars."

Spit retreated to his bedroom, leaving Donna alone and confused and unable to sleep. It was nearly midnight. Donna lay in bed and stared at the ceiling, imagining a starry canopy. She checked her watch. 12:09. She rolled over, determined to sleep. She lay first on one side and then the other. She checked her watch. 12:23. She pulled the blanket up around her neck. She kicked the blanket down to the floor. She checked her watch. 12:42. She sat up in bed, trying hard not to think. She walked around the room. She climbed back into bed. She checked her watch. 1:04.

Donna climbed from bed and walked over to Spit's bedroom door. She stood there, debating her next move. She checked her watch. 1:07. Knocking on Spit's door, she walked in without waiting for an invitation. Spit was snoring lightly.

"Spit?" Donna spoke softly at first and then again, louder. "Spit?"

Donna hoped she was not out of line, as she shook Spit awake.

"Hunnnh?"

"Does it count if I leave the pontoon boat tied up at the dock?"

And so it came to pass at 1:11 in the morning that Donna Carter ventured out Spit's front door onto the old wooden deck, climbing with care down the ladder to the waterline some eight feet below and to Spit's pontoon boat, tied to one of the wooden stilts that elevated Spit's home above the saltwater.

Checking to make sure that the boat was tied securely to the stilt, Donna boarded the boat, stretched out on the platform and stared at a sky filled with stars. The night sky was magnificent, Donna told herself, but neither Orion nor Cassiopeia, not the Big Dipper nor the Little, brought her knowledge or sleep. She checked her watch. 1:28. Donna threw her timepiece overboard and watched by moonlight for the ever-expanding concentric circle of time.

Donna rolled over and stretched. Reflexively she checked her watch before she remembered that she no longer trapped time on her wrist. Judging by the position of the sun, it was mid-morning. Herons waited patiently among the sedge grass. Donna watched the sunlight sparkle on the water. She climbed the ladder and walked back up to the house. Spit was squeezing orange juice in the kitchen. He handed Donna a glass.

"Good morning, Donna."

"And a very good morning to you too, Spit."

"You look different."

Donna held out her naked wrist for inspection. "I feel different."

"I'm gonna scramble up some eggs. Are you hungry?"

"No."

Spit tried to remember how long Donna had been his houseguest. Three days? Four? Spit needed to spend the day behind the wheel of his cab, earning a living. He was satisfied that he could safely leave Donna behind. He explained as much, between bites, and Donna quickly agreed.

"I'll be fine."

Donna grabbed a note pad and began scribbling furiously. "Could you stop at my apartment? I need a few things. You know, clean clothes, toothbrush. It's all on the list, okay?" She handed Spit the note and the key to her apartment.

As Spit got up to leave, Donna remembered one more item for the list. "Could you stop at the drugstore for me? I need tampons."

Spit's face turned red. "Yeah, okay."

Donna jumped up and kissed Spit's scarlet cheek. "You're a doll."

Cleanup in Aisle Three

Detective Sububie's colleagues on the White Sands police force generally avoided surveillance assignments, unless, of course, in season, on the beach. The endless hours of bitter coffee and stale leads rarely led to anything more than a reprimand for abuse of the department's overtime policy. Detective Sububie, however, embraced the long period of inaction as an opportunity to refine her theory of the crime. After three days in her car, keeping watch on Donna Carter's apartment, the detective had constructed an elaborate theory of the missing persons case.

Heather Dean died on the pitcher's mound of natural causes while she was masquerading as the team mascot. Natural causes, yes, but questionable circumstances to be sure. Meanwhile, the real mascot had gone missing. As the newest member of the squad, Detective Sububie knew that the missing persons case was a low priority, but before she was finished, the detective was confident she would be solving a sensational double murder. This was the sort of case on which a young black detective could build her career.

Mavis Sububie sat in her Chevy, in a far corner of the parking lot, sipping coffee: the solitary life of a detective waiting for her big break.

Spit drove past the drugstore four times before he could bring himself to stop. He sat in the parking lot and visualized the challenge that lay ahead. Surveying the layout, he told himself that he could handle the transaction, but down deep he knew the truth. This would be worse than that time at the age of fifteen when he first tried to buy condoms. Spit forced himself to take ten deep, even breaths before getting out of the cab.

Spit approached the counter, mumbling. "Where can I find the feminine hygiene products?"

The cashier looked up. "I'm sorry, sir. What was that?"

Spit stared at his shoes. "Where can I find the feminine hygiene products?"

The teenage girl behind the counter giggled and directed Spit to aisle three. When he got there, he did his best to ignore the other shoppers. He planned to grab a box, throw his money on the counter and get out fast. Then he took a closer look. Regulars. Supers. Super plus. Ultra. Spit figured Donna for a regular. Then he noticed the slender regulars. Cardboard applicators. Plastic applicators. Soft plastic applicators. Grabbing a pretty pink multi-pack, Spit tried not to think. Turning quickly, he bumped the shelf, sending a rainbow of pastel protection—regular and slender regular alike, super, super plus and ultra—tumbling to the floor.

Over the loudspeaker, Spit listened for the announcement. "Cleanup in aisle three."

By the time he was safely back in the cab, he realized he was hyperventilating. To settle his nerves, Spit lit a cigarette—a Virginia Slim left on the back seat by his last fare.

Spit still had to make a stop at Donna's apartment. He drove slowly, smoking the cigarette. Checking his odometer, Spit knew he had come a long way, baby.

Spit turned left into the garden apartment complex, following the signs to building six. The parking lot was crowded, but a spot opened up just in front of the building. Spit located Donna's ground-level apartment and let himself in.

Sitting at the far end of the lot, Detective Sububie put down her coffee.

Inside the apartment, Spit tried not to think as he went down Donna's list. He found her blue jeans and t-shirts without difficulty. He found her sweatshirt and socks. When he opened her panty drawer, not thinking became an unmentionable challenge. He tried not to think about Donna in her yellow bikini panties. He tried not to think about her in black lace. He especially tried not to think about Donna in her red thong. Shutting his eyes, Spit reached into the drawer. Grabbing random panties he tossed them into a suitcase along with her toiletries and the rest of her clothes.

Leaving her apartment, Spit compulsively checked that he had turned off the lights. He jiggled the doorknob to be certain the door had locked behind him.

Sitting at the far end of the lot, Detective Sububie watched as Spit tossed the suitcase in the back of the cab. It had been the detective's experience that a dead girl rarely had need of luggage. Mavis Sububie started up the Chevy.

When Spit pulled out of the parking lot, he was grateful to be heading home. His day on the mainland had been difficult. He hoped that his encounter with Donna's panties would not continue to intrude on his thoughts.

Detective Sububie followed from a respectful distance. Traffic was sparse and the detective had no problem keeping the cab in view without making her intentions obvious. Focusing her attention on the taxicab up ahead, Detective Sububie didn't notice the car that had pulled out of the adjacent parking lot several hundred feet to her rear.

Twenty minutes later, less than a mile from the ocean, Spit turned off the main road. Detective Sububie hesitated to follow the cab down the unmarked one-lane roadway. Leaving her car parked on the shoulder, the detective proceeded on foot. She could see Spit's cab, not more than a half-mile ahead where the road dead-ended at the water. She used the scrub along the narrow road to provide cover as she moved cautiously toward the taxi. She crouched in the sedge grass and watched as Spit got out of the cab and struck off on foot. She continued to make her way carefully toward the car, uncertain what she might find in this isolated corner of the world.

When Detective Sububie reached the water's edge, she spotted the narrow wooden planking, an elevated boardwalk extending for several hundred yards over the marsh. At the far end of the boardwalk, she could see Spit carrying the suitcase that he'd removed from Donna's apartment. The detective was startled to realize that there were a couple of ramshackle cottages hidden in the marshland. She watched until Spit disappeared into the marsh.

Detective Sububie considered her next move. There was no cover to be had once she stepped out onto the boardwalk. If she chose to follow Spit, she would be exposed to anyone who might be watching. She could call for backup and wait, but it seemed to the detective that Spit was likely to have a boat available to make a water escape. Detective Sububie considered her options and stepped out onto the boardwalk.

Another time, under other circumstances, she might have stopped to marvel at the desolate beauty of this spot, but this was no nature walk. Her stride was purposeful, her senses on alert. Suddenly she heard voices coming from up ahead. With no place to run and no time to think, Detective Sububie climbed down under the boardwalk, clinging awkwardly to a support beam on the underside of the planking, suspended in midair some eight feet above the marsh. She waited, hanging from the wooden beam like a piñata. Peering through a crack in the planking, Detective Sububie watched as Donna Carter walked down from the cottage. The support beams shook as Donna passed overhead and, for a moment, Detective Sububie worried that she might lose her grip on the wooden beam.

Detective Sububie realized that Donna was heading for the car. Having tracked Donna to this isolated cottage, the detective was not prepared to let her get away. Watching from under the boardwalk, she waited until Donna neared land and then she climbed up onto the boardwalk. Moving with surprising speed, she caught the startled young woman just as she was reaching for the car door, reaching out with her own hand from behind to grasp Donna's forearm. Donna screamed, but made no attempt to escape.

"Excuse me, Ms. Carter, isn't it?" She held out her detective's badge for Donna's inspection.

"Omigod. You scared the crap out of me." Donna looked around expecting something more than one lone detective.

"People are worried about you, Ms. Carter."

Donna wasn't sure what she should say. "I'm fine. On vacation, sort of."

Detective Sububie considered how she wanted to proceed. "So the man I saw earlier … the man with the suitcase … he isn't holding you against your will?"

"Of course not." Donna laughed.

Detective Sububie made a mental note that Donna's laugh seemed forced. "And you weren't trying to take his car and escape?"

Donna laughed a second time, and this time the detective knew the laughter to be genuine. "I came up here to get something out of the car." And Donna reached in through the window to retrieve the pink multi-pack.

"We need to talk, Ms. Carter."

"We can talk at the cottage, detective." Donna set a brisk pace as the two women headed back along the boardwalk.

Ten minutes later the two women were sitting comfortably on the dock, looking out at the ocean. After four days in hiding, Donna was grateful for the police protection and happy to answer the detective's questions.

"Your friend covered for you at the ballpark. She died on the pitcher's mound in front of five thousand fans. Meanwhile you're here, 'on vacation, sort of,' as you put it. If you don't mind my saying, it just doesn't make sense."

"Billy—that's my boyfriend—anyway, Billy had two tickets to a concert in Philly. He was pressuring me to skip the ball game and go with him to the concert."

Detective Sububie nodded. "I guess I can understand boyfriend pressure. So why didn't you just skip work? I mean, no offense, but it's not like the world needs a Skeeter."

Donna was offended by the detective's remark. "Maybe the world doesn't, but the fans in White Sands Beach sure do. Mr. MacTavish has been good to me …"

Detective Sububie interrupted. "You mean Andy MacTavish, the team owner?"

"Yeah, I didn't want to disappoint him."

"Okay, I understand. So instead of disappointing him, you decided to try to deceive him."

Donna cringed. "It doesn't sound very nice when you say it that way."

"It isn't." Detective Sububie returned to her questions. "So whose idea was it to get Heather to cover for you?"

Donna tried to remember who said it first. "I think it was my idea. Maybe Billy suggested it. I'm not sure."

"But at some point, you asked your friend Heather and she agreed, because … ?"

Donna knew that the real answer was complicated. "Because it would be a hoot."

Detective Sububie thought Heather got more than she bargained for, but the detective bit her tongue. "So did you enjoy the concert?"

Donna stood up and walked to the edge of the dock. "I never went to the concert. Me and Billy had a fight. Heather died for nothing."

The detective wondered, had Donna gone to the concert, would that mean that Heather had died for something? "So you had a fight with your boyfriend and the next thing you know your friend Heather is dead at the ballpark. So what do you do? You 'take a vacation, sort of.' "

Donna didn't like the way it sounded, but the detective was essentially correct. "Yeah, pretty much."

Detective Sububie decided to press the issue. "I still don't understand. Your friend died and you went into hiding. What am I missing here, Donna?" Detective Sububie didn't think she was missing anything, but she wanted to hear Donna say it.

Donna struggled to explain. "Can I ask you a question, detective?" Without even a pause to catch her breath, Donna asked, "Do you think

Heather's death was an accident?"

Detective Sububie was impressed by Donna's question. "No, Ms. Carter, I do not."

Donna appreciated the detective's honest appraisal. "Neither do I, detective."

"So you went into hiding because you were worried you could be next?"

"I went into hiding, as you put it ..." Donna stopped, doubtful that the detective would understand about the Tarot, and certain the detective would not appreciate the importance of Blue Moon Odom.

Donna started over. "I figured no one knew that Heather was filling in for me at the baseball game. I figured maybe it was supposed to be me."

Detective Sububie tried to soften her response. "Your boyfriend knew."

Donna was crying now. "That's why I'm hiding. Look, I know I've made mistakes, but I haven't broken any laws, have I?"

Detective Sububie locked eyes with Donna Carter. "Not unless you murdered Heather Dean."

Donna dared not look away. "No, detective. I did not murder my best friend."

The detective answered with authority. "Then you haven't broken any laws."

Donna was relieved. "So no one needs to know that you found me here?"

Detective Sububie had been weighing that same question since they first sat down together on the dock. Until she could determine whether Donna was the next victim or the prime suspect, it would benefit the detective to keep Ms. Carter in hiding. "No, Ms. Carter, no one needs to know."

"Thank you, detective."

Detective Sububie walked back across the boardwalk to the dead-end roadway. She walked along the narrow roadway until it connected with the main road, where she found her Chevy waiting on the shoulder. Detective Sububie was pleased with her day's effort. Starting up the Chevy, the detective failed to take note of the car pulling onto the county road on the opposite side of the street.

Our Next Guest

Andy said goodbye to his attorney, the rotund Mr. Garibaldi, and returned the telephone to its base. He motioned for Cassie to turn on the television. Cassie found the remote and tossed it back to Andy, who turned the set to channel sixty-two. Mrs. Patterson, dressed in her wool plaid business suit, sitting straight and tall, was being interviewed by a soft-spoken gentleman with perfect hair and teeth.

"Mrs. Patterson, when the Sand Skeeters first proposed to locate in White Sands Beach, your group opposed their application. Could you explain the basis for your objection?"

Mrs. Patterson, already sitting ramrod-straight, pulled herself up in the chair. "Thank you, yes. My concern was for the safety of our migratory flocks. Do you realize that nearly every hawk on the Eastern seaboard passes over this site during the annual migration?"

Watching at home, Andy MacTavish was talking back to the TV. "And do you realize how much bird crap my stadium staff has to clean during the damn migration?"

The newsman, however, was only listening to Mrs. Patterson. "I didn't realize that."

"Not to mention that the heron and the cormorant rely on the salt marsh for their food supply."

"And my hot dogs, my grilled chicken and the salted peanuts."

"So your objection was based on your assessment that the birds would be negatively impacted by the baseball team?"

"That is correct."

"What about the negative impact the birds have on my team?"

"And you were joined in your opposition by other birders?"

"Every major birding organization joined in our complaint."

"And yet, Mrs. Patterson, I understand that those other organizations no longer object to the baseball stadium. Why is that?"

"Yes, Mrs. Patterson, why is that?"

Mrs. Patterson looked directly into the camera. "I cannot speak for the motives of any other group. I can only say that I continue to object to the presence of the baseball team."

"And why is that, Mrs. Patterson?"

"Because she's an effing lunatic."

"When I testified against construction of the baseball stadium, I predicted that a minor league baseball team in White Sands Beach would lead to the death of shore birds." Mrs. Patterson paused for effect. "Even I didn't anticipate that putting a minor league baseball team in White Sands Beach would result in the death of birders."

"What the …"

The TV newsman did his best to disguise his glee at the direction of the interview. "I assume you are referring to the recent dizzy bat accident."

Mrs. Patterson looked through the TV camera, imagining Andy MacTavish watching from the comfort of his sofa. "I am referring to the dizzy bat homicide."

"Homicide?"

The soft-spoken newsman turned toward the camera. "We'll be right back with our next guest after this short commercial break. I hope you'll join us."

During the commercial break, Andy dialed up his attorney. "She's a freakin' lunatic, that woman is."

Andy barely had time to yell at his attorney before Cassie called him back to the television.

"Our next guest," the newsman explained, "has his own perspective on recent events at the ballpark. Please welcome Mr. William MacTavish."

"Billy!" He didn't know whom to yell at first. "I'll call you back." Andy threw the phone across the room.

Billy sat there smiling into the camera, his hair green, his t-shirt burnt orange. "Please call me Billy."

"Okay, Billy. I should explain to the audience that Billy MacTavish is the brother of Andy MacTavish, principal owner of the Sand Skeeters. Is that right, Billy?"

"Yes. Andy is my older brother."

"And I understand that you yourself have an ownership interest in the team?"

Watching from the comfort of Andy's home, Cassie was startled by the question and even more so by the answer.

"Only in the sense that buying one share of stock in Bell Telephone makes you an owner of the phone company."

The newsman was not entirely satisfied with Billy's answer. Watching at home, neither was Andy.

"But the Sand Skeeters is not a publicly traded company, is it?"

Billy was not a businessman, but explained as best he could. "The baseball team is owned by a group of investors under the direction of my brother Andy. I own a two percent share of the team, courtesy of my brother. For all intents and purposes, Andy MacTavish is the Sand Skeeters."

"Damn right!"

The newsman continued to press for some clarification. "So you would have us believe that you are a part-owner of the team, the younger brother of the principal owner, but you are not here today as an official team representative. Is that right?"

"I am not here tonight to represent the team or my brother."

"Thank heaven."

"I understand that the dead girl, Ms. Heather Dean, I believe, was a friend of yours. Is that correct?"

"Yes."

"And like Mrs. Patterson, you and Heather were birders?"

Billy smirked. "I don't think Mrs. Patterson would appreciate the comparison. She bird watches by day; we do it all night long."

The newsman laughed uncomfortably. "Nocturnal bird watching, that's a new one on me."

Billy explained. "I guess it's more like bird listening. We sit up all night in the salt marsh, listening for nocturnal bird calls."

The newsman had been waiting for the right opportunity to ask his next question. "As a birder, do you share Mrs. Patterson's opinion regarding your baseball team?"

"Shit. Here it comes."

"My brother and I disagree on many things, but I don't believe that the baseball team is responsible for the death of birds or of birders …"

"Hallelujah!"

Billy completed his thought. "… at least not deliberately."

Andy MacTavish, watching at home, was so busy yelling at the television, he nearly missed the conclusion of the interview.

"And the other girl, the one that's still missing, Donna Carter, what is your relationship with Ms. Carter?"

"Donna is my girlfriend."

The newsman did his best to sound sympathetic. "So this last week must have been extraordinarily hard on you."

"Yes, it has."

"Could you explain to the audience why you agreed to come on the show tonight?"

"Yes, Billy, why did you go on the damn show?"

Billy looked straight into the camera, his green-tipped hair sparkling in the klieg lights. "Most of the media attention concerning this incident has focused on the tragic death of Heather Dean. And it certainly was tragic. But it is not the whole story. As you know, the team's regular mascot, Donna Carter, is missing. I hope that by coming on TV, I can bring some attention to Donna's case. I hope that someone in the TV audience has seen her this week."

Billy looked directly into the TV camera. "Donna, if you're watching, don't worry. I'll find you."

Tugging at the Edge of Cassie's Consciousness

There was a great deal about Andy that Cassie had yet to learn, but when she rolled over in bed early the next morning, she knew she would find his side empty. Andy would already be in his office, listening to doo-wop and planning his response to the television interviews. Pulling on a nightshirt, she wandered down the hall, surprised only by Andy's choice of morning music. Sitting in his retro 'fifties office, talking on the rotary phone, Andy was listening to her Savoy jazz CD.

Andy looked up at Cassie as she entered the office. "Some of it's not bad."

Cassie gave him a kiss. "I'll make a pot of coffee."

While the coffee brewed, Cassie hopped in the shower. With her shampoo and conditioner, her creams and lotions, Cassie marveled at how completely Andy had lost control of his bathroom. Life was good.

When Cassie walked back into Andy's office, she was dressed in black low-rider jeans and a Princeton T, her hair was wrapped in a bath towel, and she was carrying two cups of coffee. Andy put aside his work and followed her to the enclosed deck overlooking the ocean.

He took a long pull on the coffee. "You look wonderful."

"You'd say that to any girl that brought you a morning cup of coffee."

Andy grinned. "If she could fit into that pair of jeans."

"Do you have to go to the ballpark today?"

Andy thought for a moment before answering. "People call me a workaholic, and I guess I am. I love going to the ballpark. All season long, whether or not it was a game day, I'd get up early and head to the park. But now that the season is over and I have a good reason to stay home …" Andy looked at Cassie and blushed. "I would love to take some time off and spend more time with you, but I can't right now … Heather, Donna, Billy, the birders …"

Cassie and Andy sipped coffee and looked at the water.

"So what will you do today while I'm at the ballpark?"

Cassie didn't respond right away. She was still trying to formulate a plan. "I thought I'd pay a visit to your brother Billy, if that's okay with you."

"Better you than me."

Later that morning, dressed in her black low-rider jeans and Princeton T, Cassie knocked on the door of Billy's apartment. She waited patiently before knocking a second and then a third time.

Billy was pulling on his blue jeans as he opened the door. "Yeah?"

"Billy MacTavish?"

"Who wants to know?"

"I'm sorry. My name is Cassie O'Malley. I'm a friend of Andy's."

Billy smiled. "Are you the new girlfriend? I don't see Andy with a looker."

"Do you mind if I come inside?"

Billy motioned for Cassie to come in, allowing her to pass so he could watch her butt as she walked into the apartment.

Billy tossed a pile of clothes off the sofa, clearing a spot for Cassie to sit. "I thought I might hear from Andy today. Did he like my TV appearance?"

"Your brother is worried …" Cassie stopped mid-thought, distracted by the girl in panties and a t-shirt who stepped out of the bedroom.

"Your brother is worried about Donna."

Billy seemed to miss the irony. "So am I."

Cassie looked at the half-dressed girl in Andy's apartment. "I guess we each deal with worry in our own way."

Billy grinned. "Oh, that's Cheryl. She's just sex."

Cassie was appalled. She decided it was her job to teach this rude young man some manners. "Listen to me, Billy MacTavish. It's bad enough you think about this girl that way, bad enough you're willing to talk about her that way, but it's unacceptable to do so where she can hear you."

Billy didn't share Cassie's concern. "Don't worry about Cheryl. She's deaf."

Cassie needed Billy's cooperation if she was going to find Donna. "Whatever. It's really not my business."

Billy realized he still didn't know what Cassie wanted. "Just what is your business?"

"I'm looking for Donna."

Billy made an elaborate show of looking around the room before responding. "She's not here."

Cassie struggled to mask her mounting frustration. "Relax, Billy. You say you're worried about Donna. Andy's worried too. Give me a chance here, okay?"

Billy stood up and walked over to Cheryl, touching her lightly on the cheek to get her attention, looking her straight in the eye as he spoke to her. Cassie couldn't hear what Billy was saying, but when he was finished, Cheryl nodded and went back into the bedroom. Billy walked over to the sofa and sat down next to Cassie.

"Maybe you don't approve of me having sex with Cheryl. Under the circumstances, maybe I don't approve of me either. Look, I am worried about Donna. If you're serious about finding her, I want to help."

"Thank you, Billy. What can you tell me about the night that Donna disappeared?"

"I had two tickets to a concert in Philly. Donna didn't want to miss the final game of the season, but I talked her into it." Billy recounted the events of the day, leading up to the argument at the ballpark.

Cassie interrupted. "So you drove off, leaving Donna standing in the parking lot?"

Billy nodded, remembering the stupidity of the fight. "Yeah."

"Do you know where she went, Billy?"

Billy remembered watching her in his rearview mirror, driving slowly so he could watch until she was out of sight. "She went back inside the stadium."

Cassie struggled with her own dizzy memories of the night at the ballpark. "She went back inside? You're sure?"

Billy was sure. "Yeah."

Something about the dizzy bat race had been tugging at the edge of Cassie's consciousness since the tragic evening, something fleeting and discordant, ethereal, a dream. She could not retrieve the memory that lurked just beyond reach of her conscious mind. She could barely remember that she was trying to remember. Something about Donna …

Billy studied Cassie's reaction. "Is that important?"

Cassie had forgotten about Billy. "Is what important?"

There was something at the ballpark, something that would jog her memory. So Cassie told herself, driving to the stadium, repeating it like a mantra, focusing on the phrase, clearing her mind of all else, even turn signals and traffic lights, arriving somehow at the ballpark, her mind centered and her Mustang undented.

There was something at the ballpark. Cassie wondered, would she find it in time?

The Dead Girl, the Missing, the Birders, the Police

When Andy arrived at the ballpark, the mood was grim. A skeleton crew was packing away memories of the inaugural season of Sand Skeeter baseball. The equipment manager was taking inventory. It seemed to Andy that he counted the same box of baseballs three times. The director of ticket sales was staring at the ceiling in the ticket office, reviewing attendance figures for the year. In the gift shop, the promotions manager considered what to do with the souvenir bats. In the office suite, youthful staffers were talking quietly. There was an awkward silence when Andy joined the conversation.

"What's the matter?"

After a lengthy pause, one of Andy's aides met his gaze. "Donna?"

Andy pulled up a chair. "It'll be okay. You'll see."

A second aide now spoke up. "There's a rumor going around that the team won't be back next year."

Andy knew what they needed to hear. "The team'll be back next year."

"And Donna?"

"Donna will be back."

Andy got up and walked into his private office where he spent the rest of the morning going through E-mail. His inbox was clogged with messages about the team, the birders, the dead girl and the missing. Andy was surprised to find an E-mail from Mrs. Patterson, an E-mail hinting at a possible solution to their year-long dispute. Andy read the E-mail carefully and then forwarded a copy to his attorney, the rotund Mr. Garibaldi. There was even a message, Andy noted with disgust, from a psychic looking to take advantage of the tragedy, offering her assistance to locate Donna.

Andy was reading messages, occasionally crafting responses, but mostly just hitting delete when Detective Sububie appeared in his doorway.

"May I come in?"

"Of course." Andy waved her to a seat. "What can I do for you?"

"Do you mind if I look around?"

"That depends. What are you looking for?"

"I'm not sure."

Andy had nothing to hide. Still, he did not want the police believing the dead girl was a free pass to examine his business activities.

Andy stood up and walked toward the detective. "Maybe I can help you figure it out."

When Andy and the detective walked out of his private office, Andy made a point of stopping to joke with the staffers talking in the outer office. His aide looked over, a subtle gesture obvious only to Andy, silently asking if the boss needed assistance. But Andy was back in control. The dead girl, the missing, the birders, the police—bring them on, Andy told himself, all of them.

When Andy and the detective walked by the gift shop, Andy saw that the promotions manager was still agonizing over the souvenir bats. "Send them back."

The promotions manager looked over. "What?"

"Send them back. They don't meet Sand Skeeter standards."

When Andy and the detective walked by the ticket office, the ticket manager was still staring at the ceiling. "Let me see that report."

The ticket manager gave Andy the spreadsheet.

"You did good."

"Thanks, boss, but we were below the target."

"Next year."

When Andy and the detective reached the locker rooms, the equipment manager was still counting baseballs. "Is there a problem?"

Startled, the equipment manager dropped the box, sending baseballs bouncing around the room. "I'm sorry, boss."

Detective Sububie toured the stadium with Andy MacTavish, the public areas and the private, gaining an appreciation for the intricacies of Sand Skeeter baseball, but finding little that might lead her to the missing girl.

"Where do you keep the mascot stuff? Did Donna have an office?"

Andy explained the operation. "The promotions manager is responsible for the team mascot. You met him in the gift shop. Donna had a changing room."

"Could I see the changing room?"

"Of course."

The room was barely larger than a walk-in closet, but it was Donna's and it was private. "When was the last time Donna was in here?"

Andy tried to remember the last time he had seen Donna. "The team was out of town for a week before the final home game. I don't know. I guess she came in sometime that week, but I really can't be certain."

Detective Sububie looked around the room. "Has someone been cleaning in here?"

Andy hadn't really thought about the room. "We have a cleaning service. Is that a problem?"

Detective Sububie didn't bother to answer. She pointed to a door in the back of Donna's changing room. "What's back here?"

"Just a closet." Andy realized he had no idea what Donna kept in her closet.

Detective Sububie opened the closet door in the rear of the changing room. There was a costume hanging from a hook in the closet. "Is that the mascot costume?"

Andy had forgotten about the spare Skeeter costume. He quickly considered the most plausible explanation.

He had gone to the morgue to pick up the real costume, the one Heather had died in, and he had seen Heather's family grieving for their dead daughter. The trip to the morgue had made him pessimistic about the team's future, certainly about the team's name and its mascot, if not the team itself. He remembered how the mascot intruded on his dreams that night. And he remembered getting out of bed and throwing the costume into the ocean. He remembered watching until the costume sank. Andy had forgotten about the spare in Donna's closet until the moment that Detective Sububie opened the closet door.

He could tell all that to Detective Sububie but the real answer, he decided, was unnecessarily complicated. "Yes, that's the mascot costume."

"When the morgue asked you to pick up the costume … I don't know how to say this … but they screwed up." Andy could see the embarrassment in the detective's eyes, could hear it in her voice.

"They should have run a lab test on the costume. I mean, it's not a problem or anything, but I was wondering if you could do me a favor." Detective Sububie rushed ahead with her request. "We know that Heather's death was an accident, but they should have run a test on the costume. It's not going to change anything, but it doesn't look good, the record incomplete like that. Not good if there's a lawsuit. Not good for us and not good for the team. You see what I mean?"

Andy considered the civil suit that Mr. Garibaldi had warned him to expect. He pictured Heather's family attorney asking questions, implying some conspiracy between the Sand Skeeters and the local police. "It's okay, detective. You can borrow the costume. That is what you're asking me, isn't it?"

"Yes, thank you." Relieved to have the team's cooperation, Detective Sububie explained her plan. "I'll take the costume back to the coroner's office and ask the lab to run a routine test on the fibers. They'll add a note to Ms. Dean's report and that'll be the end of it."

The Way the Sun Sparkles on the Water

As the attorney of record for the Sand Skeeter Baseball Club as well as for Andy MacTavish's other business interests, Mr. Garibaldi had done substantial background work for the team. By the time he arrived at his office, his paralegal had already retrieved the file on Mrs. Jodi Patterson and placed it on his desk, complete with Post-its marking those passages that she especially wanted Mr. Garibaldi to read first.

Mrs. Patterson was in her mid-forties, married to a highly successful mutual fund manager, with no children. She was a formidable woman who might have been pretty, with a little effort and fashion advice. She had a deep and abiding interest in the fate of New Jersey's shore birds. With the support of her husband, she had formed a nonprofit organization devoted to birds and birders. It was unclear whether her organization had any other members, but she had a title and letterhead and, with the advent of the Sand Skeeters, she had a cause. When Mr. Garibaldi read the E-mail that Andy had forwarded, he realized that she also had an appreciation for the fine art of blackmail.

Mrs. Patterson wanted to establish a bird sanctuary in White Sands Beach. Her E-mail suggested that the Sand Skeeter Baseball Club might be inclined, as a gesture of goodwill and civic responsibility, to finance said bird sanctuary. In exchange, the E-mail implied, or perhaps Mr. Garibaldi inferred, she would suspend her public attacks on the team. Mr. Garibaldi was relieved to discover that the proposed site for the bird sanctuary would not interfere with Sand Skeeter operations. The attorney placed a call to Jodi Patterson, suggesting that they arrange a meeting. Mrs. Patterson was not only willing to meet, but she offered to show Mr. Garibaldi a potential site for the bird sanctuary that very afternoon. Mr. Garibaldi juggled another appointment and accepted Mrs. Patterson's invitation.

Mr. Garibaldi drove his Cadillac Seville up and down the county road, unable to find the turn that would lead him to the property and a waiting Jodi Patterson. On the third pass he spotted the unmarked road partially obscured by a car that had broken down on the shoulder, its hood propped open, a red rag tied to its antenna. He drove down the unmarked road until it reached a dead end at the water. Mrs. Patterson was sitting in her Lexus at land's end, waiting. She stepped out of the car to greet the attorney. Mr. Garibaldi was impressed by her squared shoulders and wool blazer. Mrs. Patterson was impressed by his exquisite tailoring and extraordinary girth.

Mr. Garibaldi looked beyond Mrs. Patterson's shoulders at the elevated boardwalk that spanned the marshland. It didn't look like it would support the attorney's weight. "Where are we?"

Mrs. Patterson smiled. "I don't think this place has a name. Do you like it here?"

Mr. Garibaldi was surprised by his response. "It's a very pretty spot. The way the sun sparkles on the water ... it brings out the blue in your eyes."

Mrs. Patterson's cheeks flushed. "Oh, Mr. Garibaldi. You are a scamp." Mrs. Patterson hoped the attorney understood this to be a compliment. "I could get in trouble with a man like you."

It was Mr. Garibaldi's turn to redden. "Don't tease me, Mrs. Patterson." The attorney tried to bring the conversation back to the business at hand. "How did you find this place?"

"I followed the birds here. It's not an easy place to find, is it?"

Mr. Garibaldi agreed. "Damn near impossible. Especially when there's a broken-down car blocking the turn."

"Yes, the poor man. You know, I always feel bad that I don't stop and try to help, but a woman by herself can never be too careful. Do you know how many women were sexually assaulted last year by men pretending to run out of gas?"

It did not occur to Mr. Garibaldi that she expected him to answer.

"Take a guess, then."

Still, Mr. Garibaldi stood there mute, at a loss for words.

"According to the Internet, more than one thousand women were sexually assaulted last year in such auto-related incidents."

The attorney in Mr. Garibaldi began to dream of a class-action lawsuit. "You were smart not to stop. Besides, there's really very little you could do to help the man."

Mrs. Patterson snorted. "Don't be silly. Of course I could help the man."

Like a moth drawn to a flame, Mr. Garibaldi was drawn to ask, "How could you help?"

"I always have a sealed container of synthetic fuel in the trunk. Do you know how many women are sexually assaulted every year because they run out of gas?"

Mrs. Patterson watched a great blue heron gracefully land in the sedge grass at water's edge. "Do you think Mr. MacTavish would consider buying this land and letting me create a sanctuary for these birds?"

Mr. Garibaldi was grateful for a question he felt equipped to answer. "Perhaps he will." Mr. Garibaldi hoped he was reading Mrs. Patterson correctly. "Especially if a bird sanctuary will permit a more congenial partnership between your organization and the ball club."

Mrs. Patterson reached out and touched Mr. Garibaldi's arm. "I think I would like that, Mr. Garibaldi. A more congenial relationship. Yes, I think that would be better for us all."

Mr. Garibaldi needed more information about the property. "How much does the owner want?"

Mrs. Patterson batted her eyes. "I don't even know if the land is for sale, but really, look at those abandoned shacks. Wouldn't you sell if you got a bona fide offer?"

Mr. Garibaldi found himself agreeing with her logic. "Who is the owner?"

Mrs. Patterson gave the attorney a girlish smile. "I was hoping you could find out for me."

Mr. Garibaldi chuckled. "I guess I have some work to do. Tell you what, let me do some research and then we can talk again. Is that okay with you, Mrs. Patterson?"

It was clearly okay with Mrs. Patterson. "Would you like to go get a cup of coffee, Mr. Garibaldi?"

An unexpected huskiness in her voice suggested to Mr. Garibaldi something more dangerous than café latte. Stumbling over his words, the attorney declined her invitation and walked back quickly, a large man in a suddenly too-tight suit, and sat down heavily in the Cadillac Seville. "Perhaps next time."

"Next time then."

Mr. Garibaldi drove back up the unmarked roadway, faster than the conditions allowed. As he turned onto the county road, he was relieved to see that the stranded car was now gone. He would not have stopped to help, but it would have made him feel guilty. Mr. Garibaldi did not want to feel guilty about driving by without offering to help. It was enough to feel guilty about a mostly innocent flirtation with Mrs. Jodi Patterson.

From the car, Mr. Garibaldi called to update his client.

"Mr. MacTavish, I just met with Jodi Patterson. You were right, sir. This may be an opportunity to make peace with the birders."

"Excellent. What's it going to cost me?"

Mr. Garibaldi gave it some thought before responding. "I wonder what the going rate is for a bird sanctuary."

"A bird sanctuary?" Andy MacTavish was intrigued. "Can I do that?"

Mr. Garibaldi was prepared to offer an opinion. "Of course you can. We structured everything so you'd have complete control. With your approval, the team can buy the land and use it for any purpose you see fit."

Even so, Andy wondered if it were wise to involve the team in the transaction.

Mr. Garibaldi was already contemplating another course of action. "You may be right, sir. It may be easier if we use one of your other corporations."

Andy was ready to fast-track the deal. "See what you can find out, okay?"

"I'll get right on it when I get back to the office."

"Call me when you have something more." Andy hung up the telephone.

Mr. Garibaldi was old enough to remember when this sort of research would mean days, sometimes weeks, poring through dusty tomes in the basement of the county office, thumbing through public records looking for names, dates and numbers. The Internet had changed everything and Mr. Garibaldi was old enough to marvel at the possibilities. He placed a call to his office with instructions for Doris, his paralegal.

By the time he pulled into the parking space with its sign, *Reserved for Louis A. Garibaldi, Esq.,* Doris had tracked down the name of the property owner. As he entered the office, Doris handed him a printout. The undeveloped marshland, with the ramshackle cottages and extraordinary view, with its spotted sandpipers, green-winged teal and its great blue herons, belonged to a gentleman by the name of Perry S. Pettigrew.

Doris was not satisfied with her rapid research results. "The thing is, Mr. Garibaldi, I can't seem to find a current address for Mr. Pettigrew."

A Very Public Embarrassment

Leaving Sand Skeeter Ballpark, Detective Sububie was feeling good about her day's work. Her visit to the stadium had not resulted in a lead regarding the missing girl, but gaining temporary possession of the mosquito outfit was a big deal. It was clear that Heather Dean's death had been an accident; it was a tragic, meaningless death, but nonetheless, it was an accident. When the Dean family eventually filed a lawsuit (they always do, the detective told herself), the investigation record would now be complete. Maybe the baseball team would offer to settle, maybe a jury would find in favor of the family, but, in any event, the case would not become about the failure of the police lab to conduct a simple test. And Detective Sububie understood that the lab and, more importantly, the police brass, would recognize that it was Detective Sububie who had saved the department from a very public embarrassment. All in all, it had been a good day's work.

Hurrying back to her parked car, carrying the costume, the detective nearly collided with a woman hurrying toward the stadium entrance. The detective took a step back, fumbling to hold on to the mosquito costume.

"I'm sorry, ma'am, I didn't …" and then Detective Sububie recognized the woman in her path. "Ms. O'Malley?"

Cassie, on her way to meet Andy MacTavish, was even more surprised than the detective. "Officer Sububie?"

Mavis Sububie beamed. "Actually, it's Detective Sububie now."

Cassie was genuinely happy for the policewoman. "Congratulations. What brings you to White Sands Beach?"

Detective Sububie explained. "I work here now. After the Wehnke case, I made detective. I guess I have you to thank for the promotion and transfer. What about you? Are you here to cover the story?"

Cassie liked the policewoman. Still, Cassie warned herself, Mavis Sububie was a policewoman. "Sort of."

"I understand that your friend, Ms. Harbrough, is running for mayor now."

"Yes, she is. And I think maybe she's going to win." Cassie made a mental note to call Cheyenne as soon as possible. She did not want to miss the final mayoral debate. "You know, I never had an opportunity to ask you this, but when you investigated the Wehnke murder, did you ever really believe that Cheyenne was the killer?"

Detective Sububie considered how much she was willing to reveal. "It's my job to follow every lead, regardless of my personal opinion. Let's just say there was sufficient evidence to treat her as a suspect."

The two women stood in the parking lot chatting, useful adversaries pretending to be friends. As they spoke, Detective Sububie tried to gauge Cassie O'Malley's interest in the Sand Skeeters.

"Omigod," blurted the detective, replaying a snippet of videotape in her head. "The dizzy bat race!"

Cassie reddened. "Yes. That was me."

"We need to talk."

"Is that why you're here, detective? Are you investigating the death of Ms. Dean?"

Detective Sububie explained her involvement in the case. "I'm sure you must be aware that Ms. Dean's death was ruled an accident. No, I'm here about the other girl, the missing one, Ms. Carter."

Cassie was cautiously optimistic about the policewoman's involvement in the case. "Do you know where she is?"

Detective Sububie was cautiously optimistic about Cassie O'Malley's interest in the case. "Do you?"

Cassie smiled. "If I learn anything about the missing girl, you'll be the first person I call." Cassie turned to leave.

"Actually, Ms. O'Malley, while we're here, there is something you could help me with." Detective Sububie had an idea. "Perhaps you could walk me through the dizzy bat incident."

"If it'll help you find the missing girl ... sure, what do you want me to do?"

Detective Sububie put the mosquito costume in her car and began walking back toward the stadium entrance. "Let's go down on the field and see what happens."

As they walked into the stadium, Cassie frantically considered how best to explain her relationship with Andy MacTavish. The less the detective knew of their personal relationship, the better. She stopped the detective before heading inside.

"There's something I need you to know. The team has been good to me since the incident. I guess they see me as another potential lawsuit. Anyway, they don't know that I'm writing a story. I haven't told them what I do for a living. I'm sure you understand."

Detective Sububie appreciated the heads-up. "Just follow my lead."

Cassie would follow the detective's lead. She wondered, would Andy MacTavish follow her lead?

"Mr. MacTavish?"

Andy looked up from his desk, surprised to find Detective Sububie again standing in his doorway, and even more surprised to find Cassie standing just behind the detective.

"I'm sorry, detective. I thought you left."

Detective Sububie explained. "I did, sir. But I met someone in your parking lot. I believe you know Ms. O'Malley." The detective pulled Cassie into the doorway.

"Ca—"

Cassie interrupted Andy's greeting. "Mr. MacTavish, how nice to see you again."

Andy decided to play along until he could talk privately with Cassie. "Ms. O'Malley, how are you?"

"I'm doing well."

"That's wonderful. What can I do for you?"

The question was directed at Cassie, but Detective Sububie answered. "I've asked Ms. O'Malley to walk me through the dizzy bat incident."

Andy had no idea what was going on. "If you think it will help." He looked at Cassie for a clue, but she was following the detective's lead.

Detective Sububie asked Andy to have two bats sent down to the field. "Of course, you are welcome to join Ms. O'Malley and me down on the field if you'd like."

Andy MacTavish had no desire to prolong the charade. "Thank you, no. I'll be here at my desk if you need anything more."

Detective Sububie led Cassie down to the infield. The equipment manager met them behind home plate with two bats.

"Mr. MacTavish said you needed these."

The detective nodded. "Thank you, yes." When the equipment manager lingered, Detective Sububie added, "I'll let you know if I need anything more."

As the equipment manager headed out through the dugout to the lockers, Detective Sububie turned to Cassie.

"As I understand it, they draw a ticket stub at random for the dizzy bat race and your ticket was chosen. Amazing."

Cassie was uncertain whether Detective Sububie's comment was intended for her ears. "Yes, my seat number was announced over the PA and I came down onto the field."

"Ms. Dean—that is, Skeeter—was already waiting for you?"

"Yes, Skeeter and a couple of staff were waiting down here behind home plate."

"At that point, they gave you a bat and you started to spin?"

"That's right."

"I'll be Ms. Dean. You can be you, okay?"

Cassie agreed she could be herself. Detective Sububie handed her a bat and the two women began to spin. They spun slowly, re-creating the event at a safe speed. Nevertheless, Cassie found herself feeling queasy, not from the spinning so much as from the memory of spinning.

"And at some point, you dropped the bats and began racing toward first base?"

"Yes."

"Only Skeeter doesn't make it down the base path. Skeeter staggers out toward the pitcher's mound, like this, right?"

Detective Sububie dropped her bat and pretended to stagger out toward the mound. She motioned for Cassie to run toward first. Speaking loud enough for Cassie to hear her at first, Detective Sububie stood on the pitcher's mound and continued to verbally rehash the event. "At this point, Skeeter collapses on the mound."

"That's what I understand. I was pretty dizzy. I think I must have been on the ground as well by then, down by first base."

Cassie, queasy from the re-creation or from the recollection, started walking toward the mound to continue talking to the detective. The policewoman waved her back toward first base.

"So far, everything that happened followed the script, right?" And Detective Sububie pretended to collapse, lying down in the dirt.

"That's what they tell me." Cassie sat down at first base. As Cassie looked over at Detective Sububie, prostrate on the pitcher's mound, the scene grew hazy. She struggled to regain focus, but Cassie was back at the final game of the season, at the final dizzy bat race in Sand Skeeter history. She tried to focus, but her field of vision would not stay fixed. As the ballpark spun, Cassie saw Skeeter lying on the mound, she saw the trainer running from the dugout, she saw the stunned fans, suddenly silent in their seats and she saw…"

"Holy shit!"

On the pitcher's mound, Detective Sububie jumped to her feet. "What is it, Cassie?"

Cassie's head gradually cleared. "It was … nothing … I'm sorry, it was nothing."

Detective Sububie walked over to Cassie O'Malley as she stood up at first base. "You saw something that night. What was it?"

"It was Donna. I saw Donna. I remember I saw Donna in the aisle, over there near the concession stand." She pointed. "At the time, I thought Donna was inside the Skeeter outfit. I was racing Donna. I mean, I was racing Skeeter and I thought Donna was Skeeter. You know what I mean."

"What was she doing?"

Cassie tried to remember. It was like waking from a disturbing dream. She knew there was something else, but she couldn't retrieve the image. The harder she tried to focus, the less clear it all seemed. "I don't know."

Detective Sububie assessed the situation. "You would tell me if you knew, wouldn't you?"

Cassie was barely listening to the detective. "I don't know."

Cassie tried to remember. It wasn't about what Donna was doing. It was about who was with Donna. Cassie tried to remember. "I don't know."

Pan-Seared Steak with Twice-Baked Potatoes

When Detective Sububie announced that she was satisfied with the dizzy bat re-creation, Cassie didn't dare go looking for Andy. She assumed that Detective Sububie was still watching her every movement. Rather than follow her heart back to Andy's office, Cassie walked out to the parking lot, where she climbed into her Mustang, popped a Count Basie–Duke Ellington CD into the player and drove back to Andy's oceanfront home. It had been an amazingly long day since Cassie had left the house that morning heading for Billy's apartment and, she guessed, long for Andy as well.

Letting herself into the house, Cassie kicked off her shoes and poured herself a Tullamore Dew. It felt good to be home. Cassie smiled, realizing that she now considered Andy's house to be her home. She dialed Andy's extension at the ballpark.

"Hi, sweetheart."

It thrilled Andy to hear Cassie call him her sweetheart. "What happened to Mr. MacTavish? How about a little respect here?"

"I'm sorry, Andy. I didn't think it was a good idea for Detective Sububie to know too much about you and me."

"What were you doing with the cop, anyway?"

Cassie couldn't think of a simple answer to such a complicated story. "I'll tell you all about it when you get home. Will you be home soon? I'm going to make you supper."

Cassie rarely cooked, content to eat take-out Chinese or pepperoni pizza washed down with a shot of Irish whiskey or a glass of Merlot. She rarely cooked, but in a pinch, Cassie could make a delicious pan-seared steak with twice-baked potatoes. She checked the supplies in Andy's kitchen and drew up a short list of groceries. At the market, Cassie counted fourteen items in her cart. Looking around at the other shoppers, Cassie decided to stretch the rules and pulled her shopping cart into the express check-out.

By the time Andy got home, Cassie had finished the prep work. She was ready to sear two steaks.

"The steaks can wait, Cassie." Andy kissed her deeply, pressing lightly into all of her curves.

"Mmmm...But I want to tell you about my day."

"And I want to hear all about it." Andy kissed her again. "Later."

"Mmmm. Later." Cassie took Andy by the hand and led him to the bedroom.

Lying in bed afterward, naked with her lover, Cassie had to remind herself that it had only been six weeks. She understood that love has a way of warping the ebb and flow of linear time. She'd known Andy for barely six weeks, but it was the "bare" knowing that made her feel like she had known him forever. She knew his lips and his arms, his shoulders and back, she knew the extra five pounds at his waist, she knew the hollow of his knee and the curve of his foot, she knew…In the face of such knowledge, what is the measure of a day?

Andy stroked her cheek. "So how was your day?"

Cassie kissed him lightly on the chest. "I love you, Andy MacTavish."

"Do you love me enough to make me that steak now?"

"Enough to make you the steak and the potatoes."

Andy grinned. "I'm a lucky man."

Cassie threw on a robe and headed for the kitchen. "And don't you forget it."

Between bites of steak and potatoes, Cassie and Andy eventually got around to telling each other about their day. Cassie told Andy of her visit to Billy's apartment as well as her chance encounter with Detective Sububie.

Cassie explained what happened when they re-created the dizzy bat race. "Donna was inside the ballpark during the dizzy bat race."

Then she realized that she needed to back up. She needed to explain her history with Mavis Sububie.

"She was Officer Sububie when I met her, during the Bill Wehnke case."

"Bill Wehnke?"

"I'm sorry, Andy. Sometimes I forget that you don't know all my secrets yet. Bill Wehnke was the dead deer story. I told you about the dead deer."

"Of course, the dead deer." Andy took a moment to remember. "Harrison loved your dead deer stories."

Cassie smiled, remembering the first time that Andy told her how much Harrison liked her stories. They were sipping hot cocoa with minimarshmallows. "And as I recall, you thought the stories were kind of trashy."

Andy was quick to change the subject, telling Cassie about the bird sanctuary and about his own encounter with Detective Sububie.

Cassie looked forward to a time when their lives would be as one, but for now she needed to tell Andy about the mayoral race in Doah. "When I was talking to Detective Sububie, I was reminded that it'll be election day in two weeks. I know the timing is bad, Andy, but I need to go home for a few days. I promised Cheyenne I'd be at the debates. I already missed the first two. I can't miss the last debate."

"Of course you can't, Cassie. When do you need to leave?"

Cassie wasn't sure. "Soon. Not tomorrow. Maybe the day after."

Andy had an idea. "What if I come with you?"

Cassie gave Andy a kiss. "I love you, Andy MacTavish."

When Andy completed his account of the day, there was still one piece of the story that Cassie found troubling.

"How did you give Detective Sububie the Skeeter costume?"

Andy didn't understand Cassie's question. "She asked me for it."

Cassie tried to explain. "No, that's not what I mean. Look, I understand why she wanted it. I even understand why you want to cooperate with her. What I don't understand is where the costume came from. Didn't you tell me you threw the costume into the ocean?"

Andy looked away. "I did."

"You did what? Throw it away? Or just tell me you threw it away?"

Andy looked out the window, remembering that night. "I was depressed about the future of the Sand Skeeters. Remember? We talked about changing the team name, changing the mascot. We said fans wouldn't want to see Skeeter on the field next season. Remember? I threw the costume over the retaining wall and watched it sink offshore."

Andy paused. "Now I see what you mean. If I threw the costume into the ocean, where did I come by the one that I gave to the detective? Is that it?"

Cassie nodded yes.

"It's a spare. More of a prototype, really. Donna wore it at the start of the season. The truth is, I had forgotten all about it until Detective Sububie found it this afternoon in Donna's changing room. She wanted the costume, something about a missing lab test."

Cassie tried to follow Andy's logic. "Wouldn't it have been smarter to tell Detective Sububie that it's not the same costume?"

"Think about it, Cassie. You know why I tossed the costume into the ocean, and I know why I tossed it into the ocean, but to the police it would sound suspicious. The truth is complicated, Cassie. In my experience, the police don't like complicated."

Cassie wasn't convinced. "I guess you're right, Andy. But won't it look even worse if the police find out later that you lied about the outfit?"

"Look, Cassie, the lab screwed up. They forgot to run a test. All they want to do now is cover their behinds. They can't run the test if the costume doesn't exist anymore. So really I'm doing them a favor. They'll run the test and file away the report and that'll be the end of it."

Cassie remembered what it was like when Officer Sububie believed that Cheyenne was guilty of a crime. "I hope you're right, Andy."

Mr. Pettigrew's Address

"**D**on't worry, Doris. You did a great job just finding a name." In truth, Mr. Garibaldi was ill-equipped to judge whether Doris had done a great job searching the database, for he himself had no particular computer skills. He appreciated her ability to pull a name out of the computer in much the same way that he appreciated when a magician pulled a rabbit out of a hat. He knew there was a trick; he just didn't know what the trick was. But Mr. Garibaldi understood that where the magician found one rabbit, in another moment, he was likely to find a second. "C'mon, Doris, let's see if we can find an address for Mr. Pettigrew."

An hour later, they had Googled a few dozen Pettigrews, but none of them appeared to be a match. Doris got up from the computer station, stretching her back, her fingers and her mind. "Maybe we should take a short break."

"Whatever you say, Doris. You're the expert."

But Doris knew that what Mr. Garibaldi meant was, "C'mon, let's get back to work." She liked Mr. Garibaldi immensely, but not when he looked over her shoulder at the computer screen, expecting instant hits. "I need to go to the ladies' room, sir, if that's okay with you."

"Of course, Doris. You should know by now you don't need to ask my permission." It made Mr. Garibaldi feel fair-minded to pretend he didn't keep track of her breaks.

Doris went into the ladies' room and lit a cigarette. She delayed as long as she dared, tossing the butt in the john and freshening the room with pine-scented room deodorizer, before heading back to the office. Mr. Garibaldi was sitting in front of the computer screen waiting for a Web site to load. "Thank God you're back. I can't get this machine to do anything." The attorney nearly leapt from the chair, making room at the computer console for his paralegal.

Doris smiled at her boss. "Let's see what we can find."

But the rest of the afternoon slipped away without a match. They tried every search engine with which Doris was familiar, every database likely to produce an address for the mysterious Mr. Pettigrew. Five o'clock came and went, but the attorney showed no signs of slowing. "We're getting closer, Doris. You're doing great."

At six o'clock, Mr. Garibaldi considered ordering in dinner for the two of them, but he didn't want Doris to think he planned to keep her at the office late. "By the time the food gets here, you'll be home."

At seven o'clock, Doris announced that she was leaving.

"That's a good idea, Doris. We both need some rest. We'll get a fresh start in the morning."

Doris was at her desk by 8:00. When Mr. Garibaldi arrived at 9:15, she had Mr. Pettigrew's address.

Mr. Garibaldi was delighted. "I knew we'd find it."

"Actually, sir," and Doris grinned, "we had it all the time."

"What do you mean?"

"I mean he lives there, sir."

Mr. Garibaldi worried sometimes about Doris. "What do you mean he lives there? He lives where?"

"There, sir. On his property."

Mr. Garibaldi was stunned. "But I saw the place. It's just a couple of ramshackle cottages threatening to fall into the water. No one could live there, Doris."

Doris was not to be swayed. "He does, sir. Mr. Pettigrew lives in one of those ramshackle cottages."

Mr. Garibaldi rubbed his expansive stomach with delight. "This is going to be fun. Doris, could you please get me Mr. MacTavish on the telephone. And if you're not busy, would you mind brewing a fresh pot of coffee?"

Andy MacTavish was pleased to know that his attorney was working hard to settle his dispute with the birders. He listened carefully to Mr. Garibaldi's report before providing his attorney with clear direction.

Donna Carter was sitting at the card table. From time to time, when the mood was right, she picked up a puzzle piece and added it to the jigsaw. Spit was outside on the dock, enjoying the cool October morning. Inside, the phone was ringing. Donna called out to let Spit know, "I'll get it."

"Hello."

On the other end of the phone, Donna heard a smooth baritone voice. "Hello. My name is Louis Garibaldi. I'd like to speak to Mr. Pettigrew, please."

Donna decided not to disturb Spit. "I'm sorry, sir. I believe you have the wrong number."

Mr. Garibaldi tried again. "Are you sure, Miss? Mr. Pettigrew. Perry Pettigrew."

Before Donna could hang up on the persistent caller, Spit ambled into the cottage. "Who's that on the telephone?"

Donna shrugged. "Wrong number."

"Who are they looking for?"

Donna stifled a laugh. "Perry Pettigrew."

Spit reached out his hand. "I'll take it."

Donna handed Spit the receiver. "Hello."

Mr. Garibaldi tried a third time. "Mr. Pettigrew?"

"Speaking."

"Mr. Pettigrew, sir, I am an attorney here in White Sands Beach. Perhaps you've heard of me?"

Spit seemed embarrassed to admit that he was not familiar with Louis A. Garibaldi, Esquire.

"That's all right, sir. Anyway, I represent a businessman who has expressed an interest in purchasing your waterfront property."

Spit had no particular interest in selling the land, but Mr. Garibaldi was persistent and, finally, in order to get off the phone, Spit agreed to meet with the attorney. Of course, when Spit hung up the telephone, Donna had a question of her own.

"Perry Pettigrew? You have got to be kidding."

Spit pretended to take offense at Donna's teasing. "What do you think, my parents named me Spit? I was born Perry Stephen Pettigrew, Jr., and I remained Perry Pettigrew until I went to Iraq."

"I'm sorry, Spit. Or should I call you Perry? Or Mr. Pettigrew? How about Junior?"

Spit waited patiently for Donna to finish making fun of his name. "The last person who called me Perry was my grandmother. And, except for the DMV, no one ever called me Mr. Pettigrew."

"Okay, I'll stick with Spit. What'd the guy want anyway?"

Spit had already forgotten about Louis Garibaldi, Esq. "What guy?"

"On the phone, Spit. The guy on the telephone."

Spit laughed. "Oh him…nothing, really. He wants to buy the land."

Spit might drive a taxicab and live in a shack, but Mr. Perry Stephen Pettigrew, Jr., was apparently a land baron, owner of one of the last undeveloped pieces of oceanfront real estate in south Jersey. Donna was impressed.

"What are you going to do?"

Spit wasn't sure he understood Donna's question. "I'm gonna go back out on the dock and enjoy the fall weather."

Donna smacked Spit upside the head. "About the land, silly. Are you gonna sell?"

"Nah. I like it here."

Donna had heard Spit offer to meet with the attorney. "But you agreed to take a meeting."

"Don't worry about it, Donna. I was just being polite."

Donna gave Spit a hug. "Okay then. When is this big meeting?"

Spit shrugged. "I told the attorney I'd come to his office tomorrow morning."

A Good Influence

When Donna awoke, she found Spit standing at the kitchen sink dressed only in his boxer shorts and Dallas Cowboys t-shirt, trimming his hair and cursing.

"#&*#@!"

"And a good morning to you too, Spit."

Spit jumped, nearly poking his eye out with the scissors. "Shit, Donna. Don't do that."

"I'm sorry, Spit." Donna watched for a minute as Spit battled to assert control over his spaghetti hair. "Would you like me to help you with that?"

Staring uneasily at the random clumps of hair accumulating in the kitchen sink, Spit was grateful for the offer. "Thanks, Donna. I'm glad you're here."

Donna chuckled. "Yeah, it's almost fun. Gimme the scissors."

Donna examined Spit's head, looking for a safe place to start. Slowly she worked her way in, like a gardener attacking an overgrown hedge. Neither of them spoke until the pruning was complete. Finally, Donna stood back, admiring her handiwork. "There."

Spit stared in the mirror. "Thanks."

"Now that we trimmed your hair, how about a shave?"

Spit took another look in the mirror. "Do you think so? It's only been a couple of days."

"Whatever. It's up to you. Why'd you decide to cut your hair anyway?"

Spit adopted a serious pose. "I'm not sure. The attorney, I guess. I don't want him taking one look at me and thinking I'm just some loser he can dick around with. I need to work on my look."

Donna imagined Spit on one of those TV makeover shows. She tried to look at Spit with a queer eye. "What are you going to wear?"

"This…" Spit thought about his answer for a moment. "…And my jeans."

"Tell you what, Spit. While you shave, I'll take a look in your closet."

Donna knew it would take more than a queer eye to make sense of Spit's wardrobe, but in the back of the closet, behind the stained blue jeans and the olive drabs, behind the army surplus and the thrift shop bargain rack, Donna found a black wool-blend three-piece suit. The vest was beyond repair, but the jacket was still serviceable.

Spit walked in as Donna was examining the slacks. "I haven't worn that since my grandmother's funeral."

"It's a good suit for your meeting with the lawyer. How about a shirt and tie?"

Spit had to draw the line somewhere. "No tie."

"What about a shirt?" Donna rummaged through Spit's closet, but the best she could find was a clean blue denim work shirt. "This'll have to do then. Get dressed, Spit."

Donna stood there and for a moment Spit believed that she planned to supervise him while he changed.

"I'll be in the kitchen when you're ready." Donna exited the bedroom, leaving Spit alone with his wardrobe. Ten minutes later Spit emerged from his bedroom, the makeover complete, wearing his black suit, blue shirt and red Converse sneakers. "I'm sorry, Donna. I don't own a pair of dress shoes anymore."

Donna smiled. "It's okay, Spit. You look fabulous."

Spit grinned. "I do, don't I?"

When Spit was ready to head for the attorney's office, Donna gave him a peck on the cheek and sent him out the door. "Remember, Spit, just don't sign anything."

Half an hour later, Spit was pulling up in his cab at the office condominium belonging to Louis A. Garibaldi, Esquire.

Doris greeted him warmly at the door. "You must be Mr. Pettigrew."

"No, I'm…" Spit snuck a peek at his wardrobe. "…Actually, yes, I am Mr. Pettigrew."

Doris opened an inner office door. "You can wait in here."

Spit found himself alone in a large, oak-paneled conference room, imbued with the scent of pipe tobacco and successful litigation. Several minutes passed before Mr. Garibaldi squeezed in through another private door at the far end of the conference room.

"Mr. Pettigrew, thank you for coming."

Despite the red sneakers, Spit felt good about the image he projected. "Thank you for inviting me."

"Let me get right to the point then." Mr. Garibaldi did his best to explain his client's interest in the property, without actually divulging either the client or the intentions.

Spit was thoughtful. "The thing is, Mr. Garibaldi, that spot is very special to me. I would hate to see yet another condo community go up on my grandmother's land."

Mr. Garibaldi made a show of winking conspiratorially at Spit. "I'm not supposed to tell you this, but I'm sure I can trust you. My client intends to use the land to create a bird sanctuary."

Spit returned the wink. "I like birds, Mr. Garibaldi. However, it seems to me that the property is already a spot where birds congregate. I mean, it's not like your client can attract more birds by advertising. So how exactly do you create a bird sanctuary?"

Mr. Garibaldi chuckled. "No, you're correct, Mr. Pettigrew. I misspoke. It's not that my client intends to create a bird sanctuary. Your property is already teeming with birds. My client wants to protect the land as an official bird sanctuary, a safe spot for birds and birders."

"That's very interesting. Do you know why I like birds, Mr. Garibaldi?" Spit didn't wait for a response. "Because I don't like people. And do you know what people I don't like most of all?"

This time Spit waited, but Mr. Garibaldi offered no guess.

"The people I don't like most of all are other birders, mainstream, respectable, broomstick-up-their-butt birders. I'm sorry, Mr. Garibaldi, but I think I will hold on to the property."

"I can certainly respect that. May I ask you a question, Mr. Pettigrew? Is it true that you currently live on the property?"

Spit nodded quickly. "Yes."

"In one of those…cottages?" Mr. Garibaldi didn't want to insult the prospective seller by referring to his home as a shack.

"Yes."

Mr. Pettigrew recalled his first view of the property from land's end with Mrs. Patterson. "It must be very peaceful out there."

"It is." Spit had an idea. "Would you like to go out there with me?"

"Excuse me, but did you mean now?"

"Sure. Now's fine."

"I think I'd like that, Mr. Pettigrew."

As the two men exited the conference room, Doris barely looked up from her computer screen.

"Doris, I'll be back in an hour or two. I don't think I have anything on the schedule today that can't be changed."

Doris rolled her eyes. "I'll take care of it for you, Mr. Garibaldi."

"What would I do without you, Doris?" The attorney closed the door behind him before his paralegal dared to respond.

Mr. Garibaldi took Spit into his confidence. "Honestly, I don't know what I'd do if I didn't have Doris to take care of me. A man in your position, Mr. Pettigrew, I'm sure you understand."

Spit ran a hand across his neatly trimmed hair. "I know what you mean, Mr. Garibaldi."

Spit offered the attorney a ride in the taxicab. There was a moment of awkwardness as each man privately considered the matter of cab fare. Mr. Garibaldi tactfully suggested it would be easier for them both if he followed behind the cab in his Cadillac Seville.

Mr. Garibaldi was relieved to have a guide leading him to the isolated spot. Spit found the unmarked turn leading down to his property on his first try. When they parked their cars at land's end, the attorney took a closer look at the rickety wooden walkway spanning the marsh.

Spit set out on foot along the wooden path. Mr. Garibaldi, an exceptionally large man with dainty feet, had second thoughts about accepting Mr. Pettigrew's invitation. Still, there was no turning back. Moving carefully, he followed his host along the path.

"It must be hard living out here all alone."

Spit waited for Mr. Garibaldi to catch up. "Right now it feels kind of crowded."

Spit realized that Mr. Garibaldi might not understand. "I'm sorry. I didn't mean you. I have a houseguest this week. A very nice girl…a good influence…still, I'll be glad when everything gets back to normal."

Something was bothering Spit, but try as he might, he could not remember what it was.

From the cottage, Donna could hear two men talking. She looked out the window, spotting the men as they made their way across the marsh. She had spent enough time with the Sand Skeeters to recognize the team's rotund attorney.

Donna didn't want Mr. Garibaldi to stumble upon her hideout. Had Spit forgotten she was in hiding? She was in a state of panic. She couldn't stay in the house without being found out, but there was no place to go without risk of being seen. Standing at the window, Donna sneaked another peek. The two men were getting closer.

In Her Summer-Weight Wool Bikini

Donna knew that she had to make a decision. Moving to the back room, where the house itself would shield her actions from view, Donna clambered out the window and followed the path from the rear of the cottage, moving quickly, heading deeper into the marsh. Donna stopped some thirty yards behind the cottage, crouching in the mud along with the gnats and the mosquitoes, hidden from view by the tall marsh grass waving in the wind.

She could no longer see the two men and was fairly certain they could not see her, but she could hear their voices carrying from the dock.

"I don't think I could live here, but there is something romantic about the idea." The two men stood on the dock, watching a colony of common terns.

Mr. Garibaldi continued to be surprised by his reaction to this desolate spit of land jutting out into the ocean. "I can respect your decision not to sell…Still, I can't help but wonder whether you shouldn't consider my client's offer. Can I tell him that you'll think about it?"

Spit had begun the day nervous about meeting Mr. Garibaldi, but he realized he had something that the attorney wanted—not the real estate, but the way of life. He pictured the oversized Mr. Garibaldi living on the water, dressed in his custom-tailored suit, and on his dainty feet, in place of the expensive Italian loafers, a pair of tiny red sneakers.

"I'll think about it."

Mr. Garibaldi watched as a tern suddenly snatched a small fish from the water. Meanwhile, a sea gull watched Mr. Garibaldi. "I should be heading back to my office." Mr. Garibaldi made no attempt to leave.

When Donna moved in, Spit managed to adjust to the doubled occupancy. He had a sudden uncomfortable vision of the trebling of the local population. "Would you like me to walk you back to your car?"

Mr. Garibaldi had got Mr. Pettigrew's commitment to think about the offer. It was time to leave. "No, thank you. I can find my way back to the car. I'll call you in a few days, okay? We can talk some more about my client's offer." Mr. Garibaldi turned and headed back over the marsh.

Spit opened the door to his home and stepped inside. It took him a moment to realize the house was empty. Scratching his head, Spit stepped out onto the dock. He was startled to see Donna coming around from behind the house.

"Are you okay?"

Donna scratched at a mosquito bite on her cheek. "I'm fine, Spit." She scratched at a bite on her neck. "How was your meeting with the attorney?"

"Okay, I guess."

"Did you sign anything?"

From his car, Mr. Garibaldi called Andy MacTavish and briefed him on his meeting with Perry Pettigrew. "I'm going to talk to him again in a few days, but when all is said and done, I don't think he'll sell you the land, sir."

Andy's experience had taught him that some of the best deals begin with a "no." "You may be right, Mr. Garibaldi, but our Mr. Pettigrew sounds like a shrewd businessman. I bet you he's got a counterproposal the next time you hear from him."

Mr. Garibaldi had learned to respect Andy's instinct for the deal. Still, Andy had not met the eccentric Mr. Pettigrew. "We'll see. In the meantime, with your permission, I'd like to reach out to Mrs. Patterson. Perhaps she knows something more about our Mr. Pettigrew than she has let on."

"That's a good idea, Mr. Garibaldi. Let me know what you find out."

When Mrs. Patterson answered the telephone, she was pleased to hear Mr. Garibaldi's strong baritone voice.

"It's so nice to hear from you, Mr. Garibaldi. Have you made any progress locating the owner?"

Oozing male pride, Mr. Garibaldi briefly explained the situation. "Not only have I identified the owner, but I've met with him already."

"Is he willing to sell?"

"We'll see." Mr. Garibaldi knew this was a conversation he needed to do face to face. "Perhaps we should get together to discuss it."

Mrs. Patterson eagerly accepted the offer. "I'm meeting my husband for a late lunch in town. I can meet you on the boardwalk at three o'clock."

"On the boardwalk?"

"Yes. The coffee shop on the boardwalk. Three o'clock."

When Mr. Garibaldi approached the coffee shop, Mrs. Patterson was standing on the boardwalk, tall and stiff, a vision in glen plaid, watching the laughing gulls scavenging on the beach.

"It is a pleasure to see you again, Mrs. Patterson. You look lovely."

Mrs. Patterson giggled. "Oh, Mr. Garibaldi, how sweet of you to say so."

Mr. Garibaldi ordered one black coffee and one mocha latte with raspberry syrup. "The back deck has a lovely view of the beach." Mr. Garibaldi held the door for Mrs. Patterson. Off-season, they had their choice of seating on the deck.

Mrs. Patterson sipped her black coffee. "Don't you just love the beach this time of year? In season, everyone flaunts their sun-tanned bodies. It's all so in-your-face, don't you think?"

Mr. Garibaldi said nothing. He liked those sun-tanned bodies.

Mrs. Patterson continued. "The way everyone stares at you…I mean, one look at the men and it's obvious what they're thinking, and the women are even worse…I won't walk on the beach anymore."

Mr. Garibaldi tried to imagine Mrs. Patterson, in season, walking on the beach in her summer-weight wool bikini. "Would you like to hear about my meeting with Mr. Pettigrew?"

Mrs. Patterson caught Mr. Garibaldi discreetly checking her out, before he changed the subject. She thought she wouldn't mind with Mr. Garibaldi.

"I would like that very much." Mrs. Patterson could feel the warmth in her cheeks. "Hearing about your meeting, that is."

Mr. Garibaldi described his appointment with Mr. Pettigrew. "He's really quite eccentric…you know, he lives on the property."

"You mean he actually lives in one of those shacks? I thought the place was abandoned." Mrs. Patterson considered that *eccentric* was not a strong enough adjective for the man who would choose to live in such a dwelling.

"Yes, he does. And he drives a vintage taxicab."

"How unusual."

Mr. Garibaldi agreed. "Yes. He is a most unusual gentleman. I fear, however, that he may not be swayed by matters of finance."

Mrs. Patterson weighed the attorney's words. "Perhaps it is just a negotiating ploy."

"Perhaps. Mr. MacTavish thought the same thing."

Mrs. Patterson knew that Andy MacTavish was a clever businessman and a worthy adversary. She was confident that he would recognize the advantage of declaring an end to their season-long hostilities. Still, her recent attack on the team might have gone too far. She was concerned that she had made the dispute too personal. She was concerned that she had angered Mr. MacTavish to the point that he might ignore the business benefits of a truce. So she was pleased to hear that Andy MacTavish was considering the economics of the deal. "Mr. MacTavish is willing to buy me the property?"

Mr. Garibaldi nodded. "If we can convince Mr. Pettigrew to accept a reasonable offer, I believe that Mr. MacTavish is likely to sign off on the arrangement."

Mrs. Patterson was not worried about Perry Pettigrew. "It is an unusual man indeed who is not swayed by large sums of money, but if money does not motivate our Mr. Pettigrew, then we simply need to find out what does." Mrs. Patterson made it clear that by "we," she was referring to Mr. Garibaldi.

The attorney chuckled. "I guess I have some work to do. I'd better be getting back to my office."

Mrs. Patterson stood up. "Would you mind walking me to my car? A woman can never be too careful."

As they strolled down the boardwalk, Mr. Garibaldi pointed to the Om Depot, its neon eyeball blinking in the sunlight, open for business and attracting a small crowd of curious customers. "I guess there's never an off-season for psychic readings."

Mrs. Patterson snorted. "What's wrong with these people?"

Mr. Garibaldi could tell from her tone that she was not asking a question. "It's just harmless fun. Maybe we should get a reading. Maybe she can tell us how to motivate our Mr. Pettigrew."

Again, Mrs. Patterson snorted. Mr. Garibaldi felt like a novice *torero* in the ring with a determined bull. "I guess not."

Mrs. Patterson pointed to her Lexus. "That's me, over there. Thank you for the coffee." She smiled warmly. "May I call you Louis? Yes? Let's do this again, Louis, okay?"

Mrs. Patterson turned to leave. Almost as an afterthought, she looked back at Louis Garibaldi. "You say he drives a taxicab?"

A Line Began to Form Outside Andy's Office

Cassie didn't want to leave White Sands Beach without Andy. She had delayed her return to Doah for as long as she could. She intended to be in the audience for Cheyenne's final mayoral debate and she wanted Andy to be there with her. Andy had declared his intention of going with her to Doah, but now that it was time to leave, he explained that Sand Skeeter business made it impossible for him to get away.

"I can't, Cassie. There's just too much going on." Andy knew his decision did not sit well with Cassie, but there really was a lot he needed to handle, what with the dead girl, the missing girl, the bird sanctuary and the police.

They were building a life together. Andy understood that required give and take. But he also understood that they were building their life on the foundation of his continued business success. If the business faltered, so would their relationship. It seemed obvious to Andy, and it bothered him that Cassie did not seem to understand.

"I'm sorry, Cassie, but I have to spend some time at the ballpark today." Andy considered his options. "What if I meet you in Doah later tonight? With a little luck, I'll get there in time for the debate."

Cassie threw her arms around him. "I love you, Andy MacTavish."

Andy gulped down his coffee. "The sooner I get to the ballpark, the sooner I can leave."

By the time Andy arrived at the ballpark, there was a stack of phone messages leaning like a paper Tower of Pisa. Andy sorted the slips and returned a call from Mr. Garibaldi.

"Louis. What have you been able to find out?"

Andy pictured Mr. Garibaldi on the other end of the telephone line, leaning back in his oversized chair, his tiny feet propped up on the edge of the desk.

"I don't know, sir. She's an odd one, all right."

"She? Don't you mean he? Or is our Mr. Pettigrew married?"

Mr. Garibaldi clarified his message. "No, I don't believe he is married and, yes, he is an odd one, but, no, I wasn't referring to him just now. I was referring to the other odd one, Mrs. Patterson."

Andy wasn't interested in her personality profile, except as it might relate to their ability to do business together. "Will we be able to deal with her?"

The attorney believed that, yes, they probably could. "As long as we can motivate Mr. Pettigrew to sell."

Mr. Garibaldi was troubled by some of Mrs. Patterson's remarks. "I get the feeling she knows more about Mr. Pettigrew than she is letting on."

"Good work, Louis. Keep on it. Perhaps we can motivate Mr. Pettigrew to talk figures." Andy looked at his watch. "I'm pressed for time today, Louis. Call me back if you make any progress."

Before Andy could place another call, the switchboard patched through an incoming call. Andy didn't recognize the name.

"Mr. MacTavish?"

"Yes."

"Mr. Andy MacTavish?"

The unfamiliar caller with the pushy telephone voice already annoyed Andy. "Who is this?"

"I'm looking for Cassie O'Malley."

At the mention of Cassie's name, Andy took another glance at his watch. "I'm sorry, but I'm kind of busy today. Have you tried her cell phone?"

The caller laughed, spitting phlegm on the receiver. "I've been trying her cell phone for days. That's why I'm calling you."

Andy was growing frustrated with the caller. "Before I hang up on you, why don't you tell me who you are and what this is all about?"

It seemed to the caller that Andy MacTavish was acting like a jerk, but then, in an uncharacteristically self-reflective moment, the caller allowed for the possibility that it was he who was the jerk, jealous of Andy MacTavish, who had both money and Cassie. "I'm sorry. My name's Morris. I'm Cassie's editor. Perhaps she's told you about me."

"I'm sorry if I was brusque, Morris. Cassie's on her way home to Doah. I'm going to join her there as soon as I can get away. Would you like me to tell her anything?"

Morris wasn't sure whether he wanted to leave a message. "Is she still looking for that girl who went missing?"

"Do you know where she is? Did you find her? Is she okay?" Andy silently said a prayer of thanks for Donna and for Morris.

Andy raced through the work remaining, but the more quickly he attempted to finish his work, the more work there was to finish. Detective Sububie appeared unexpectedly in Andy's doorway.

"Detective…" Andy tried to disguise the irritation in his voice. "How nice to see you again."

Detective Sububie was in no mood for small talk. "Who had access to the Skeeter costume?"

"Huh? Is there a problem, detective?"

The policewoman had yet to smile. "I'll ask the questions, Mr. MacTavish. Again, who had access to the costume?"

"Let's see…Donna, of course."

"Of course. Who else?"

Andy ticked them off on his fingers. "The promotions manager, the equipment manager, the laundry service, the cleaning crew. They would all have routine access. I don't think Donna locked the door to the changing room unless she was actually changing, so I guess just about anyone on the staff could have access."

"That's very interesting. Until we have a way to narrow it down, I'll need to talk to everyone on your list."

"Now?"

Detective Sububie glared at the team owner. "Unless you have something more important to do than to cooperate with a police investigation."

Andy glanced at his watch. "Of course not. The Sand Skeeters are never too busy for a local peace officer."

Andy dialed up his executive assistant and within minutes a line began to form outside Andy's office.

The detective set about her work. "I'd like to use your conference room for the interviews." It wasn't a request. "You can send people in one at a time."

Andy had hoped for an early getaway on the drive to Doah, but he no longer had control of the schedule. "In any particular order?"

Detective Sububie finally smiled. "Whatever."

Andy decided to start with Donna's immediate supervisor. The interview was brief, not more than ten minutes and when it was over, Andy asked his promotions manager what it was all about.

"I don't know, boss."

Andy wondered aloud whether Detective Sububie had instructed him to say that.

"No, boss. Really. I don't know." And he didn't.

The equipment manager went next, with similar results. One by one staff went into the conference room and one by one they came out, unable to give Andy a clear picture of the detective's intentions.

The language barrier prevented Andy from asking the laundry staff.

When Detective Sububie completed her interviews, she sat down with Andy MacTavish in his office.

"Please thank your employees for their cooperation. I realize this was probably uncomfortable for people, but we have a problem we need to deal with." Detective Sububie emphasized the shared nature of their problem.

"You have a job to do, detective. I can respect that. Perhaps the staff could be of more help to you if we understood the nature of the problem."

"The nature of the problem…" Detective Sububie shook her head. "The lab found malathion on the fibers."

Detective Sububie watched closely for Andy's reaction. His surprise, to her trained eye, seemed genuine. "I don't understand."

"Then let me explain. Heather's death was determined to be an accident, the result of extreme heat inside the costume mixed with excessive alcohol consumption. When I took the costume in for testing, I didn't expect to find anything. I was looking to make points by saving the squad the embarrassment of a missing lab report. No more, no less. Instead, the lab finds some kind of toxic insecticide and now all hell's gonna break loose. And somehow it's all gonna be my fault. It's not fair."

Andy tried to make sense of the detective's tirade. "Are you saying that Heather was poisoned?"

The detective was grim. "I'm saying, however she died, accident, murder—hell, old age—I need to figure it out, and I need to do it fast."

Andy made a mental note to ask Mr. Garibaldi if a murder case would lessen his exposure in a civil lawsuit. "If there's anything I can do to help, detective."

Detective Sububie had to ask. "Do you know how the insecticide ended up on the Skeeter costume?"

What Andy knew was that the malathion, however it ended up on the costume, was not a factor in Heather's untimely death. Andy remembered

Cassie's advice. Was it too late to tell the detective that Heather hadn't worn the tainted costume?

"I don't know, detective. So what happens now?"

Detective Sububie sighed. "I imagine the department will decide to exhume Ms. Dean's body…Damn, it's gonna get crazy around here."

Her Unfinished Tale of Sabotage

Cassie gathered the few belongings she had brought with her to Andy's home and threw them in her overnight bag. Then she considered leaving some of her stuff at Andy's. They hadn't discussed living together. How long did she plan to be in Doah? For the night? Until the election? Would it be presumptuous, she wondered, to leave things at Andy's, as though the beach house was now her primary home? Would it send the wrong message, she countered, to take her things back to her condo, as though her time at the ocean were now ending? What would Miss Manners say? Cassie didn't want to be a Mr. Bungle.

She sat on the deck, enjoying the view and rethinking her packing decision. As she sat, a light rain began to fall. She listened to the staccato tap of raindrops on the deck until the morning sky began to darken. She realized she should get on the road before the weather turned ugly. Cassie opted for presumptuous. Leaving her overnight bag where it lay, she locked the beach house behind her and climbed behind the wheel of her rebuilt '67 Ford Mustang, taking only her CDs.

Cassie loved the way the driver's seat conformed to the contours of her body. She slid Thelonius Monk into the player and turned on her windshield wipers, the rhythm of the wipers a perfect counterpoint to Monk's bebop piano and Coltrane's tenor sax. Cassie imagined Thelonius Monk composing during a driving rain.

Puddles formed on the back roads. There was little traffic on these roads, but what little there was, was beginning to bunch up, slowed by the conditions. Still, Cassie preferred these small roads to the highway. Popping another CD in the player, Percy and Jimmy Heath, she made her way home to Doah. It seemed to Cassie that the sky cleared even as she passed the sign welcoming her to historic Doah Township.

Cassie pulled the Mustang into her reserved parking space. Opening the door to her condo, she was greeted with a rush of stale air. She walked from room to room, opening windows, breathing in the fresh scent of pine forest.

Cassie poured herself a Jameson and water and started to clean house. She would not have Andy MacTavish see her condo dirty. It had been nearly fifteen years since Rob died, nearly a decade and a half that Cassie had endured a half-empty bed. She needed the condo to be perfect.

Cassie kept one photo of Rob on her bureau. It was the only visible reminder of her young love. She picked up the photo, slipped it into the top drawer and continued cleaning. She changed the bed linens and tidied the closet. She cleaned the bathroom and put out fresh towels. She put Rob's photo back out on the bureau.

She wiped down the kitchen counters and the stovetop. She inspected the refrigerator, disposing of past-dated milk and wilted lettuce. She walked back to her bedroom and returned Rob's photo to the drawer.

Cassie vacuumed her carpets and organized her desk. She separated her bills from the mass of new junk mail. She read the latest issue of "Princeton Alumni Weekly." For the six hundredth consecutive time since graduation, she was not mentioned in her class notes. She retrieved Rob's photo from the drawer and stood it proudly on the bureau.

Cassie poured herself a second glass of Jameson and dialed Cheyenne's number.

"Still answering your own phone? I bet that stops when you become Mayor Harbrough."

"Cassie! Where are you? How are you? Is Andy MacTavish giving you the high hard one?"

Cassie made sure to respond to each of Cheyenne's questions. "Home. Great. And yes."

Cheyenne was nearing the end of a surprisingly effective mayoral campaign. She was busily preparing for the final debate, reviewing her talking points and selecting her footwear. Still, all that could wait. "What's he like, Cassie?"

Cassie pretended not to understand Cheyenne's question. "He supports all the right causes, Chey. Gives money to the local charities. Helps old ladies cross the street. A real gentleman."

Cheyenne wanted to reach through the telephone line and smack Cassie upside the head. "Shit, girl. You know what I mean. Is he good?"

Cassie laughed heartily. "He's good, Chey. He's good two, sometimes three times a night."

Cheyenne was thrilled that Cassie finally had a love life. "I'm happy for you, Cassie. So when do I get to meet this good-lucking, wealthy stud-muffin?"

"How about tonight?"

Cheyenne was disappointed. "I can't, Cassie. The debate's tonight. Remember?"

"I know, Chey. That's why I'm home. We want to be in the audience tonight."

"You're bringing Andy MacTavish to the debate? That's hot."

"If he gets here in time." Cassie explained the plan to Cheyenne. "I'm looking forward to seeing you, Cheyenne. I'm really proud of what you're doing."

"I'll see you tonight, Cassie. Don't forget to check out my shoes."

It felt good to be home. When Cassie hung up the phone, she noticed her folder of story ideas.

Cassie realized she had no idea what Morris needed from her. She hadn't done any writing in weeks. She dialed her editor's number and left a message on his voice mail. She reread her unfinished tale of sabotage on Black Tom Island and recognized her problem—she was allowing facts to intrude on her storyline. She freshened the Jameson.

It all began with the mosquitoes (if you believe the official German version of events). Imagine. You are working as a night watchman in a warehouse. It's a lonely job, making your solitary rounds in the dark, tired and bored, and worst of all, under constant attack from hordes of blood-crazed mosquitoes. There are millions of mosquitoes on Black Tom Island and you're the only human host on the island overnight. It's like you're the last early bird special and the mosquitoes have all arrived with their senior citizen discount cards.

If you really were the last early bird special, you could outrun an angry mob of senior citizens with their walkers and their canes (even motorized wheelchairs fail to achieve racing speed). But if you were the night watchman on Black Tom Island, you were the guest of honor at an all-you-can eat mosquito buffet. There would be no escape.

If you were a night watchman in a warehouse on Black Tom Island, you might want to carry a can of mosquito repellent, perhaps a spare can in your utility belt. But this was 1917. Mosquito repellent was a night watchman's wet dream.

So what do you do? According to the Germans, you grab a smudge pot and start swinging it at the mosquito cloud.

Now suppose that the warehouse serves as the storage center for a manufacturer of fine ladies' undergarments. The smudge pot accidentally sparks and a small fire spreads. The next day we read a humorous account in the newspaper and until the manufacturer can restock his wares, there is a noticeable increase in feminine droopage.

But what if the warehouse were actually a top-secret Army munitions depot, sending covert aid to Great Britain prior to our entry into the First World War? (You don't believe that clandestine military operations began during the Reagan administration, do you?)

When the smudge pot sparked, according to the Germans, a chain reaction was started, explosions ripping through the night sky, spreading quickly across the island, shock waves jumping across the water all the way to New York City, shattering glass, interrupting coitus (masculine droopage,) and otherwise playing havoc with business and recreation throughout the metropolitan region.

It all began with the mosquitoes.

Cassie saved the file and logged off the computer. It was time to head for the mayoral debate.

Cheyenne would be disappointed when she walked in sans escort. Cassie glanced at her watch. What was keeping Andy?

The Next Mayor of Doah Township

"**W**elcome to the third and final debate among our candidates for mayor, Beverly Becht, Democrat, Cheyenne Harbrough, Independent, and the incumbent, Mayor Big Jim Donovan, Republican." Mr. Caputo, the boyish attorney and tireless self-promoter, was once again moderating the debates.

"Tonight's format will be somewhat different. Each candidate will make a brief opening statement. Questions tonight will be posed by you, the audience and citizens of our fair town."

There was a noticeable buzz in the room at the invitation to participate in the evening's political proceedings. Mr. Caputo waited for the buzz to subside.

"In order to maintain a proper sense of decorum, the candidates have agreed that members of the audience who wish to pose a question will write down their question on one of these index cards"—Mr. Caputo waved a packet of cards in the air—"and then I will read the questions as submitted."

"Earlier today the order of the candidates' opening remarks was selected at random. Councilwoman Becht, Democrat, will go first. Ms. Becht?"

Beverly Becht stood at the podium, looking out at the fifty or so citizens sitting in the audience and the additional citizens of Doah watching at home on local access cable. She considered whether to read her prepared statement. Ms. Becht's campaign had derailed at the outset because of her strident, some would say xenophobic, vision of a white, Christian township. The Democratic Party publicly denounced their own candidate and denied her access to party resources. Nevertheless, Ms. Becht was on the ballot and on the podium.

"My friends, there are some who would maintain that the citizens of Doah are interested in electing a local government that will fix potholes, collect garbage, manage development, that will support fire safety and emergency services, preserve open space, plow the roads and reduce the local tax burden. However, I believe that local government has a higher calling. I believe that there are many of you who agree with me. Our enemies twist our words and make fun of our beliefs. Therefore, let us not speak openly tonight of that higher calling. Let us simply take comfort in knowing that it is not too late to send a message to the heathens and the homosexuals, the liberals and the lesbians. On election day, let us reclaim Doah Township. Thank you."

As Councilwoman Becht spoke, angry citizens scribbled furiously on their index cards. Mr. Caputo looked up at the podium. "Thank you, councilwoman. Next to speak will be the incumbent, Mayor Big Jim Donovan."

For all his difficulties, Cassie knew that Mayor Donovan was still a decent man. She wondered how Cheyenne could overcome the mayor's likeability factor. Big Jim rose to speak, looking tanned and fit, thinner than Cassie remembered.

"My friends, unlike my worthy opponent, I happen to believe that it is exactly the business of local government to fix the potholes, collect the garbage and manage the development, to support fire safety and emergency services, to preserve open space, plow the roads and reduce the local tax burden. During my first term, we did these things well and I pledge to you here, now, that in a second term we will do them even better. There is no higher calling for local government than to serve its citizens. It saddens me to have to make the point that as mayor, I am committed to insuring that our government treats every member of this wonderful community with respect, even the heathens and the homosexuals, even the liberals and the lesbians. Even the developers." Mayor Donovan turned and looked at Cheyenne before returning to his seat. "Your turn, Ms. Harbrough."

As Cheyenne rose to speak, Cassie made sure to get a good look at her stiletto-heel, pointy-toe, Italian mid-calf boot. The audience waited, anticipating Cheyenne's opening remarks.

"Did you hear the one about the traveling salesman and the developer's daughter?" Even Mr. Caputo chuckled, before encouraging the room to quiet down. Cheyenne smiled broadly.

"During Mayor Donovan's term in office, this town has been witness to extraordinary scandals. We have been witness to fistfights among local officials; we've seen the planning board and council threaten each other with lawsuits. Hell, we watched as the mayor attempted to sue himself.

Big Jim is a good man, a likeable man, a decent man. If you are satisfied with the status quo, by all means reelect Mayor Donovan. But, if you are embarrassed by the shenanigans, if you want to restore civility to public discourse, if you want to watch council meetings in order to hear honest debate of important issues, then you know that it's time for a change. On election day, I ask you to go to the polls and elect Cheyenne Harbrough the next mayor of Doah Township."

Cassie hardly listened to the question-and-answer portion of the evening. It had been her experience that people rarely asked a question at one of these events because they wanted to hear the answer, they asked because they wanted to hear their question. It seemed to Cassie that all three candidates had used their opening remarks to articulate their position and that no voter was likely to change their mind based on the Q and A.

Even Mr. Caputo seemed bored by the question-and-answer format. After the first few questions, he read mechanically, without regard for the content. One question, in particular, did grab Cassie's attention, precisely because it must have escaped Mr. Caputo's attention.

"In this time of unprecedented homeland security considerations," read Mr. Caputo in a question directed to the mayor, "what is the significance of baba booey, baba booey, baba booey?"

Mayor Donovan stared at the moderator, while the audience roared. Mr. Caputo stared at the index card, trying to comprehend the question, before directing his anger at the audience.

"Do I need to remind you that the strength of our democracy depends on the will of serious-minded citizens? Wasting time and energy on such foolishness is as much a threat to our way of life as are the terrorists."

Mr. Caputo's reprimand failed to quiet the room. "Let's take a short recess. And I would ask you not to return if you do not intend to participate in a responsible fashion." Mr. Caputo jammed the index cards into his jacket pocket and marched out of the room.

Cheyenne located Cassie during the break. "Where is he?"

Cassie had been asking herself the same question all night. During the Q and A, she had even scribbled that very question on an index card. At least she hadn't turned the card in to Mr. Caputo. "I don't know, Chey. I guess he ran into a problem at the ballpark."

"Do you think he's still coming tonight?"

Cassie knew that Andy wouldn't let her down. "He's probably sitting outside the condo even as we speak, waiting for me to get home. I know the debate's not over yet, Chey, but would you mind terribly if I left now?"

"Go. Go find your missing man. Shit, I'd go with you if I could."

"Thanks, Chey. By the way, the boots look great."

Cheyenne grinned. "Tell you what, Cassie. How about we meet for breakfast? That is, if you and Mr. Two, Sometimes Three Times a Night are able to get out of bed."

Collecting Stars, Like Fireflies

When it began to rain, Donna realized how much she had changed since she first set foot in Spit's home in the marsh. Without thinking, she retrieved the buckets and placed them strategically to catch rainwater leaking in through the roof. Then she returned to her seat at the card table and the latest jigsaw challenge.

"I think I'm finally getting the hang of this place."

Sitting alongside Donna, Spit didn't bother to look up from the puzzle. "Yeah, I think so too."

Donna pulled her chair back from the table. "I'm gonna make myself a cup of tea. How about it, Spit? Should I make you a cup?"

Again, Spit answered without looking up. "Yeah. Red Zinger. Thanks."

Donna went into the kitchen, returning a few minutes later with two cups of Darjeeling. "Sorry. It's all I could find. You know, I've been thinking …"

This time Spit looked up. "Yeah?"

Donna struggled to find the right words. "I'm starting to think that I may have overreacted."

Spit weighed her words, sensing that Donna was seeking his opinion. He was hesitant to offer one without an idea what it was she might have overreacted to. "Yeah."

Donna began to laugh. "You don't have a clue what I'm talking about, do you, Spit?"

Spit ducked his head, sheepish in his confusion. "Not really."

"That's okay, Spit. It's my fault, not yours."

Spit still had no clue. "Okay."

Donna hoped Spit would understand. "I think it's time for me to go home. Not that you haven't been a wonderful host. I just think maybe it's time for me to end the melodrama. Blue Moon Odom or no Blue Moon Odom, there's no one out there trying to do me harm."

Spit thought for a moment. Until Donna reminded him of the reading, he had completely forgotten about Madame Alexina. "I'd feel better about letting you leave if I knew you would be safe."

Donna sipped her Darjeeling. "It's okay, Spit. No one is trying to hurt me."

"But…"

"It's okay, Spit. Really." Donna watched the raindrops bounce in the bucket near her feet.

Spit had grown accustomed to Donna's company. It was hard for him to admit that he enjoyed having a friend around the house. "When were you thinking about leaving?"

Donna didn't answer right away. "It depends on the weather." Donna sipped her tea. "I was thinking about something you told me when I first got here. You told me I should spend a night alone on the pontoon boat."

Spit liked that Donna remembered. "And then you did. It helped you adjust to the place."

But Donna remembered more clearly. "I didn't really, Spit. I mean, I slept on the boat and you were right, it helped a lot. But I never took the boat out. It was tied to the dock the whole time."

Spit dismissed Donna's correction. "It doesn't matter. It worked."

Donna remembered how the sky overflowed with stars. "Before I leave, I want to spend another night alone on the boat. This time in the middle of the channel. If you trust me with the boat."

Spit was impressed with Donna's resolve. "Sure."

Donna sipped her tea. "If it stops raining, I thought I'd like to take the boat out tonight. Tomorrow I'll call a cab to take me home."

"You don't have to call a…" Spit paused, feeling foolish. "I get it."

Now that Donna had made the decision, she watched the rain, looking for evidence of clearing. She rotated the buckets as they filled with rainwater. As the afternoon sky lightened and the rain moved south, Donna sat on the dock trying, without success, to calculate the length of her stay in this isolated outpost. Heather's untimely death and Madame Alexina's bizarre reading had convinced her that her own life was in danger. Suddenly, it all seemed so foolish.

Spit joined Donna on the dock. "I love the sky after a good rain."

"I bet you'll be glad to get rid of me."

Spit thought about the night when Madame Alexina had dumped Donna in his cab. At first he had resented the intrusion. "Would you like me to show you how to operate the pontoon boat?"

"Is it hard?"

Spit showed Donna how to work the controls and explained how to read the channel markers. Donna cooked them a light supper of shrimp fried rice. They ate in silence. After supper, Spit watched the sky gradually darken. "It's going to be a beautiful night on the water tonight. Are you sure you'll be okay?"

Donna stepped off the dock and onto the pontoon boat. "I'll be fine." She turned the ignition and listened for the motor to catch.

Spit tossed her an old woolen blanket. "It's gonna be cold out there."

Easing back on the throttle, Donna unhitched the line and slowly pulled away from the dock. "Don't worry about me, Spit. I'll see you in the morning." Donna guided the pontoon boat toward the first channel marker. Spit stood on the dock, scanning for maritime hazards. When Donna saw him keeping watch, she waved him back inside the house. Alone on the water, Donna wiped a tear from her eye and smiled.

In the darkening sky, stars began to pop up, just one or two at first, gradually increasing in number and forming their immutable patterns and then suddenly the night sky teemed. Donna thought that God must be a small child collecting stars, like fireflies in a jar stolen from His mother's cupboard, a jar that we like to call the universe.

Donna thought about the men in her life. She had few memories of her father, who left home when she was barely five years old. She remembered how he hated to fish, but loved to take his little girl fishing. She would sit at the edge of the man-made pond, dangling her pole in the water, a dough ball for bait. She never caught a fish, but Donna remembered how they would always stop at the market on the way home. She would walk in the house proudly carrying her fillet of flounder or bluefish. She would show her mother the prize fish, her father explaining excitedly how Donna had caught the big one, how she had nearly been dragged out to sea by the fish, how she had stood there bravely reeling in the monster. And then her mother would take the prize fish and cook them a family feast. Donna wished there were a fishing pole on the pontoon boat.

She thought about her boyfriend Billy and his heavy-metal, spiked-hair, take-no-prisoners, moshpit philosophy of life. Was Billy worried about her? Did he miss her? More to the point, Donna wondered, did she miss Billy? She should have let Billy take Heather to the concert. They had more in common anyway. She wondered: if she had stepped aside, would Heather still be alive?

She thought about Spit. The confused taxicab driver, this disabled veteran of Desert Storm, this radical activist and conspiracy theorist, this fragile intellect living alone in a condemned shack in the marsh, was perhaps the most responsible man in her life.

Donna allowed the boat to drift farther down the channel, just far enough from land to be utterly alone in the universe. She listened to the pontoons as they slid through the swells. She watched the water for glints of silver, party fish out for a night on the town. With neither mattress nor pillow, wrapped in a stained and scratchy blanket, Donna fell asleep and dreamt of dolphins and mermaids, of seahorse and starfish. She dreamt of Spit.

Sometime during the night, Donna dreamt of an extraordinary sea serpent, gliding along the surface. Its head rose up high, fire belching from its nostrils, heat waves emanating across the surface of the sea.

Donna dreamt and all the while the pontoon boat drifted. When the sea serpent roared, she shook off the dream and found herself adrift in the Atlantic in the middle of the night. Under other circumstances, she might have struggled to find her bearings, but not on this night. Donna lifted her gaze toward the shoreline, scanning for the tiny piece of earth jutting out into the ocean. There it was, her landmark, ablaze in the night sky.

"Omigod! Spit!"

Smelling of Wood Smoke and Saltwater

When the unidentified caller reported the blaze, the fire department responded with dispatch. Volunteer firefighters throughout the coastal region jumped out of bed. Leaving their homes and sleeping families, they sped through the dark night to the firehouse and their civic duty. Within minutes, fire trucks were rolling, sirens blaring, the pumpers roaring down the county road. Their response would have been quicker had the trucks not missed the unmarked turn that would lead them to the site of the reported blaze.

Still, acting with a response time that would have been the envy of paid professionals, the volunteer firefighters soon were setting up their equipment at land's end. Looking out over the marsh, they could see flames leaping from the ramshackle cottages. They could see the far end of the elevated boardwalk collapsing in flames. The fire called out to them, mocking them, but they could not respond. There was no way for the firefighters to bring their equipment in close enough.

They set up at land's end, the water cannons unleashing a torrent out over the marsh, soaking the near end of the boardwalk, but falling far short of the blazing cottage. The firefighters debated tactics, argued and experimented, determined to do more than merely watch as the fire spread quickly, devouring everything in its path. Gradually they came to accept, man by man, the futile nature of their efforts. The firefighters were consoled by the knowledge that these shacks had long since been abandoned.

Even in the middle of night, even in the middle of nowhere, a fire demands attention. A local news crew pulled up in their van, thrilled by the chance to shoot exclusive footage of the blaze. A small crowd formed at land's end, bystanders, insomniacs, the fire paparazzi. There was a brief commotion when a middle-aged woman came out of the crowd, with hair like fire itself and a trace of moustache like burning embers, insisting that one of the shacks was inhabited.

Adrift in the Atlantic, Donna turned the boat toward shore, pushing the throttle forward, begging the little motor for speed. Slowly, the pontoons cut through the water, inching the boat toward land.

Watching the flames rip through the night sky, Donna desperately tried to quell the panic in the pit of her stomach. She pulled to within several hundred yards of the shoreline and eased up on the throttle, bringing the boat to a halt. Fire raged out of control, the cottage engulfed in flames, the dock collapsed, large sections of boardwalk missing, charred and burning pilings jutting up out of the marsh. Donna watched in silent horror. She thought she might be sick.

The pontoon boat bounced lazily in the offshore swells, gently swaying, peaceful, serene. Suddenly the boat pitched. Donna lost her footing, nearly falling, stumbling head first as an exhausted Spit, sooty and waterlogged, slightly singed, smelling of wood smoke and saltwater, pulled himself into the boat.

He was shaking, unable to talk. "You're freezing." Donna wrapped him in the blanket, holding him close. She hugged him, sharing her warmth, unwilling to let him go. They huddled together in the pontoon boat. Donna was talking, could not stop talking, seeking in her words refuge from the turmoil, the fear and the guilt.

Heather had died. Spit, very nearly, had died. Donna hugged him tighter, overwhelmed by the grim joy of survival. She wanted to protect him, to take care of him, to let him know it would be okay. She took his hand. She struggled to make sense of her feelings. Spit struggled to stop himself from shaking.

Spit watched as fire consumed his home, his thoughts his own, his emotions locked inside his shivering body. "We need to get out of here."

Where can you go, Donna wondered, when you have already retreated to the very end of the earth?

"I'm going to take us down to the Point." Spit turned the boat around and headed back out to the channel. "It's not very far. Of course, this old boat's not very fast."

Donna stared at the fire. "What about your house?"

Spit shrugged. "What house?"

He eased the throttle forward. The pontoon boat picked up speed, leaving the charred remains churning in its wake. Donna took one final look back.

At land's end, the volunteer firefighters stood by helplessly while the fire raged out of control. Sometime during the night, the fireboats arrived. Working at close range, the fireboats contained and finally extinguished the dramatic fire. Coming in behind the boats, fire investigators began the work of unlocking the secrets of the blaze.

The investigators were extremely tight-lipped. They made no official comment, but by morning, rumors were already circulating widely.

Some Men Could Make Your Heart Race

When Cassie turned her Mustang into the condo lot, she recognized Andy's Lexus in a visitor's parking space. Then she noticed Andy sitting on her stoop, leaning back against her door. She pulled her car into the first available space, bumping the curb in her haste. Jumping from the car, she ran to give Andy a kiss.

"I knew you'd be here."

Andy stood up, stretching to unkink his aching back. "I'm glad you're here. I was starting to wonder if I was in the right place."

"Tough day?"

Andy smiled. "I'll tell you all about it. Can we go inside?"

"I'm sorry. Of course. By the way, Andy, you look like shit."

"I feel like shit. Or I did."

Cassie unlocked her door, allowing Andy to enter her condo and another part of her life. "I love you, Andy MacTavish."

It seemed to Andy that Cassie was more relaxed in her condo, but at the same time, nervous. She gave Andy a quick tour. In the bedroom, she slipped Rob's photograph back inside the bureau. Andy wisely decided it was not time to crack wise.

"I'm sorry I missed the debate. How'd she do?"

"She did real good."

"I tried to call you. Your cell was turned off."

Cassie tried to remember where she'd last seen her cell phone. "I think I left it in the glove compartment. I guess I should take the phone out and charge it. If I can find the charger."

Andy laughed. "It does work better that way."

Cassie and Andy sat down at the kitchen table with a pint of black raspberry ice cream.

"I had another visit from Detective Sububie." Andy explained about the lab results. "They think they found something on the costume. Apparently, the detective believes it has something to do with Heather."

"Did you tell her?" Cassie had warned Andy about this.

Andy took a large spoonful of black raspberry ice cream.

"Andy, whatever Detective Sububie thinks she found, you know and I know it has nothing to do with Heather. Did you tell her?"

Andy stared at the black raspberry. "I wanted to."

Cassie recognized how messy this was going to get, how unnecessarily messy. "You should have told her the truth, Andy."

Andy knew that she was right, but he managed to rationalize his decision. Andy explained to Cassie that the police planned to exhume Heather's body. "So you see, when they test the corpse, they'll realize that whatever they found on the costume, whatever they think they found, it has nothing to do with Heather. So it'll all be okay and I won't have to tell them they tested the wrong costume."

Cassie was unconvinced. "You should have told her the truth, Andy."

Andy was not ready to surrender the point. "Can we talk about it tomorrow?"

"I'm sorry, Andy. Of course it can wait until tomorrow. You're exhausted. Why don't we go to bed?"

"First I'm going to get your cell phone, Cassie. It'll charge overnight."

Andy retrieved the phone from her Mustang, located the charger and plugged the phone in on her bureau.

By the time Andy was finished with the phone, Cassie was under the covers. All afternoon, she had worried about this moment. Would it be different in her bed? At Andy's house, Rob's hold on her had been weaker. Would she feel like Andy had taken Rob's place? Would she feel like she was cheating? She and Rob had married so young, children almost, playing house. Surely Rob would not want her to be alone. She watched as Andy got ready for bed. He was a good-looking man, but not excessively so. Some men could make your heart race, Cassie thought; Andy would make your heart race walk. He was a modest man, but he moved with a graceful confidence. He had warm eyes and soft lips. He had a smile that he saved for Cassie and Cassie alone.

Andy climbed into bed, wearing a pair of black pajama bottoms. Cassie rested her head on Andy's bare chest and fell asleep listening to his heart.

That night, Cassie dreamt of rockets launching, of volcanoes erupting. She dreamt of submarines rigged for silent running, torpedoes set to fire in the torpedo bay.

She dreamt of Andy, and when she awoke, she awoke with Andy, with his warm eyes and soft lips and … Outside her condo, at the edge of the pine forest, Cassie heard the unmistakable sound of waves crashing on the shore. It thrilled her to know that Andy had brought the ocean surf with him from his bedroom in White Sands Beach.

When the surf finally subsided, Cassie announced she was ready for breakfast. Half an hour later, Andy in the passenger seat, Jay McShann in the CD player, Cassie drove her Mustang to the Eggery. The morning after a debate, Cassie was surprised to find that Mayor Donovan was absent from his regular table. Cheyenne also had yet to appear for breakfast. Cassie and Andy found a table in the rear of the large room.

"You want a cup of—grr—coffee, yes?"

Andy studied the waitress, with her heavy pancake makeup, herky-jerky style and good-morning growl. He waited for Cassie's reaction.

"Two cups of regular."

As she poured the coffee, Andy studied her tics, impressed when the waitress got most of the coffee into their cups. It was, it seemed to Andy, another example of the triumph of the human spirit. She flung one menu at the table, a second onto the floor. "I'll be—grr—back in a minute to take your order."

Andy waited for the waitress to disappear into the kitchen. "One time when I was in Mexico, I saw a mariachi band on blotter acid…"

Cassie was surprised. "I can't picture you dropping acid."

"Don't be silly, Cassie. You know me better than that. I don't mean I dropped acid and went to see a mariachi band. I was straight. The band was high."

Cassie was still confused. "Is there a point to the story?"

Andy thought it was obvious. The waitress reminded him of that mariachi band. "Never mind."

Andy ordered Belgian waffles; Cassie ordered pecan pancakes. Breakfast arrived with maple syrup and an occasional growl, but otherwise without incident.

In the rear of the room, a television was mounted on the wall. The TV had been purchased mainly to placate the local football crowd, but was also used on rare occasions to keep an eye on breaking news. This was such a morning.

Andy's seat faced the set, so he saw the footage first. The sound was muted, but Andy didn't need to hear the report. Cassie turned her chair to watch the report—a dramatic nighttime fire somewhere along the coast. Cassie hoped that no one had been hurt in the blaze.

There was brief footage of a commotion among the bystanders. A woman was pushing her way through, yelling at the firefighters.

"Holy shit, Andy! I know her. I wrote a story about her."

Before Cassie could tell Andy all about Madame Alexina, her cell phone began to vibrate. Cassie looked at Andy for an explanation.

"When I charged your phone, I must have switched it from ring to vibrate."

Cassie didn't like people who sat around in restaurants and theaters, in grocery stores and coffee shops, living their lives attached to a cell phone. Cassie was about to become one of those people.

"Hello."

"Huh?" Morris had not expected Cassie to pick up. "Cassie, sweetie, it's me."

"I want to finish my story, Morris."

"Huh?"

"You remember, the explosion on Black Tom Island. I want to finish it. How much time can you give me?"

"Huh?"

It was not like Morris to be confused about a story.

"Are you okay, Morris?"

Morris had not called her to talk about the magazine. "Cassie, have you seen the news this morning? The fire?"

Cassie glanced up at the TV. The morning news show had moved on to a cooking segment.

"I just saw the footage. What's up, Morris? A story for the magazine?"

"Forget about the magazine, Cassie."

Forget about the magazine. Cassie knew this was serious.

"What's going on, Morris?"

"The girl, the one you're looking for..."

"You want—grr—more coffee, yes?" The waitress suddenly appeared at the table with a fresh carafe, spilling coffee along the edge of the table.

Cassie grabbed a couple of napkins, mopping up the small coffee spill.

"I'm sorry, Morris. What were you saying about the missing girl?"

"I think she was hiding in one of the shacks. I think she may have been caught in the blaze."

"Are you sure, Morris?" Cassie didn't want to believe her editor.

Morris didn't want to believe it either. "Do you think the fire had something to do with your missing girl?"

Cassie didn't know what to think. "I'll call you right back, Morris."

Andy could only hear Cassie's half of the telephone call. Still, he could tell it was important. He waited for Cassie to hang up the phone.

"What's that about the fire?"

Cassie didn't answer right away. "Ten minutes ago, I didn't even know that there was a fire last night. Then, we're watching the footage and I recognize Madame Alexina at the scene. I can't help but wonder what she's doing there in the middle of the night. Now I get a phone call from Morris talking about the fire."

Cassie tried to finish making her point, but she was interrupted when Andy's cell phone began to ring. "You better get that."

Andy picked up. "Hello."

"Mr. MacTavish, this is Louis Garibaldi. I think we may have a problem."

Andy groaned. "I know, Louis. Detective Sububie came to the ballpark yesterday."

But Andy's attorney was calling about another problem. "Not that. There was a fire, sir. Have you seen the news this morning?"

Andy wished he could spend a quiet morning with Cassie. He wished they had never got out of bed. "What's the fire have to do with me, Louis?"

"It's the Pettigrew property. The land that Mrs. Patterson wants us to buy for her bird sanctuary."

"Would you hold for just a moment, Louis?" Andy put the phone down and looked across the table at Cassie. "Do you have any aspirin with you?"

Andy rubbed his forehead while Cassie rummaged through her purse. He swallowed a couple of extra-strength pain relievers and picked up the phone.

"I'll call you back, Louis."

Mr. Garibaldi had one question before he let Andy off the phone. "Do you think the fire could have something to do with the bird sanctuary?"

"I'll call you back, Louis."

Andy thought about spending a quiet day in the Pine Barrens with Cassie. He pictured them enjoying the fall foliage, antiquing, hiking, making love.

"I'm afraid I have to go back to work, Cassie. Mr. Garibaldi thinks the fire may be related to our plans to buy the land."

Cassie was thinking about Madame Alexina. "That's odd. Morris thinks the fire may have something to do with your missing mascot."

A Simple Moment of Clarity

As soon as she got word of the fire, Madame Alexina rushed to the scene, hoping for good news regarding Donna and Spit. She hung near the fringe of the fire activity, looking for information, trying not to draw attention to herself. She could not get the firefighters to tell her anything. The news crew, filming the disaster, were themselves pestering the firefighters, with the same lack of results. But it was obvious that the damage was extensive. It was unlikely that Spit and Donna could have survived the carnage.

Madame Alexina tried to achieve a trance state. As a younger woman, she had been able to slip in and out of the trance state effortlessly, with the grace of a middleweight boxer slipping punches. With age had come osteoarthritis, weight gain and a certain calcification of the trance state. Like a pugilist unable to make weight, nearing retirement, Madame Alexina was unable to admit that her skills were diminishing with age.

When the trance state failed, Madame Alexina sat in her van, listening to the chatter on her police scanner. There were reports of the fire, but none of the reports made mention of people, dead or alive, neither victims nor survivors. The authorities were describing the fire scene as an abandoned waterfront property.

Getting out of her van, Madame Alexina pushed her way through the small crowd of bystanders, trying one last time to get someone's attention, needing to let the firemen know there were lives at stake. Looking across the marsh, Madame Alexina was forced to accept that there was nothing to be done for Donna and Spit. If they had not found a way to save themselves, no one else would be able to save them.

Madame Alexina stood at land's end, watching the flames against the backdrop of the night sky. She watched as the fireboats arrived, imposing control on the raging fire. She watched the fireboats and finally it came to her, not in a trance, not in a police report, but in a simple moment of clarity. She remembered Spit's pontoon boat.

Madame Alexina thrilled at the possibility that Donna and Spit might be alive, somewhere out on the water—scared, no doubt; injured, perhaps; but alive. No one else knew about Donna and Spit. No one else would look for them. Madame Alexina understood that she and she alone would need to find the unlikely pair.

Where would Spit take them in the pontoon boat? Madame Alexina worried that a confused Spit might make landfall just about anywhere. She had to think like Spit.

Madame Alexina's head hurt from all the smoke. Where was Spit heading? She knew Spit as well as Spit allowed himself to be known. She was confused. Where would he go? Madame Alexina tried to remember their many conversations, hoping to unearth a clue hidden in his words. She pictured them at the Point, midnight birding and talking politics. Where would Spit make landfall?

"How much farther?" Donna hopped up and down in the pontoon boat. She needed to feel solid ground under her feet. She needed to wear warm, dry clothes. She needed to sleep in a real bed. Donna needed to pee real bad.

Spit peered at the shoreline, looking for landmarks as the sky began ever so gradually to lighten. "I can't be sure. It can't be too much longer."

Donna knew how easily Spit could get confused. "Are you sure? It seems like we've been on the boat for hours. By car, it's only about fifteen minutes to the Point."

"It's okay, Donna. We're almost there. I can feel it. Wait and see."

"Okay, Spit." Donna wanted to believe. "What are we going to do when we get there?"

Spit peered at the shoreline, without answering.

"There it is." Spit turned the boat in toward land. He had gotten them safely to the Point. What was next, he wondered.

Madame Alexina parked her van in the empty parking lot. The chilly nights had brought midnight birding season to an end. They would not be back until spring, sitting in the salt marsh in the dark, listening for the migrating flocks. The midnight birders would not come back to the Point until spring, but Madame Alexina held out hope that two of them would make an appearance before morning. She stood at water's edge, sending her prayers out in ripples on the water. When she saw the pontoon boat approaching, Madame Alexina jumped, nearly falling in the surf, yelling in joy and relief. She ran into the icy cold water, up to her knees, nearly dragging the boat the final few feet.

She helped Donna and Spit climb off the boat. They could barely walk. They lay on the ground, soaking wet, exhausted, covered in soot and oil. Madame Alexina thought they looked wonderful.

Spit sat up, still wrapped in the army surplus blanket. His corporeal form may have arrived safely at the Point, but Madame Alexina could see reflected in his eyes that Spit was sitting in a foxhole in Iraq.

She turned to Donna for help. "C'mon. Help me get Spit to the van."

The two ladies helped Spit to his feet and they walked slowly back to the van, Madame Alexina crooning softly in his ear.

Donna stopped to use the Porta Potti in the parking lot and then they were safely on their way.

Donna cracked the window open. The air seemed to revive Spit's spirit. He had made a promise to Madame Alexina the night she put Donna in his cab. He had promised to keep her safe. He looked at Madame Alexina behind the wheel of her VW minivan.

"I kept my promise."

Spit lapsed back into silence. Madame Alexina was worried.

From the rear window, Donna stared at the familiar landmarks. She could see the boardwalk and the ballpark. It seemed odd to her that nothing had changed in her absence.

"Where are we going?"

Madame Alexina turned toward Donna in the back seat. "Om Depot."

The boardwalk was deserted, the attractions shuttered for the winter. As the sun came up over the ocean, Madame Alexina unlocked her storefront.

"There's a tiny apartment in back."

Donna looked around at the psychic's place of business. "Do you live here?"

"No. I'm not much of a beach person. I live inland."

She led them to the back. As she said, there was a small apartment. "The zoning officer thinks it's a storeroom. You can stay here while we figure things out."

Donna looked around. There was a bed and a sofa, a hot plate, a microwave, a coffee pot, a television, a card table and in the rear corner, there was what appeared to be an office cubicle, with its modular three-quarter wall. Donna peeked into the cubicle and found a full bath. "It's perfect."

"In a couple of hours, when the stores open, I'll bring you clean clothes and food. In the meantime, why don't you take a nice hot bath?"

Donna thought that a hot bath would be wonderful. "But maybe I should wait until I have a change of clothes."

Madame Alexina offered up a solution. "I have two kinds of customers in my business—the ones who want a reading and the ones who want a show. You know what I mean; they want a reading like they've seen in the movies."

Donna wanted to be polite, but she was not in the mood for a story. "I don't think I'm following you."

"I'm sorry. It's just some of my customers want me to do this whole medieval sorceress thing so I keep a couple of long black robes in the closet. They're clean and they're comfortable."

Madame Alexina looked in the closet. "Excellent. One for each of you."

She had been so busy worrying about Donna and Spit, Madame Alexina had barely stopped to consider her own needs. "You should be okay here. I'm going to go home for a few minutes. On my way back, I'll stop at the store. Do you have any special requests?"

Spit was sitting at the card table, largely ignoring the ladies' conversation. "A jigsaw puzzle would be nice."

Madame Alexina departed, locking the door behind her as she left. Donna ran a bath. Crouching down behind the partial wall, she began to disrobe.

"No peeking, okay, Spit?"

Donna submerged herself, relaxing in the hot water.

At Spit's cottage, they had spent weeks alone together. They had grown close, but not intimate. Donna thought of Spit as a platonic friend, a male girlfriend if you will—a well-meaning, but embarrassing, somewhat addled male friend. Donna hadn't a clue how Spit thought of her, but she was pretty sure it wasn't sexual. Still, there had been a moment on the pontoon boat … Donna wondered what would happen if she asked Spit to soap her back.

But Donna didn't ask. She told herself, by way of excuse, that it was better that way. She soaped up. She soaked in the tub. She allowed the moment to pass. She climbed out of the tub. Crouching down inside the cubicle she toweled herself dry. It was at that moment, clean and dry and smelling of soap, that Donna realized she had forgotten the sorcerer's robe.

"Spit, would you hand me one of those robes?"

"Yeah, sure."

"Remember, Spit, no peeking."

Standing a full arm's-length from the cubicle with his eyes averted, Spit draped a black robe over the wall.

Donna emerged from the cubicle, dressed like a sorceress (like a sorceress without underclothes), drying her hair with the towel. Spit couldn't help but notice the way Donna's body moved inside the robe.

"You should try it, Spit. You'll feel great."

Spit blushed, caught thinking about just how it might feel. "I don't know. I'm not much for baths."

But Donna was persuasive, and lying in the tub, Spit admitted that she had been right. Spit also admitted, at least to himself, that he liked it when he caught her peeking.

When Madame Alexina returned, she found the two of them in their robes, freshly scrubbed, smelling of Ivory soap and black magic.

"Sorry I took so long. I had a flat."

Spit looked through the bag of provisions. "You forgot the jigsaw puzzle."

Closing Arguments

Leaving their half-eaten breakfast at the Eggery, Cassie and Andy raced back to her condo. Andy kissed her deeply, mourning the loss of a tranquil day in the Pine Barrens. Grabbing his overnight bag, Andy jumped into his Lexus and pulled out of the lot, heading for the parkway. How was it, he asked himself, that when his personal life was so unbelievably good, his business life could spin so horribly out of control.

Andy got his Lexus up to seventy on the parkway and made great time heading for White Sands Beach. He was nearly home when he caught up to a stopped line of cars. Sitting in his luxury car, cursing at the traffic gods, Andy called his attorney, arranging to meet at the ballpark. It took half an hour to inch past the VW minivan with the flat tire.

Andy recognized Mr. Garibaldi's Cadillac Seville sitting in the Sand Skeeter parking lot. Mr. Garibaldi was waiting in the outer office.

"C'mon in, Louis. Can I get you something?" Andy barely slowed down, disappearing into the inner office.

Mr. Garibaldi climbed slowly off the sofa and followed Andy into his private office. "An iced tea would be nice."

Andy buzzed for two glasses of iced tea. "What do we know about the fire, Louis?"

Louis did his best to explain the situation, both what he knew and what he suspected. Andy listened closely, interrupting the attorney and repeating back the key points.

"Let me see if I have it straight, Louis. The fire occurred on the land we're trying to buy, a couple of days after you met with the owner. Also after you met with Mrs. Patterson about your meeting with the owner."

Mr. Garibaldi nodded. "That's right, sir."

Andy continued. "The authorities seem to believe that the property was abandoned. Why don't they know about Mr. Pettigrew, Louis?"

"I'm not sure, sir. All I can tell you is, when I saw the land, I thought it was abandoned too. It sure didn't look like anyone was living way out there."

Andy considered the attorney's explanation. "Maybe. In any event, it would be nice to know what has happened to our Mr. Pettigrew."

Mr. Garibaldi admitted that he, too, was troubled by the whereabouts of the eccentric Mr. Pettigrew. "Yes, it would, sir. I'll keep working on that."

Andy stood up, walking around his office, thinking out loud. "What I don't understand is why you believe that Mrs. Patterson is involved. Couldn't it just be coincidence?"

Mr. Garibaldi watched as Andy paced. "I'm sorry, Mr. MacTavish. Was that question meant for me?"

Andy returned to his chair. "Yes, Louis, it is. Explain to me again why you suspect Mrs. Patterson."

"To begin with, sir, I have been an attorney far too long to believe in coincidence. Coincidence is the explanation of choice when you don't have an alibi."

With that, Louis pulled himself up from his chair, buttoned his suit coat and smiled warmly, the experienced litigator making closing arguments.

"We know that Mrs. Patterson wants the land, wants it badly. When I told her that Mr. Pettigrew wasn't interested in moving off the land, she would not accept my answer. She told me she would do whatever was necessary to motivate Mr. Pettigrew to sell."

It still seemed to Andy that Mr. Garibaldi did not have sufficient evidence to draw the conclusion that Mrs. Patterson had torched the property.

But Mr. Garibaldi had not yet finished his summation to the jury. "As yet, there has been no official announcement of findings, but unofficially, the fire investigators are already calling it arson. The details are sketchy, but it is apparent that the investigation has turned up evidence of an accelerant."

Mr. Garibaldi paused for effect. "I may be mistaken, sir, but I will trust my gut on this. My considerable gut tells me that they will find the accelerant in the trunk of Mrs. Patterson's automobile."

As Louis turned to sit, Andy imagined he could hear the attorney announce, "I rest my case."

Andy weighed his options, assessing the risks and benefits were he to act on his attorney's gut instinct. "So what is our next move, counselor? Do we report your suspicions to the police?"

Mr. Garibaldi nodded. "I am an officer of the court. I believe it is my legal and moral obligation to report this information to the appropriate authorities."

Andy decided to place a call to Detective Sububie.

When the detective understood why Andy was calling, she agreed to meet him at the ballpark.

"Mr. MacTavish."

Andy was growing accustomed to seeing the grim-faced Detective Sububie standing in his doorway. "Please come in, detective."

"Thank you, Mr. MacTavish."

Andy introduced the policewoman to his attorney, the rotund Mr. Garibaldi.

Detective Sububie ignored the attorney, speaking instead to Andy MacTavish. "I wondered how long it would take before you lawyered up."

Mr. Garibaldi smiled expansively, at ease dealing with the police. "I am here, detective, as an officer of the court. Mr. MacTavish called you, and I am here, because we have information about the fire, information that the police can use as the basis for bringing criminal charges. Wouldn't you like to be the detective who gets credit for breaking the case?"

Detective Sububie again chose to ignore the attorney. "Mr. MacTavish, I am not in a good mood today. I'm warning you, sir, don't mess with me."

Andy MacTavish told the detective his story, Louis Garibaldi filling in the details. Detective Sububie revealed little of her thinking, interrupting just one time to ask Mr. Garibaldi about the accelerant.

"What exactly will we find in her car?"

Mr. Garibaldi explained. "Mrs. Patterson believes she'll be assaulted by a pervert if she breaks down on the road somewhere."

Andy hadn't heard this part before.

"She's so consumed with fear that she carries a canister of synthetic fuel in the trunk."

Detective Sububie was taking no chances. She didn't entirely trust Andy MacTavish or his attorney. "And you know this how?"

Mr. Garibaldi leaned back in his chair. "Mrs. Patterson told me all about it. Look, maybe I'm wrong, but it should be easy enough for you to find out. If the synthetic fuel matches the accelerant…"

Detective Sububie nodded, allowing just the slightest trace of a smile to cross her face. "I see what you mean."

The way that Mr. Garibaldi handled the detective reminded Andy just why he had chosen to retain the attorney's services. The fire might yet work to his advantage. Andy walked the policewoman to the door. "Thank you for coming out to the ballpark."

But Andy was not yet rid of the detective.

"We're not done yet." Detective Sububie turned and faced Andy. "We still need to talk about Ms. Heather Dean."

Andy looked over at his attorney. Mr. Garibaldi said nothing.

Detective Sububie continued. "I need your assistance, Mr. MacTavish."

Andy smiled uneasily. "I'm always happy to help the police, detective."

Detective Sububie wasn't smiling. "Thank you. So, can you explain to me how come the lab can find traces of malathion on the Skeeter costume, but not a single trace of that same toxin on the dead body?" Detective Sububie shook her head. "Not a trace."

Andy didn't know what to say. "I gather the department exhumed Ms. Dean's body then?"

"Yes, we did. Based on information that I developed. And what do we have to show for it? Her death remains an accident, but now it's an accident complicated by a mystery. The department looks incompetent and the family is calling for an investigation of our handling of the case. And I'm caught right in the middle."

Detective Sububie glared at Andy. "Is there something you want to tell me, Mr. MacTavish?"

Andy glanced at his attorney. "I wish I could be more help, detective, but I've told you everything I know."

Detective Sububie tried again. " 'Cause if you know something that you haven't told me, it might look like you're obstructing a police investigation."

Andy again turned to his attorney. Mr. Garibaldi rose to his feet. "My client told you he doesn't have any further information. I think we're done here, detective."

"For now." Detective Sububie turned and walked out the door.

Second Best

Cassie sat in her empty condo watching more tape of the fire. She knew very little about the fire, but what little she did know, didn't make sense. Cassie watched the part again when Madame Alexina caused a commotion among the bystanders. What was she doing there? And how was it that Morris appeared to know more about the fire than the reporters on the scene?

Cassie picked up the phone, thinking, one day, she should learn how to program her frequently called numbers. She dialed the phone. An answering machine said, "Hello."

"Morris. It's me. Pick up the damn phone."

The machine invited Cassie to leave a message.

"Listen to me, Morris. I need to see you. I'll come by the office at…"

"You're coming to the office? Damn, this is important." In more than a decade of writing for the magazine, Cassie had been to the office just three times.

"Thanks for picking up, Morris."

"Sorry I couldn't get to the phone quicker. I was checking proofs."

Morris had built a small but successful printing business on Staten Island before moving to New Jersey and buying the nearly bankrupt (morally as well as financially) magazine. His original plan for the rag sheet was to transform it into a journal of serious political analysis. He opened an office in the state capital to have access to the state's power brokers. Although he never did succeed in transforming the magazine's subject matter, he did bring a certain style to the magazine's questionable content and a very respectable profit margin to the annual operating budget. By all accounts, the turnaround could be traced to a day, almost fifteen years past, when a recently widowed Cassie O'Malley wandered into the Trenton office, looking for a job covering the state legislature.

Cassie's ability to take a hodgepodge of outlandish events and construct a plausible cover story, coupled with Morris's ruthless editorial cynicism, had been an instant hit with the readers.

After so many years living and working in New Jersey, Morris liked to maintain he was a native, born and raised in Atlantic County. Cassie winked and played along, but the truth was, every time Morris talked about growing up at the beach, the natives knew him for an impostor.

Cassie made her second trip to the office six years into her employment, when she first investigated the secret tunnels underneath the state capitol. Her third visit occurred one evening en route to a hockey game when Cassie stopped to use the office bathroom. When Cassie announced her fourth visit to the magazine's office, Morris knew that she was more than a little worried about the fire.

Morris cleared a spot for Cassie among the piles of paper, the photos, stories and research, the ad copy and correspondence.

"Cassie, sweetie, you look wonderful." Morris pushed aside another pile of paper. "Here, sit. Can I get you a cup of coffee?"

"Thanks." Cassie looked around the small office. There was even more paper than she remembered. "How's the conversion coming along?" Cassie was referring to Morris's technology plan to create the paperless office.

"I'm almost there. So what brings you into the office today? The fire?"

"Yeah, the fire. What can you tell me about it?"

"The fire started shortly after midnight, quickly consuming the cottages and boardwalk. According to the authorities, the property was abandoned."

"But you believe Donna Carter was hiding there?"

Morris nodded.

Cassie had a million questions about the fire and one very specific question about her editor. "How do you know so much about the fire?"

"I called it in." Morris saw the puzzlement on Cassie's face. "Maybe I'd better start at the beginning."

"You called me a couple of weeks ago and asked me if I had heard anything about the missing girl. Remember?"

Cassie thought about that night at Andy's oceanfront home. She was missing him already. "I remember."

"Well, I hadn't heard anything, but I decided to check it out myself."

Cassie was startled. "Why'd you do that?"

"I thought there might be a story." Morris knew the real answer would make him sound jealous or pitiful, or both. "Anyway, I sat on Donna's apartment, waiting for something to happen. It didn't take long."

"What didn't take long?"

"A cab pulled up to the apartment. The driver let himself inside and came back out a few minutes later carrying a suitcase. I followed the cab to land's end. Since then, whenever I can clear my schedule, I've been keeping an eye on the place."

"And you did all that for a story?" Cassie knew Morris better than that. "Yeah."

Cassie let him slide. "So why'd you wait so long to call me?"

"You told me to call your cell, remember? I don't think you wanted me to know about Andy. Anyway, I tried to call you for days. This morning was the first time you picked up."

Cassie wondered what else Morris might have learned. "There was a piece of footage on the news…a commotion among the bystanders at the fire…did you see it, Morris?"

"Not when it happened, but this morning on TV, yeah, I saw it."

"The red-haired lady at the center of the commotion…what do you know about her?"

Morris recalled the middle-aged lady with the wild hair. "Sorry, Cassie. I don't know anything about her at all."

"But I do. Do you remember the story I wrote about the psychic spy?"

Morris grinned; the story about remote spies working for the CIA was sure to be an instant classic. "Of course. You don't mean…?"

"Yeah, Morris. That was her. Madame Alexina. Don't you think that's a strange coincidence?"

Morris reached for a file on his desk, sending random papers fluttering to the floor.

"Damn. If you think that's strange, wait till you hear this. The guy who lived in the shack, the cabbie who was helping Cassie hide out…you know him too."

Cassie was stunned. "I do?"

"Yeah." Morris thumbed through the old file. "When you investigated the Wehnke case…do you remember the night at the train station?"

"Holy shit, Morris. You mean the cabbie we met at the train station, the one who identified the mayor's wife, that guy?"

Morris showed her the old file. "Yeah, that guy, Spit."

Cassie glanced at the folder. "Spit lived out there? This is getting really strange, Morris. He can't possibly own the place, can he? It's gotta be a rental."

Morris didn't see where she was heading. "I don't understand, Cassie. What difference does it make?"

Cassie had been careful to avoid bringing Andy's name into the conversation, but there was no other way to explain. Morris would just have to get over it. "You know I'm seeing Andy MacTavish, right?"

Morris wanted to be happy for Cassie. Really. Only deep down he wanted her to be happy with him. And he knew that she knew it too. "Yeah. I'm happy for you, Cassie."

That was a conversation for another time. "Anyway, Andy has been getting pressure from the president of the local birding society. She wants Andy to buy the property and donate it for a bird sanctuary. His attorney has already met with the owner."

Cassie refilled her coffee. "The mascot, the psychic, the cabbie, the bird lady…what's the connection, Morris? What am I missing?"

Morris struggled to make the pieces fit. "You're the finest researcher I've ever met, Cassie. And a lot of this stuff has got to be in the public record. Why don't you pay a visit tomorrow to the county clerk's office? If there's a connection, maybe you'll find it there."

Cassie gave Morris a hug. "You're the best, Morris."

Second best, Morris told himself. "I really am happy for you, Cassie."

A Box of Coffee

When Donna awoke, it took her several minutes to remember where she was. She looked around at the one-room apartment. Spit was sleeping comfortably on the sofa. Donna marveled at his ability to sleep anywhere. She longed for the rest that came with her own mattress, her own comforter.

Hiding at Spit's, Donna had discovered the simple pleasure of a daily routine. She had not found that rhythm on the first day, but with time she had learned the secret of a solitary life. Donna told herself to give the Om Depot time, but she felt more trapped now than she had at Spit's.

Donna turned on the television, keeping the volume down low, just in time for the local weather. The television promised a gorgeous fall day; the weatherman urged everyone to spend the day outdoors. Donna changed the channel. There was an extraordinary shot of the moon reflected on the ocean. Donna was impressed by the unusual shot. "Wow. It's blue."

"What's blue?"

Donna screamed.

Spit bolted upright on the sofa. "What's that?"

Donna looked at Madame Alexina, standing in the doorway with a box of coffee and a bag of donuts. "You scared me."

"I'm sorry. I just stopped by with breakfast." Madame Alexina put the donuts and coffee on the card table. "What's blue?"

Donna felt foolish explaining. "Nothing. A shot of the moon on the water."

Donna poured herself a cup of coffee and selected a jelly donut. Spit joined her at the table for a chocolate-covered donut. Madame Alexina explained, "I've already eaten breakfast," before choosing a vanilla crème donut.

Munching on donuts, they watched the morning news. Before cutting to a commercial, the local anchor read the tease. "Local birder behind bars, after the break."

Donna looked at Madame Alexina. "What do you think that's about?"

The first story after the commercial break was a soft news story about a south Jersey student competing in the national spelling bee. The next story profiled activities at the local food pantry. Finally, the anchor returned to the teaser item.

"Early this morning, an arrest was made in the case of the spectacular waterfront fire." The TV ran a short piece of film of Spit's cottage in flames.

Donna put down her donut and stared at the screen. "Holy shit!"

Spit looked up from his coffee. "That looks familiar."

The TV cut to a reporter standing outside the police station. Looking into the camera, the reporter began her carefully scripted story. "Mrs. Jodi Patterson, president of a local birding group, was arrested this morning and charged with arson in connection with the case."

In a box in the background, the TV ran a photograph of Mrs. Patterson, dressed in a wool skirt and jacket.

Spit nearly spat up his coffee. "That's…that's…what's her name, you know, the lady with the broomstick up her butt…what's her name, you know…"

"That's right, Spit." Madame Alexina patted Spit on the arm.

"Shhh, I want to hear this." Donna was glued to the TV.

"I am here with Detective Sububie, the officer who broke the case." The reporter managed to turn toward the policewoman, all the while maintaining eye contact with her TV audience.

"What can you tell us, detective?"

Detective Sububie adopted her official police business face. "Yesterday we received a tip that pointed us in the direction of Mrs. Patterson. We obtained a warrant to search the suspect's car. In the trunk of the car, we found a can of synthetic fuel. Preliminary reports indicate that the synthetic fuel is a match with the accelerant found in the debris by the fire investigators. Based on this evidence, we have arrested Mrs. Patterson and charged her with arson."

"Can you tell us anything about Mrs. Patterson's motives?"

Detective Sububie suppressed an urge to smile into the camera. "Mrs. Patterson was interested in establishing a bird sanctuary on the property. Apparently the fire was her way of encouraging the owner to relocate."

The reporter was genuinely surprised by the detective's answer.

"Excuse me, detective, but I understood that the property was abandoned."

Detective Sububie weighed how much she was permitted to reveal. "Most everyone shared your understanding. Most everyone was wrong."

It was rare that a local reporter had an opportunity to break real news. "No bodies were found at the fire. Do you know where the owner…" The reporter stopped and looked at the detective. "How many people are we talking about?"

When Detective Sububie failed to offer a number, the reporter continued, pressing for details. "Anyway, do you know if the residents are safe? Do you know where they are now?"

Detective Sububie looked into the camera, speaking directly to Donna. "All I am permitted to tell you is that it's over. It's safe for you to go home."

Donna grabbed her donut and jumped up from the table, singing. "We're going home! We're going home! We're going home!"

She looked at Spit, sitting quietly at the table. "It's over, Spit. We can go…Omigod, Spit. I'm sorry."

Madame Alexina turned to Spit, quietly inquiring, "What are you going to do now?"

Spit was confused by Donna's apology and Madame Alexina's question. "It's okay, guys. I'm going to rebuild."

Donna looked at Spit with renewed admiration. "Sometimes you amaze me."

Spit reddened. "It's not such a big deal. I've been thinking it might be fun to build one of those log homes, from a kit, you know what I mean?"

Donna didn't have a clue what Spit meant, but it did sound like fun. "Maybe I could help."

Spit looked at Donna, surprised by her offer. "You would do that for me?"

Donna was reminded that men were truly oblivious life forms. "Of course. And in the meantime, I've got a two-bedroom apartment. Why don't you come home with me?"

"Are you sure that's okay?"

Donna tried to find the words to explain. She had spent more than a month in hiding in Spit's cottage and not once had he complained about her. She didn't know where to begin.

"Yes, Spit, it's okay."

Spit stared at his feet, smiling. "Okay then."

Donna danced around the room with her donut. "We're going home! We're going home! We're going home!"

Number Forty-Two

For more than a decade, Cassie had been waking every morning in a half-empty bed in her condo in Doah. Once again, she was waking in a half-empty bed, only suddenly, it was a different half-emptiness. Cassie lay in her bed, staring at the ceiling, adjusting to Andy half-emptiness. It was, she decided, not the same as Rob half-emptiness. Rob half-emptiness was a dull ache, an emotional pain that stretched out into the infinite. Andy half-emptiness was a sharper pain, more physical than emotional, but the pain was tempered by the promise of a deep and abiding fullness.

Cassie climbed from her half-empty bed. When the county clerk's office opened, she wanted to be there. She was ready to spend a day in the stacks at the record room, breathing the dry, dusty air and browsing through the public record. She was eager to get started building a paper trail, making sense of the unanswered questions and getting back to the important business of banishing half-emptiness from her life and from her bed.

At 9:00 sharp, Cassie was standing at the front door of the county clerk's office. She was surprised to discover the record room would not open until 10:00. There was a note on the door encouraging visitors to take advantage of the county Web site to initiate their record request.

At 10:00, Cassie returned to the record room. She was the only visitor. There was an elderly gentleman nearing retirement in charge who patiently explained to Cassie that she would not be permitted to browse through the stacks.

"But if you fill out one of these forms," he explained, "and bring it back to this window, I'll pull the file for you. You can use that table," he pointed, "over there." Cassie tried to tell the clerk that she wasn't certain which files she needed to see, but the clerk was unmoved by her dilemma. "I'm sorry, ma'am, it's the rule."

Cassie knew better than to argue. "I understand." At least she knew where she needed to start. Her only hope was that as she worked her way through the documents, they would lead her each to the next. She asked the clerk for the title to the property.

"Have you filled out your form?"

Cassie filled out the form and placed it in the "form box" at the clerk's window. The clerk then went to his box, examined the form and disappeared briefly in the stacks. Five minutes later he returned.

"Number forty-two?"

In the empty record room, Cassie realized she was number forty-two. She signed for the file and sat down at the vacant table. There were no surprises and no new information. The land was owned in the name of Perry Pettigrew, Jr. The question, Cassie reminded herself, was whether Perry Pettigrew, Jr., and Spit were one and the same.

It seemed like a long shot, but Cassie knew that sometimes it was useful to go back a generation. What could she learn from Perry Pettigrew, Sr.? What would Senior have to say about his son and where in the public record would he say it? Cassie filled out a form requesting a copy of the last will and testament of Perry Pettigrew, Sr. If she were lucky she would find a disillusioned father's parting shot at his ne'er-do-well son…"To my son Perry Jr., the taxicab driver, I leave my road atlas and my car deodorizer." But Cassie had no such luck. The last will and testament of Perry Pettigrew, Sr., was a dead end.

Cassie wondered what name was printed on Spit's hack license. She could drive to the motor vehicle office, but Cassie didn't relish the idea of standing in line and bribing a motor vehicle clerk to check the records for a hack license issued to Perry Pettigrew, Jr. She thought about veteran's records, but the federal office would be even worse than the DMV.

Cassie had an idea. She approached the clerk, seeking his advice. "I'm interested in information regarding county residents who served in Desert Storm. I was wondering if I could find that information in the county records."

For the first time that day, but not the last, the elderly clerk took an interest in Cassie's record search. "Give me a few minutes. Perhaps I can locate something."

It took the clerk nearly half an hour to return, but when he did he was waving a folder proudly. "When the troops returned from Desert Storm, everyone wanted to honor the soldiers."

The clerk remembered his own experience decades earlier. "When I came home from 'Nam…I think maybe we all wanted to exorcize our collective guilt about the way we treated our Vietnam vets. Anyway, we held a ceremony here to honor all of the county residents who served in Desert Storm. Here's the file. Maybe it'll have what you're looking for."

Cassie thanked the clerk for his help and returned to her worktable. She flipped through the program, stopping at a photograph of seven young soldiers smiling for the camera. The third face from the left was identified as Pfc. Perry Pettigrew, Jr. Cassie studied the photo. He was younger, leaner, less hirsute, but the third face from the left was unmistakably Spit.

Cassie pushed her chair back away from the table and smiled. She loved feeling the rush of a good paper trail. What might she find in the public record about one Jodi Patterson?

Cassie knew that Mrs. Patterson was the president of a nonprofit organization dedicated to advancing the needs of birds and birders. Nonprofits leave a substantial paper trail with the state and with the IRS. Unfortunately, they do not file papers with the county. Unless, Cassie suddenly realized, they receive any grants from county government. Cassie grabbed a form and went up to the clerk's window, requesting the file on Mrs. Patterson's organization.

It took the clerk a while to find it, but several years past, the group had indeed filed an application for county funds. Although the proposal was rejected by the county, the application and supporting materials remained on file in the dead records room.

Cassie read the file with care. Apparently, long before she asked Andy MacTavish to buy her a bird sanctuary, she had made the same request of the county. Cassie read the application. She reviewed the certificate of incorporation and the IRS approval of their nonprofit status. She glanced at the project budget and the letters of support. The papers revealed a woman with a grim determination to realize her vision. This was a woman for whom the ends most certainly might be used to justify the means. Perhaps to justify arson.

Her researcher's instinct told Cassie to keep looking. She read the organization's annual report, with its feel-good stories about birds and its list of donors. Most of the names on the list were unfamiliar to Cassie. A few were familiar, but bore no special meaning. One name jumped out at her from the donor list...one name that tied it all together.

Cassie grabbed another form and hurried over to the clerk's window, scribbling her request on the paper—the last will and testament of Harrison T. Dicke.

Spilling Coffee Down the Front of Her T-Shirt

Donna unlocked the door and stepped inside. Her aging garden apartment, with its shag rug, peeling paint and avocado appliances had never looked so good. The plumbing gurgled in excitement at her return. Donna showed Spit to his room.

"This one is mine?" Spit liked the room immediately, especially the card table in the corner. "Do you mind if I buy a jigsaw puzzle?"

"Of course not." Donna would have agreed to just about anything. She was home. It was over.

She wanted to get on the phone, to let everyone know that she was okay, but there wasn't an everyone to call. Heather was dead. Billy was… What exactly was Billy? Donna wondered. Billy was old news. Finally she called Sand Skeeter ballpark and left a message for the team.

That night, lying in bed on a mattress years in the making, Spit down the hall in her guest room, Donna felt like herself for the first time in a month. She woke late in the morning, well-rested and content. She could smell a fresh pot of coffee in the kitchen.

When Cassie tried to assemble all the pieces to the puzzle, she would build a structure in her head only to find that she was left with one piece that just didn't fit. So she would try again, starting with a different piece, constructing a scenario that could accommodate all the evidence. No matter what she tried, she would be stuck at the end with one leftover piece to the puzzle. Cassie worked and reworked the puzzle as she drove back to her condo. By the time she reached Doah, she had a long list of facts, but no truths.

Cassie poured herself a Tullamore Dew and turned on the evening news. It wasn't long before she saw the story of Mrs. Patterson's arrest. Perhaps Mrs. Patterson really was capable of committing arson to establish her bird sanctuary. The synthetic fuel was a damning piece of evidence. Still, something told Cassie there was more to the story. She watched the interview with Detective Sububie. She watched as the detective looked into the camera, announcing, "It's over."

Cassie picked up the phone and dialed the police station in White Sands Beach.

"I'd like to speak to Detective Sububie, please."

A telephone voice politely informed her that the detective was not available to take her call and offered to take a message.

Cassie chose her words with care. "Would you please tell the detective that Cassie O'Malley is on the phone? Would you tell her that Ms. O'Malley says it's not over? Could you tell her that for me?"

"One moment, please." The disembodied voice put Cassie on hold.

She waited for the click that told her someone had picked up.

"Ms. O'Malley? This is Detective Sububie."

Cassie slept poorly in her half-empty bed and woke early. She called Cheyenne and Morris. Morris surprised Cassie with big news: he was thinking about selling the magazine. Cheyenne made her promise to get back by election day.

Cassie grabbed her CDs and locked up the condo, ready for the drive to White Sands Beach. She took her time, meandering along back roads through the Barrens. Doc Cheatham and Nicholas Payton squeezed into her passenger seat, trading trumpet solos.

It was midday when Cassie pulled up to Andy's oceanfront home. No one answered the door, but Cassie knew where Andy hid the spare key. She let herself into the extraordinary beach house.

Spit was comfortable at Donna's apartment right from the start, but it wouldn't really feel like home until he had a jigsaw puzzle spread out on the card table. Donna offered to let Spit take her car into town. After a month of inactivity, the engine strained to turn over. Spit raised the hood of Donna's car. It took several tries, but the battery was not completely dead, and with a little tinkering, he was soon on his way in pursuit of a puzzle.

Donna sat at the kitchen table, enjoying another cup of coffee in the privacy of her own apartment. Suddenly she heard a scrabbling at the front door. Donna jumped, spilling coffee down the front of her t-shirt. She had to laugh, realizing it would take a good deal more time before she would truly be able to relax. She put her eye to the peephole in the front door.

"Mr. MacTavish!" Donna threw open the front door, excited to see her boss. "You didn't have to come see me. I would have driven to the ballpark later today."

Andy MacTavish was relieved to see his missing mascot. "When I heard that you were okay, I just had to see for myself. You are okay, aren't you?"

"I'm fine, sir. Only I think I owe you an apology. Would you like to come in?"

Andy wanted to spend time chatting with Donna, but he had a very busy schedule. "Tell you what, Donna. Ride with me. We'll talk in the car."

Donna was giddy. "Sure, Mr. MacTavish. That'd be fun. I'll just be a minute."

Donna started to write a note for Spit, but she stopped mid-note, feeling foolish. A note made their arrangement seem somehow more personal, more intimate. She crumpled the note and tossed it in the trash. Donna grabbed a sweatshirt, heading for the door. Andy started to open the door, but Donna stopped short.

"I better pee first. I'll just be another minute."

Andy tried not to sound impatient. "No problem."

Donna was in the bathroom when the phone rang. She called to Andy from behind the closed door. "Could you get that for me?"

Andy let the phone ring. Donna tried again. "Mr. MacTavish, could you get that?"

Reluctantly, Andy picked up the telephone. "Hello."

"I'm sorry. Do I have the wrong number? I'm trying to reach Donna Carter."

Andy tried to place the voice on the other end of the phone. "This is Donna Carter's line. Can I tell her who's calling?" Donna was yet to come out of the bathroom.

"Would you tell her that Detective Sububie is on the line?"

Without saying another word, Andy put down the phone. Donna finally emerged.

"Detective Sububie, it's so nice of you to call."

"You saw the news report, Donna?"

"Yeah. I'm so glad it's over."

Detective Sububie agreed. "Me too. Still, I'm glad to know you have a friend there with you."

"I know what you mean, detective. The whole thing still has me a little jumpy."

"I can certainly understand how you feel. If you like, I can swing by your apartment later today. There are still a few loose ends we need to tie up."

Donna just wanted to put the entire incident behind her. "Actually, detective, I'm just on my way out the door. Do you think maybe the loose ends could wait?"

When Donna hung up the phone, Andy MacTavish was checking his watch. He had not figured on the delay. Donna felt bad about keeping her boss waiting. "I'm ready now."

Andy waved off her apology. "You gave us all quite a scare, young lady. I'm glad you're okay."

Andy took her by the arm and walked her to his car. Ever the gentleman, he held the car door open as she climbed into the passenger side of his silver Lexus.

No Evidence that a Crime Was Committed

When Andy turned the Lexus into the dead-end street, he was surprised to find Cassie's Mustang parked in front of his home. He turned to Donna, squirming in the passenger seat. "Wait here. I'll only be a minute."

"But I really…"

Andy cut her off. "Wait here."

Cassie was standing on the deck when Andy let himself in. She was admiring the way the sun sparkled on Andy's ocean. "I love this view. I'm sure going to miss this place."

Andy was puzzled. "Miss it? I don't understand. Where are you going?"

Cassie didn't want to face Andy. "When you leave, I don't think I'll be happy here."

"Me? Where am I going?"

Cassie had known this moment was coming. She'd been preparing all day, but nothing could prepare her for what she needed to say. "You're going to prison."

Andy laughed uneasily at Cassie's attempt at humor. "What are you talking about?"

Cassie knew there was no turning back. She spoke slowly, through clenched teeth. "You're going to prison for the attempted murder of Donna Carter."

Andy didn't understand what was happening. "It was the birder, Mrs. Patterson. The police found the accelerant in her car."

But Cassie wasn't talking about the fire. "Maybe she did and maybe she didn't. I don't know, but that's not what I'm talking about. I'm talking about the first attempt."

Now Andy was truly confused. "The first attempt? I don't understand."

Cassie wouldn't meet Andy's eyes. "Are you going to make me say it out loud?"

"Why are you doing this, Cassie? Everything has been so good. Why?"

Cassie bit her lip. Everything had been wonderful. "The night that

Heather died…"

Andy was desperate to make Cassie stop. "Heather's death was an accident."

Cassie nodded. "Yes, that's right. Heather's death was an accident, but at the time, you didn't know it was Heather. The thing is, if Donna had gone to work that night the way you expected, she would have died, only in her case, it would have been murder."

Andy was frantic. "Cassie, sweetheart, please. What kind of craziness did that editor put in your head? I swear, sometimes I think you can't tell the difference anymore between those stories and reality."

But Cassie did know the difference. "You don't know how hard I tried to convince myself it was just my imagination, but the costume…"

"What about the costume?" Andy challenged Cassie to continue.

"You put the insecticide on the costume, expecting Donna to wear it, expecting the malathion to slowly do its work. You didn't plan for Heather. You couldn't have foreseen she'd fill in for Donna or that she'd take the old costume from Donna's closet, the one you forgot about. It was fifty-fifty, and she chose the wrong one, the clean one."

Cassie continued, afraid to look. "It's why you let Detective Sububie test the costume. Until she found it in the back of Donna's closet, you'd forgotten all about the first costume. You'd already thrown one in the ocean, so you assumed the one in the closet was clean. When Heather died, there was no reason for you to doubt that the malathion had killed her. So when the opportunity presented itself, you threw what you thought was a tainted costume into the sea. Not because you wanted to change the team's name and mascot, but because you thought you were destroying the evidence. You couldn't believe your good fortune when the morgue asked you to pick up the costume. So you destroyed the evidence when you had the chance. Then you got even luckier, or so you thought. Detective Sububie found a costume, the one you forgot about, the one you assumed was the prototype, the one you thought would be clean. You practically begged the detective to test the costume. You must have been stunned when the test revealed the insecticide."

Andy felt as though he were trapped on a runaway train. "Do you hear yourself, Cassie? Do you realize what you're saying? You're saying that when Heather died, her death was an accident, but if Donna had worked that night, if it had been Donna at the center of the dizzy bat tragedy, it would have been murder. There was no murder, Cassie. There was no attempted murder. Just a horrible accident and an overactive imagination…And if there were a murder attempt, it wasn't me."

Cassie fought to hold back her tears. "Yes, Andy, it was you."

Andy reached over to wipe her eyes, but Cassie tried to pull away. Andy's grip tightened, and for the first time Cassie felt his capacity for violence. She tried again to pull away, but Andy's cold arms had encircled her.

Suddenly the front door flew open, Donna standing in the doorway, hopping up and down. "I need to pee."

As Donna raced to the bathroom, Cassie seized the opportunity to pull free from Andy.

"Cassie, please don't do this to us. Please…before it's too late. Why would I possibly want Donna Carter dead?"

At the mention of her name, Donna stopped short. The bathroom would have to wait.

For the longest time, Cassie found herself unable to speak. "I struggled with that question. Then I remembered Billy's TV appearance."

"Billy's TV appearance? What's that got to do with any of this?"

Cassie took a perverse pride in her answer. "It's about control of the baseball team. You own the Sand Skeeters, but you're not the only owner. Your brother Billy owns a little piece of the team."

"Yes, he does." Andy did his best to look unconcerned. "So what?"

"So it made me wonder who else might own a share. Would you like to know what I found?"

Andy made no attempt to answer for her. "What?"

For the first time, Cassie locked eyes with Andy. "Harrison. I found Harrison."

Andy waited.

"Harrison owned a piece of the team. You were the principal owner, but you were gradually losing control of the team. It turns out Mr. Garibaldi's not quite as good at his job as you thought. You had control, but not the unquestioned control that you craved. Harrison was sympathetic to the birders. When he passed away, you thought perhaps you could reassert your control. And then it got even worse. Harrison left a small piece of the team to its mascot, in grateful appreciation for her love of the team. You didn't see that one coming."

Donna stared at Andy MacTavish. "Is that true? Do I really own a piece of the team?"

Andy tried to answer, but Cassie waved off his objections. "Don't bother to deny it. I've seen Harrison's will. After all, it is a public document."

Andy was defiant right up to the end. "Even if everything you say is true, Cassie, all of it, there's still no evidence that a crime was committed."

Cassie stood, her eyes a mixture of pity and contempt. "And that's supposed to make everything okay between us? No evidence…that's supposed to make me feel better? Does it make you feel better, Donna? Maybe I can't prove that you planned to murder Donna. But what if she's not the first?"

"You're out of your mind, Cassie."

"Maybe. But what if you've already killed in your attempt to maintain control of the baseball team? What if you poisoned one of your partners? What if we exhumed that partner's body and tested for malathion? Maybe you never got the chance to poison Donna, maybe Heather's death really was an accident, maybe Mrs. Patterson really did set the fire, maybe there's a lot of stuff we'll never know for sure, but what if we find malathion in the dead partner's tissue samples?"

"That's a lot of ifs." Andy slumped in his seat, head in hands. "So what do we do now?"

Cassie was exhausted. "We wait."

"What are we waiting for?"

Andy's question hung in the air, it seemed, forever. Cassie had once believed that love distorted the flow of time. She now realized that the end of love had the same effect. There was a knock on the door.

"For that."

Andy looked up. "Who's on the other side of the door?"

Wordlessly, Cassie stood up and answered the knock.

Detective Sububie stepped into the room. "Andy MacTavish, you are under arrest…for the murder of Harrison T. Dicke. You have the right to remain silent…"

The detective cuffed Andy and led him out the door.

Cassie stood on the deck, looking out at a cruel October ocean, the wind whipping in off the water, stinging Cassie's face.

Civic Duty

Cassie's bed was crowded with half-emptiness. She wanted to spend the rest of her life hiding under the covers in her twice half-empty bed. Morris and Cheyenne took turns leaving telephone messages, urging Cassie to pick up. She didn't eat. She barely drank. She lay in bed, overwhelmed by half-emptiness.

A week went by, and Cassie still had not escaped the boundaries of her bed. She might have stayed in bed forever, might never have started on the long slow path that would eventually bring her happiness and peace, were it not for her enduring sense of civic duty and personal loyalty. She put it off all day, put it off well into the evening, put it off until the last possible moment. Cassie climbed out of bed, dragged a brush through her matted hair, making a half-hearted attempt to look presentable, and drove to the local elementary school, whose gymnasium, on this day each year, doubled as an official polling place. Cassie dragged herself away from her shrine to half-emptiness in order to cast a vote, moments before the polls closed, for Cheyenne Harbrough.

Cassie drove straight home after casting her vote. She was surprised to find Cheyenne waiting for her.

"Shouldn't you be somewhere?"

Cheyenne looked at her best friend, wishing there was something she could do, anything, to ease her pain. "There is a small group of supporters, family and friends, waiting for me at the Eggery. Why don't you come with me, Cassie?"

Cassie shook her head. "I'm going back to bed."

Cheyenne barred the door. "Come with me, Cassie."

"Please, Cheyenne, I'm not ready. I just want to go inside."

Cheyenne was undeterred. "Then I'm going inside with you."

"It's election night, Chey. I appreciate what you're trying to do, but you can't stay here. You have to go."

Cheyenne showed no sign of leaving. "I'm not leaving without you,

Cassie. Go inside. Take a shower. Put on a party frock and come with me to the Eggery. I'm nervous as hell about the election. Help me wait for the results."

Cassie couldn't know it at the time, but her life was hanging in the balance. She was too tired to argue. And with that, she started on the long road back. She took a shower, put on a party frock and rejoined the world.

They were sitting together at a table in the Eggery, Cheyenne and Cassie, and a handful of friends and supporters, when Cheyenne received the call.

Everything stopped, while Cheyenne took the call. Everyone stared at Cheyenne, watching for clues. When Cheyenne hung up the phone she was smiling broadly.

Cassie was happy for her good friend Cheyenne. "Speech! Speech!"

Cheyenne stood up at the table, looking around at her family and friends. "Did you hear the one about the traveling salesman and the next mayor of Doah Township?"

About the Author

Jeff Markowitz lives in New Jersey with his wife Carol and his son Josh. Jeff is a Member of the Mystery Writers of America. The Cassie O'Malley mysteries weave elements of Pine Barrens history, geography and folklore into contemporary murder mysteries. The first Cassie O'Malley mystery, *Who Is Killing Doah's Deer?*, was published in June 2004.

Curious about other Crossroad Press books?
Stop by our site:
http://store.crossroadpress.com
We offer quality writing
in digital, audio, and print formats.

Enter the code FIRSTBOOK
to get 20% off your first order from our store!
Stop by today!

www.ingramcontent.com/pod-product-compliance
Lightning Source LLC
Chambersburg PA
CBHW072101170626
46813CB00004B/1418